# JUMPING JENNY

# JUMPING JENNY

ANTHONY BERKELEY

With an Introduction by
Martin Edwards

Poisoned Pen
PRESS

Published by Poisoned Pen Press, an imprint of Sourcebooks,
in association with the British Library
P.O. Box 4410, Naperville, Illinois 60567-4410
(630) 961-3900
sourcebooks.com

*Jumping Jenny* was originally published in 1933 by Hodder & Stoughton, London.

Library of Congress Cataloging-in-Publication Data

Names: Berkeley, Anthony, author.
Title: Jumping Jenny / Anthony Berkeley ; With an Introduction by Martin Edwards.
Description: Naperville, Illinois : Poisoned Pen Press, [2023] | Series: British Library Crime Classics
Identifiers: LCCN 2022028757 (print) | LCCN 2022028758
(ebook) | (trade paperback) | (epub)
Classification: LCC PZ3.C83829 Jv PR6005.O855 (print) | LCC PZ3.C83829 PR6005.O855 (ebook) | DDC 823/.912--dc23/eng/20220830
LC record available at https://lccn.loc.gov/2022028757
LC ebook record available at https://lccn.loc.gov/2022028758

Printed and bound in the United States of America.
SB 10 9 8 7 6 5 4 3 2 1

# CONTENTS

# INTRODUCTION

*Jumping Jenny* was published in 1933, when Anthony Berkeley was at the height of his literary powers. Under the name Francis Iles, he had recently published two highly successful crime novels, *Malice Aforethought* and *Before the Fact,* which were psychological studies respectively of a murderer going about his deadly work and a prospective victim awaiting her fate. Writing as Berkeley, he was continuing to explore the possibilities of the traditional detective novel with verve, originality, and a darkly ironic style of storytelling.

This was the ninth novel to feature Roger Sheringham, and not one of them was entirely orthodox. On the contrary, it amused Berkeley to play games with the conventions of crime writing. His previous outings had included *The Poisoned Chocolates Case,* with its dazzling array of possible solutions to a murder mystery, and *Murder in the Basement,* in which the puzzle of "whowasdunin" dominates the first part of the story; both novels have been reissued as British Library Crime Classics. In a preface to another of Sheringham's cases,

*The Second Shot*, Berkeley had prophesied that the detective novel would increasingly focus on puzzles of *character*, and although not all his own experiments succeeded, his forecast was not far off the mark.

Right from the start of this novel, Berkeley's dark humour and delight in the macabre are evident:

> *From the triple gallows three figures swung lazily, one woman and two men.*
>
> *Only a gentle creaking of their ropes sounded in the quiet night. A horn lantern, perched above the triangle of the cross-pieces, swayed in the slight wind, causing the three shadows to leap and prance on the ground in a grotesque dance of death, like some macabre travesty of a slow-motion film in silhouette.*
>
> *"Very nice," said Roger Sheringham.*
>
> *"It is rather charming, isn't it?" agreed his host.*

The setting is one of those "murder parties" which cropped up in various forms in a number of books written by leading lights of the Golden Age of detective fiction between the wars. As usual, murder rapidly becomes a reality as the hanged body of Ena Stratton is discovered. But is it really a case of murder, or did she take her own life? With most authors, the answer would be predictable, but Berkeley was perfectly capable of confounding the reader's expectations, even if, in a couple of the Sheringham books, the final surprise seems rather anti-climactic.

Ena Stratton is not a character with whom the reader is supposed to sympathise. Here, as in several of his other novels, Berkeley explores the nature of true justice (as opposed to the conventional forms of justice achieved by the law of the land). In times gone by, a hanged man was sometimes colloquially referred to as a "Jumping Jack," and Berkeley's choice of title is characteristic of his tone if arguably tasteless; this is no doubt why the book has sometimes been retitled *Dead Mrs Stratton*.

When Dorothy L. Sayers reviewed the novel in the *Sunday Times*, she said Berkeley had "kicked over the traces with glee and gusto. No infallible sleuth or cast-iron deductions for him… He is an adept at showing how, from a single set of premises, the over-ingenious mind may construct endless theories, all plausible and all wrong… If you are hard-boiled and disillusioned about detectives, you will find this tale very refreshing… The characterisation is lively, though subdued… Needless to say, Mr Berkeley has kept a cunning twist up his sleeve for the last page."

Golden Age detective fiction is sometimes referred to, in a patronising way, as "cosy." But there was nothing very cosy about the novels of Anthony Berkeley Cox (1893–1971) or indeed about his outlook on the world. Educated at Sherborne School and University College, Oxford, he was capable of great charm, wit, intelligence, and generosity. Yet he was also a complex and combative individual, a man of endless contradictions, some of which I explored in *The Golden Age of Murder*, a study of the leading figures in the Detection Club, which was founded in 1930 by Berkeley himself. He was gassed while serving in France during the First World War and never fully recovered his health; perhaps this misfortune contributed to the morbid aspects of his personality.

The final Roger Sheringham novel, *Panic Party* aka *Mr Pidgeon's Island*, appeared the year after *Jumping Jenny*.

Berkeley had been exceptionally industrious and productive, but his output began to diminish. Just three further novels (including the superb *Trial and Error*) appeared under the Berkeley name, while the third and last Francis Iles book, *As for the Woman*, made little impact.

My guess is that he was burned out, emotionally and creatively. He abandoned fiction, but any disillusion he may have felt regarding his career as a novelist did not cause his enthusiasm for the crime genre to wane. He had been a prolific reviewer during the 1930s and he continued to review regularly in the national press under the Francis Iles name, until ill-health finally intervened. His reviews show considerable insight and, although he was occasionally waspish, he was one of the first to recognise the merits of such younger writers as John Bingham, P. D. James, and Ruth Rendell, from the start of their careers.

As Berkeley and also as Iles, his influence proved significant and enduring. Julian Symons's *The Man Who Killed Himself* (1969) and Simon Brett's *A Shock to the System* (1989) are two entertaining novels which draw on the influence of *Malice Aforethought*, a book also referenced in *Eight Perfect Murders* (2020) by the bestselling American suspense writer Peter Swanson. New solutions to *The Poisoned Chocolates Case* have been devised, decades apart, by both Christianna Brand and myself. Meanwhile, the Detection Club thrives to this day, the world's oldest social network of crime writers and the brainchild of a truly extraordinary innovator.

—Martin Edwards
www.martinedwardsbooks.com

# A NOTE FROM THE PUBLISHER

The original novels and short stories reprinted in the British Library Crime Classics series were written and published in a period ranging, for the most part, from the 1890s to the 1960s. There are many elements of these stories which continue to entertain modern readers; however in some cases there are also uses of language, instances of stereotyping, and some attitudes expressed by narrators or characters which may not be endorsed by the publishing standards of today. We acknowledge therefore that some elements in the works selected for reprinting may continue to make uncomfortable reading for some of our audience. With this series, British Library Publishing and Poisoned Pen Press aim to offer a new readership a chance to read some of the rare books of the British Library's collections in an affordable paperback format, to enjoy their merits, and to look back into the world of the twentieth century as portrayed by its writers. It is not possible to separate these stories from the history of their writing and as such the following novel is presented as it was originally published with minor edits only, made for consistency of style and sense. We welcome feedback from our readers.

TO

W. N. ROUGHHEAD

*"Souvenir—very interesting"*

*The characters in this book are entirely imaginary, and have no relation to any living person.*

# Chapter I
## THE GALLOWS TREE

I

FROM THE TRIPLE GALLOWS THREE FIGURES SWUNG lazily, one woman and two men.

Only a gentle creaking of their ropes sounded in the quiet night. A horn lantern, perched above the triangle of the cross-pieces, swayed in the slight wind, causing the three shadows to leap and prance on the ground in a grotesque dance of death, like some macabre travesty of a slow-motion film in silhouette.

"Very nice," said Roger Sheringham.

"It is rather charming, isn't it?" agreed his host.

"Two jumping jacks, I see, and one jumping jenny."

"Jumping jenny?"

"Doesn't Stevenson in *Catriona* call them jumping jacks! And I suppose the feminine would be jumping jenny."

"I suppose it would."

"Morbid devil, Ronald," Roger said curiously, "aren't you?"

Ronald Stratton laughed. "Well, I thought at a

murderer-and-victim party the least one could have was a gallows. It took me quite a long time to stuff those chaps with straw. Two of my suits, and an old dress dug up from goodness knows where. I may be morbid, but I am conscientious."

"It's extremely effective," Roger said politely.

"It is, rather, isn't it? You know, I should hate to be hanged. So very ignominious, to say the least. Really, Roger, I don't think murder's worth it. Well, let's go down and have a drink."

The two men went towards the door, in a little gable of its own, which led from the big flat roof on which the gallows had been erected into the house. The little gable carrying the door projected at right angles from a larger one, and almost in the angle was a short flight of iron steps leading over the tiles and ending apparently in nothing. The glint of the bright moonlight on the metal caught Roger's eye, and he jerked his head towards it.

"What's up there? Not another flat?"

"Yes, a small one. I ran a flat across the top of those two parallel gables. They used to be an awful nuisance when there was any snow or stormy weather. I thought the flat roof would be rather pleasant as an observation point; one gets a big view from it. But I don't suppose I go up there once a year."

Roger nodded, and the two passed through the doorway and down the flight of stairs which led from the roof. They crossed the top landing of an ancient well-staircase, passed the open door of a very large room full of oak beams and dim corners in the gabled ceiling, where a dozen murderers and murderesses were dancing on a parquet floor to a very modern radio-gramophone, and walked into another room, scarcely less large, at the end of the landing.

As they stepped into the lighted area, it could be seen

that Roger's companion was picturesquely dressed in a black velvet suit and knee-breeches; he and his younger brother, David Stratton, represented the Princes in the Tower. Roger himself, clinging, like most of the men present, to the conventional dinner-jacket and black tie, had announced that he was Gentleman George Joseph Smith, of Brides in the Bath fame, who did not know that he ought to have come in a white tie and tails.

Stratton looked hospitable with bottles. "What will you have?"

"What have you got?" asked his guest cautiously.

Roger having been furnished with a tankard of old ale, and his host with a whisky-and-soda, the two men leaned their backs against the heavy oak cross-beam of the wide, open fire-place and, warming themselves pleasantly in the traditional masculine regions, continued to chat lightly upon sudden death.

Roger did not know Ronald Stratton particularly well. Stratton was something of a dilettante: a man in young middle-age, comparatively wealthy, who wrote detective stories because it amused him to do so. His detective stories were efficient, imaginative, and full of a rather gruesome humour. The idea of this party exactly carried out the light-handed treatment of death in his books. There were about a couple of dozen guests, certainly not more, and each one was supposed to represent a well-known murderer or his victim. The idea was not strictly original, but the embellishment of a gallows on the flat roof was, typically so.

The party was nominally in honour of Roger, who, with

half a dozen others, was staying in the house for the weekend; but Roger himself was not at all sure that he was not an excuse rather than a cause.

Still, he was not disposed to worry about that. He liked Stratton, who amused him; and the party, not yet an hour old, promised to be a good one. His eye wandered across the room to a far corner, where an exquisitely polished sofa-table, loaded with decanters and glasses, was doing somewhat vulgar duty as a bar. Most of the other guests were dancing to the wireless in the adjoining ball-room, but by the bar Mrs. Pearcey was telling Dr. Crippen the story of her life.

It was not the first time that Roger's eye had lingered on Mrs. Pearcey. Mrs. Pearcey seemed to invite the eyes of others to linger upon her; not, indeed, through her good looks, for she had few, nor through anything so coarse as ogling, but simply because she appeared determined that, wherever she might be, she should be noticed. Roger, always on the look-out for types, was interested. He felt, too, that it was probably significant that the lady should have chosen the dowdy but undoubtedly striking rôle of Mrs. Pearcey rather than the showier costume-part of Mary Blandy. There was a Mary Blandy, and undoubtedly Mrs. Pearcey was the more effective.

He turned to Stratton. "Mrs. Pearcey over there… I don't believe I've met her yet…it is your sister-in-law, isn't it?"

"It is." Ronald Stratton's voice had lost its usual humorous tone and become flat and expressionless.

"I thought so," Roger said carelessly, and wondered why Stratton's voice should have changed like that. It was plain that he did not very much like his sister-in-law, but

Roger thought that was hardly sufficient reason for such a very blank tone. However, it was obviously impossible to probe further.

Stratton began to ask questions about the cases with which his guest had been connected. Roger replied without his customary enthusiasm. His ears were directed towards the low conversation on the other side of the room, which was not so much a conversation as a monologue. It was impossible to hear the words, through the music which came from the ball-room, but the tone was eloquent; it meandered on and on, and Roger thought he could detect in it a note of noble endeavour thwarted, mingled with a deeper undercurrent of Christian resignation. He wondered what on earth the woman was talking about so interminably. Whatever it was, Dr. Crippen was plainly bored by it. Roger wished unblushingly that he could hear what it was all about.

The dance came to an end, and some of the dancers drifted in to the bar. A large man, with one of those pleasant, nobbly faces, strolled up to Stratton and Roger.

"Well, Ronald, my man…"

"Hullo, Philip. Been doing your duty?"

"No, yours. I've been dancing with your young woman. Perfectly charming, my dear fellow," said the new-comer, with an air of naïve sincerity which was in itself charming.

"That's rather what I think," Ronald grinned. "By the way, have you met Sheringham? This is Dr. Chalmers, Sheringham."

"How do you do?" said the doctor, shaking hands with obvious pleasure. "Your name's very familiar to me."

"Is it?" said Roger. "Good. It all helps sales."

"Oh, I didn't say I'd gone so far as to buy one of your books. But I have read them."

"Better and better," Roger grinned.

Dr. Chalmers stayed for a few moments, and then moved off to the bar to get his late partner a drink.

Roger turned to Stratton. "That's a particularly nice man, isn't it?"

"Yes," Stratton agreed. "His family and mine, and his wife's family, were all more or less brought up together; so the Chalmerses are really about my oldest friends. Philip's elder brother was my contemporary, and Philip is really a closer friend of my brother's than mine, but I like him immensely. He's absolutely genuine, nearly always says just what he thinks, and is the only man I've ever met called Philip who isn't a prig. And more I can't say for any man."

"Hear, hear," Roger agreed. "Hullo, is that the music? I suppose I'd better go and do a bit of duty. Introduce me to somebody I'd like to dance with, will you?"

"I'll introduce you to my young woman," Stratton said finishing off his drink.

"Odd," Roger remarked idly. "I always used to think you were married."

"I always used to be. Then we had a divorce. Now I'm going to do it again. You must meet my ex-wife some time. She's quite a nice person. She's here to-night, with her fiancé. We're the best friends in the world."

"Very sensible," Roger approved. "If I ever got married so that I could be divorced, I'm sure I should be so grateful to my wife that I'd want to be the best friends in the world with her."

They walked together towards the ball-room.

Roger noticed with interest that Mrs. Pearcey was just in

front of them, with an unknown man. Evidently she had torn herself away from Dr. Crippen.

"I say, Ronald!"

A low, guarded voice had assailed them from behind. Turning about, they beheld Dr. Crippen clinging, as it were desperately, to a large whisky-and-soda. No one else remained at the bar.

"Hullo, Osbert!" said Stratton.

"I say..." Dr. Crippen sidled towards them with a surreptitious air, as one not quite sure whether he is standing on solid ground again or not. "I say..."

"Yes?"

"I say," said Dr. Crippen with a confidential, guilty grin, "is your sister-in-law quite mad, Ronald? Eh? Is she?"

"Quite," said Stratton equably. "Come on, Sheringham."

II

Ronald Stratton's young woman proved to be a charming lady of about his own age, with very fair hair and a delightful smile, who admitted to two children of her own and the name of Mrs. Lefroy. She wore a seventeenth-century dress of white satin brocade, with hooped skirt, which admirably set off her fair colouring.

"You've been married before, then?" Roger asked conversationally, as they began to dance.

"I still am," replied Mrs. Lefroy surprisingly. "At least, I think I am."

Roger made an apologetic noise. "I somehow thought you were engaged to Ronald," he said lamely.

"Oh, yes, I am," said Mrs. Lefroy brightly.

Roger gave it up.

"I've got my *nisi,*" Mrs. Lefroy explained, "but not my absolute."

"This seems to be quite a modern party," Roger observed mildly, swerving somewhat violently to avoid another couple who did not seem to know what they were doing. As they passed, he saw that the couple was composed as to its feminine half of Mrs. Pearcey, who was talking so earnestly to her partner that he was able to devote little attention to the steering of her.

"Modern?" echoed Mrs. Lefroy. "Is it? Only as regards the Strattons and me, I think—if by 'modern' you mean not only readiness to recognise that you've made a mistake in your marriage, which is what most married couples always have done, but readiness to rectify it, which is what most of them still haven't the courage to do."

"And yet you're ready to try again?"

"Oh, yes. One mistake doesn't make a series. Besides, I never think a first marriage ought to count, do you? One's so busy learning how to be married at all that one can hardly help acquiring a kind of resentment against one's partner in error. And once resentment has crept in, the thing's finished. Anyhow, there one is, all nice and trained to the house, the complete article for the next comer. After all, one's got to cut one's teeth on something, but one doesn't cherish the dummy for the rest of one's life, does one?"

She laughed, and Roger laughed too. "But nature provides a second set of teeth. Haven't they to be cut on another dummy?"

"Oh, no, they just come, all ready cut. But I'm quite serious, Mr. Sheringham. One isn't the same person at thirty-four as one was at twenty-four, so why should one be expected to be suitable to the human being who fitted ten years earlier? Probably both of you have developed, on completely different lines. I think one should change partners when one's development is complete, except of course in the rare cases where the two do happen to have developed together."

"You needn't apologise for your divorce, you know," Roger murmured.

Mrs. Lefroy laughed again. "I wouldn't dream of doing any such thing. It just happens to be a subject I feel rather strongly about. What I think is, that our marriage-laws are all on the wrong lines. Marriage oughtn't to be easy and divorce difficult; it ought to be just the other way about. A couple ought to have to go up before a judge and say: 'Please, we've lived together for two years now and we're quite certain we're suited to each other. We've got our witnesses here to swear that we're terribly fond of each other and hardly ever quarrel, and we like the same things; and we're both quite healthy. We're certain we know our own minds, so *please,* can't we get married now?' And then they'd get their marriage *nisi*. And if by the end of six months the King's Proctor couldn't prove that they were unsuited after all, or didn't really love each other, or would be better apart, their marriage could be made absolute. Don't you think that's a very good idea?"

"It's the best idea I've ever heard about marriage yet," said Roger with conviction, "and I've produced a few myself."

"Oh, yes, I know. Your idea is that the best thing to do is not to get married at all. Well, there's something to be said for that. At least, I'm sure my poor brother-in-law-to-be would agree with you."

"Ronald's brother, you mean?"

"Yes. You know him, I suppose? That tall, good-looking, fair young man over there, dancing with the woman in the leg-of-mutton sleeves—Mrs. Maybrick."

"No, I don't know him. Why would he agree with me?"

"Oh!" Mrs. Lefroy looked a little guilty. "Perhaps I oughtn't to have said anything. After all, I only know what Ronald's told me."

"Is it a secret?" Roger pleaded, with unabashed curiosity.

"Well, I suppose so, in a way. Anyhow, I don't think I'd better say anything. But I shouldn't think," added Mrs. Lefroy with a smile, "that it will be a secret for long. You've only got to watch her."

"I'll watch her," said Roger. "In the meantime, do you mind telling me who you're supposed to be?"

"Haven't you guessed? I thought you were a criminologist." Mrs. Lefroy looked down, not without pride, at her billowing white skirts.

"So I am, not a costumier."

"Well, the Marquise de Brinvilliers, then. Didn't you recognise the arsenic-green of my necklace? I thought that was rather a subtle touch." She picked up her bag and white velvet gloves from the top of the grand piano and glanced round the room.

"I can see that Ronald's infecting you," Roger regretted.

He was sorry when Ronald came up, as if in response to the glance, and claimed his young woman. Mrs. Lefroy seemed to him a woman of ideas, and women of ideas are rare. So, for that matter, are men.

## III

Roger drifted, as a man will, to the bar.

His feeling that the party was going to be an interesting one was confirmed. It pleased him that ex-Mrs. Stratton should be present as well as future Mrs. Stratton, both of them all smiles and friendliness and completely unembarrassed. That is how things should be done in an enlightened age.

At the bar were Dr. Chalmers and another local doctor, who had once played rugger for England and was broad in proportion; he wore a red-and-white bandanna handkerchief round his neck and a black mask pushed up on his forehead, and his hands were splashed with red. The two were discussing, in the way of doctors, some obscene innard belonging to one of their less fortunate patients, which Dr. Mitchell had been engaged that afternoon in yanking out. Beside them stood, angrily, a thin, dark lady. Roger recognised her as the Mrs. Maybrick with the leg-of-mutton sleeves who had been dancing with David Stratton.

"Ah, Sheringham," Dr. Chalmers greeted him. "We're talking shop, I'm afraid."

"Do you ever talk anything else?" observed the thin, dark lady acidly.

"Mr. Sheringham, my wife," said Dr. Chalmers, with the greatest cheerfulness. "And this is Frank Mitchell; another of our local medicos."

Roger professed himself enchanted to meet Mrs. Chalmers and Dr. Mitchell.

"But whom," he added, scrutinising the latter's bandanna and mask, "are you supposed to represent? I thought I had them all at my finger-tips, but I can't place you. Are the two of you Brown and Kennedy?"

"No, Jack the Ripper," said Dr. Mitchell proudly. He displayed his red-splotched hands. "This is blood."

"Disgusting," said Mrs. Chalmers-Maybrick.

"I quite agree," Roger said politely. "I much preferred your methods. You used arsenic, didn't you? Or never used it, according to another school of thought."

"If I did, it's a pity I used it all," said Mrs. Chalmers, with a short laugh. "I might have saved some up, for a better purpose."

A little mystified, Roger produced a polite smile. The smile died away as he observed a significant glance pass between the two doctors: a glance which he could not quite interpret, but which seemed to convey a kind of mutual warning. In any case, both doctors immediately began to speak at once.

"I suppose you don't know many—Sorry, Frank."

"Talking of arsenic, I wonder if—Sorry, Phil."

There was an awkward pause.

This is odd, thought Roger. What the devil is going on in this place?

To fill up the pause he said: "And you still baffle me completely, Chalmers. You don't seem to be made up as anyone at all."

"Phil never will dress up," remarked Mrs. Chalmers resentfully.

Dr. Chalmers, who appeared to have remarkable powers of blandly ignoring the observations of his wife, replied heartily:

"I'm an undiscovered murderer. That's out of compliment to you. I know it's a theory of yours that the world's full of them."

Roger laughed. "I don't call that quite fair."

"And anyhow," put in Mrs. Chalmers, "Philip couldn't murder anyone to save his life." She spoke as if this was an old grievance of hers.

"Well, I'll be an undiscovered doctor-murderer if you like," said Dr. Chalmers, with complete equanimity. "I expect there are plenty of them about. Eh, Frank, my man?"

"Sure to be," agreed Dr. Mitchell with candour. "Hullo, is that the music stopping? I think I'll..." He finished off his drink and strolled towards the ball-room.

"He's only been married four months," remarked Mrs. Chalmers tolerantly.

"Ah," said Roger. The three exchanged smiles, and Roger wondered why it should be amusing when a man has only been married four months. He could not quite see why, but undoubtedly it was. Roger decided that almost anything to do with marriage was either comedy or tragedy. It depended whether one was looking at it from the outside or the in.

"Good gracious," exclaimed Dr. Chalmers, "you haven't got a drink, Sheringham. Ronald will never forgive me. What can I get you?"

"Thanks," Roger said, "I've been drinking beer."

He stood hopefully by, as one does when someone else is manipulating a bottle for our benefit. Watching, he could not help noticing the unhandy way in which Dr. Chalmers carried out that same manipulation. Instead of holding both bottle and tankard on a level with his chest in the usual way, he held them much lower; and after he had filled the latter, Roger noticed that he put down the tankard, which he had been holding in his right hand, and gave his left arm a jerk upwards with that hand before he could lift the bottle over the edge of the table. The disability was so obvious that Roger remarked on it.

"Thank you," he said, taking the tankard. "Got a bad arm?"

"Yes. A bit of trouble from the war, you know."

"Philip had the whole of his left shoulder shot away," said Philip's wife, in an annoyed way.

"Did you? That must be rather a nuisance to you, isn't it? I suppose you can't operate?"

"Oh, yes," Dr. Chalmers said cheerfully. "It doesn't bother me much, really. I can drive a car, and sail a yacht, and do a bit of flying when I can get off; and operate, of course. It's only the shoulder that's gone, you see. I can't raise my upper arm from the shoulder, but I can lift my forearm from the elbow. It might have been a lot worse." He spoke quite naturally, and without any of the false embarrassment which seems to overtake most men when forced to speak of their war-wounds.

"Rotten luck," said Roger sincerely. "Well, here's the best. Mrs. Chalmers, aren't you drinking anything?"

"Not just yet, thank you. I don't want to make an exhibition of *myself*."

"I'm sure you wouldn't do that," said Roger, a little taken aback. The remark had seemed so pointed that it could only have been directed at himself, but he could not understand why Mrs. Chalmers should have thought it necessary to be so rude.

"No, and I don't intend to," said Mrs. Chalmers grimly, and looked fixedly in his direction.

The next moment Roger saw that she was not looking at him at all, but over his right shoulder. He turned round and followed her eyes.

Several people had drifted in from the ball-room, and

among them was Ronald Stratton's sister-in-law, the woman dressed as Mrs. Pearcey. It was on her that Mrs. Chalmers's gaze was fixed.

She was standing by the bar, in company with a youngish, tall man whom Roger had not yet met, and he was evidently asking her what she would like.

"I'll have a whisky-and-soda, thanks," she said, in a voice which was just loud enough to be a shade ostentatious. "A large one. I feel like getting drunk to-night. After all, it's the only thing worth doing, really, isn't it?"

This time Roger joined in the significant glance which passed between Dr. and Mrs. Chalmers.

He finished up his beer, made his excuses to the Chalmers, and went off to look for Ronald Stratton.

"I must meet that woman," he said to himself, "drunk or sober."

## IV

Ronald was in the ball-room, twiddling with the wireless. The music to which they had been dancing had been provided by Königswusterhausen, and Ronald had decided it was too heavy; something French was indicated.

Three persons were remonstrating with him, for no particular reason beyond the strange prejudice most people have against seeing the owner of a large wireless set twiddling its knobs. One of them Roger knew to be Ronald's sister, Celia Stratton, a tall girl, picturesquely dressed as eighteenth-century Mary Blandy; the other two were Crippen, and a small woman dressed as a boy who was not difficult to recognise as Miss Le Neve.

A piercing soprano voice shot out from the wireless in one momentary shriek, instantly cut off, but not quickly enough for the manipulator's critics.

"Leave it alone, Ronald," begged Miss Stratton.

"It was perfectly all right as it was," reinforced Miss Le Neve.

"It's a funny thing," pronounced Dr. Crippen with some weight, as one who has given considerable thought to the point, "that people who have a wireless can't leave it alone for more than two seconds at a time."

"Blah," said Ronald, and continued to twiddle the knob.

A burst of jazz music rewarded him.

"There!" he said with pride. "That's a great deal better."

"It isn't a bit better," his sister contradicted.

"It's worse," opined Miss Le Neve.

"It's rotten," Dr. Crippen supported her. "Where is it?"

"Königswusterhausen," replied Ronald blandly, and with a wink at Roger walked quickly away.

Before the latter could follow him a question from Celia Stratton took his opportunity away. Did he know Mr. and Mrs. Williamson? Roger had to admit that he did not know Mr. and Mrs. Williamson. Dr. Crippen and Miss Le Neve were made acquainted with him under that title. Roger politely expressed admiration of their disguises.

"Osbert only had to put on a pair of gold-rimmed glasses," volunteered Mrs. Williamson. "He's just like Crippen, isn't he, Mr. Sheringham?"

"How unsafe you must feel, Lilian," said Celia Stratton.

"Can you wonder I want to leave the studio and get a place with a few more rooms? If the fit came on him there, I could never get away in time."

"You know perfectly well, Lilian," remonstrated her husband, "that you only wanted me to be Crippen so that you could be Miss Le Neve. Lilian never loses a chance of getting into trousers," explained Mr. Williamson with candour to the group in general.

"Why shouldn't I get into trousers if I want to?" demanded Mrs. Williamson, and sniffed.

"I hope you've got them fastened with a safety-pin at the back," said Roger fatuously.

Everyone looked at him inquiringly, and he wished he had not spoken.

"Miss Le Neve's trousers were too large for her," he had to explain, "and she took a tuck in them at the back with a safety-pin. The captain of the liner noticed it, and thought it rather odd."

"Lilian's certainly aren't too large for her," said Mr. Williamson, with a rude, husbandly laugh, "though they may be quite as odd. Eh, Lilian? What?"

"I like my trousers tight," said Mrs. Williamson, and sniffed again.

Roger, who was not so interested in these garments as the others appeared to be, turned the conversation with a jerk.

"I haven't met your sister-in-law yet, Miss Stratton," he said, in a blandly conversational tone. "I wonder if you'd introduce me?"

"David's wife? Yes, of course. Where is she?"

"She was at the bar a minute ago."

"She's mad," observed Mr. Williamson, with some interest.

"Really, Osbert!" expostulated his wife, with a glance at Celia Stratton.

"Oh, don't mind me," said Miss Stratton kindly.

Roger could not let this promising opening pass. "Mad? Is she? I like mad people. What particular form does your sister-in-law's madness take, Miss Stratton?"

"Oh, I don't know," Celia Stratton said lightly. "She's just generally mad, I expect, if Osbert says so." Roger noticed that, in spite of the lightness of her tone, there was an undercurrent of caution in Miss Stratton's voice. It was almost as if she had been glad to accept the idea of her sister-in-law's madness, in order to hide something worse.

"She wants to talk about her soul," explained Osbert Williamson with some gloom.

"Osbert isn't interested in souls," Mrs. Williamson explained. "Not having one of his own, he can't very well be."

"I'm not interested in her soul," pronounced Mr. Williamson. "But I'd keep an eye on her, Celia, if I were you. When I was with her she was swigging down double whiskies nineteen to the dozen and saying she wanted to get tight because it was the only thing worth while, or some nonsense."

"Oh, dear," sighed Miss Stratton, "is she in that mood? Perhaps I'd better go and look after her then."

"Why does she want to get tight?" Mr. Williamson asked her as she moved away.

"She thinks it clever. Mr. Sheringham, you'd better come with me if you want to meet her."

Roger went, with alacrity.

# Chapter II

## NOT A NICE LADY

### I

It was Ronald Stratton's custom to enliven his parties with charades. As he candidly explained, this was solely because he happened to like charades, and as the party was his, he did not see why he should not play them. Unfortunately for Roger, Ronald had decided upon charades at just that moment, and before the introduction could be effected, Celia Stratton had been called in to search the sitting-out places for unwilling players. Meanwhile sides were chosen out of those who were present; and since Mrs. David Stratton and Roger were on opposite sides, the acquaintanceship had again to be postponed. Roger was interested, however, to find that the lady's husband was on his side.

Although he had known Ronald Stratton slightly for some years, Roger had never before met David. As with so many brothers, the two were utterly unlike. Ronald was not particularly tall, David was quite six feet; Ronald was broad, David was slight; Ronald was dark, David fair; Ronald had a snub nose, David an aquiline one; Ronald was enthusiastic and, sometimes, rather childish in his amusements, David had a wearily disillusioned air, and his wit (for he was witty) had a cynical trend; one would have said that Ronald was the younger and David the elder, instead of the other way about.

Celia Stratton, who had been appointed captain of the side, took her duties seriously. It was their turn to perform first, and shepherding her flock out of the ball-room, she called firmly upon Roger for an actable word of two syllables. Roger instantly found his mind an utter and complete blank, and could only eye the bar with distant longing. In the end it was David Stratton who produced the word, and a neat little three-act drama to fit it, which, as an impromptu, impressed Roger considerably.

"Your brother's very much on the spot to-night," he remarked casually to Celia as they looked out props suitable to the inhabitants of Nineveh prior to the engulfment of Jonah by the whale.

"Oh, David can usually be relied on for something like that," said Miss Stratton.

"Can he? I wonder he doesn't try his hand at writing."

"David? He used to do a little before he married. *Punch,* you know, and some of the weeklies. We thought at one time that he might do something quite good. He began a book which promised very well."

"Why didn't he finish it?"

Celia Stratton bent a little lower over the drawer into which she was delving. "Oh, he got married," she said; and once again Roger felt that she was hiding something under the apparent indifference of her tone.

He looked at her curiously, but did not pursue the topic. Of two things, however, he felt quite sure: that somehow David Stratton's marriage had spoilt what might have been a successful career, and that Celia Stratton was not nearly so indifferent about it as she pretended.

More mystery, he thought.

Under cover of the general badinage he observed David Stratton more closely. At a first glance the latter looked animated enough, as he laughingly tried to persuade a pretty, plump woman whom everyone called Margot, to impersonate the whale; but it needed little more than a casual look to see that underneath the temporary excitement was an immense weariness. Indeed, the man looked tired to death, and not only tired, but positively ill; and yet Roger knew that his job of acting as his brother's estate agent was not at all an exacting one. Why, then, did he look as if he had hardly slept for a month?

Roger wondered if he were making mountains out of molehills.

The charades pursued their usual and hilarious course, and Roger found himself enjoying them absurdly. The Williamsons were on his side, and so was Dr. Mitchell and his pretty young bride, to whom her groom was as patently and as unselfconsciously devoted as any wife could have hoped. Roger found himself becoming quite sentimental in contemplation of the two of them. Jean Mitchell was dressed as Madeleine Smith, in crinoline and poke-bonnet, and looked quite charming enough to deserve all the attentions that were being poured out on her.

It was not until their own turn of activity was ended and they were sitting on a row of chairs at one end of the ballroom, waiting to deride the efforts of the other side, that a hint of drama underneath the froth began to show itself.

Roger found himself rather marooned.

On his left sat Celia Stratton, with Dr. Mitchell and his wife beyond her; on his right the plump lady called Margot, whom Roger had now discovered to be Ronald Stratton's late wife, with David Stratton separating her from her fiancé, a large and somewhat silent young man, whose name Roger had gathered to be Mike Armstrong. And almost immediately Celia Stratton had begun to engage in a low-toned and extremely earnest conversation with Dr. Mitchell, while ex-Mrs. Margot Stratton at the same time embarked on an exactly similar one with David Stratton. Roger hid his yawns, and wished that the other side would be a little quicker.

Then, willy-nilly, scraps of the two conversations began to reach him.

"But are you sure it was Ena who was responsible for it?" he heard Celia Stratton ask, in a worried voice.

"Positive," Dr. Mitchell replied grimly. "I went straight round to Mrs. Farebrother as soon as Jean told me, and she said that Ena had told her. In the strictest confidence, of course. Confidence! I told Mrs. Farebrother it was an infernal lie, of course, and I think I've stopped it going any farther in that direction, but how many other..." Dr. Mitchell lowered his voice.

Ena, observed Roger pensively to himself, is Mrs. David Stratton.

He became aware of David Stratton's voice, unguardedly loud, on his other side.

"I tell you, Margot, I can't stand it much longer. I'm about at the end of my tether."

"It's a damned shame, David," his late sister-in-law replied warmly. "You know what I thought about her. Ronald used to say I made things very awkward for him, but I couldn't help that. After that Eaves business I swore I'd never have her in any house of mine again, and I never did."

"I know," David Stratton rejoined gloomily. "It was a bit awkward, for me as well as Ronald, but I couldn't blame you. After all, as I pointed out to her, you might have done a good deal more than refuse to receive her here if you'd been really vindictive."

"That's what I told Ronald."

Roger shifted in his chair.

"I wouldn't mind if there was an atom of truth in any of it," said Dr. Mitchell, with sudden violence. "But these damnable *lies*..."

"I know. It's the way it takes her."

"Personally," broke in Jean Mitchell's small, clear voice, "I don't see that it matters. Everyone must know they're lies. What I can't understand is why she wants to do it."

"Oh, she's a pathological case, darling. There's no doubt about that. But really, Celia, something ought to be done about her. She's a danger to the community."

"Yes. But what? That's the trouble."

"I don't know, yet." Dr. Mitchell folded his arms and looked, for a pleasant man, quite formidable. "But I can promise you, she's going to be sorry she started monkeying with Jean. That's a little bit too much."

Roger took a notebook out of his pocket and began jotting down names. Among so many strangers, with so many different relationships, he found it difficult to keep his head clear.

Still the other side did not appear. Only suppressed gigglings, and an occasional hoot of laughter outside the door, testified to their continued existence.

"But why don't you *leave* her, David?"

"Money, of course. If only I could afford to keep her apart from me, I'd do it like a shot."

"Can't Ronald help at all?"

"No." David Stratton was firm enough about that.

"It's damnable." Margot Stratton stared ahead as if racking her brains for something that would help.

Celia Stratton turned to Roger.

"I quite forgot to ask you, Mr. Sheringham. Did you find everything in your room that you wanted?"

"Everything, thank you," said Roger politely.

II

Roger's list of his fellow-guests and hosts ran as follows:

Ronald Stratton *(Prince in Tower)*
David Stratton *Ditto*
Ena (Mrs. David) Stratton *(Mrs. Pearcey)*
Celia Stratton *(Mary Blandy)*
Margot (ex-Mrs. Ronald) Stratton *(?)*
Mike Armstrong *(?)*
Dr. Chalmers *(Undiscovered Murderer)*
Mrs. Chalmers *(Mrs. Maybrick)*
Dr. Mitchell *(Jack the Ripper)*

Mrs. Mitchell *(Madeleine Smith)*
Mr. Williamson *(Crippen)*
Mrs. Williamson *(Miss Le Neve)*
Mrs. Lefroy *(Marquise de Brinvilliers)*
Colin Nicolson *(Palmer)*

These, Roger considered, comprised all Ronald Stratton's intimates, and seemed to fall into a group of their own. There were a dozen or so more people present, all from the neighbourhood, but they kept more or less to themselves, and Stratton did not try to mingle the two groups. The doctors, of course, were local men, and they formed something in the nature of a connecting link between the two lots. Roger had been told by Stratton that the local group would probably leave early, and the house-party would then keep it up.

There were about half a dozen of the latter. The Williamsons, who lived in London, were staying the night, and so was Colin Nicolson, who was the assistant editor of a weekly paper for which Stratton did a good deal of work, and whom Roger had known and liked for some years. Mrs. Lefroy was staying, too, and Celia Stratton had come down to act as hostess for her brother. Roger himself had also been asked for the night.

When the charades were over at last, Roger once more tried to effect contact between himself and Ena Stratton, and once again he was foiled. Ronald himself had swung his sister-in-law on to the floor, to set the dancing in train again. Glancing round in a baffled way, Roger saw that Agatha Lefroy was sitting alone on a couch at one end of the room, and joined her.

"Do you mind if we don't dance?" he said. "I used to be considered rather good before the war, but somehow the old zest seems to have gone."

"Of course not," Mrs. Lefroy smiled. "Let's stop here. Anyhow, I'd much rather talk than dance. What shall we talk about?"

"Ena Stratton," Roger said promptly.

He was hardly surprised when even Mrs. Lefroy reacted in the usual way to that name. Her smile did not waver, she did not start or turn pale, but precisely the same guarded air showed itself to Roger's observation as she replied, brightly enough:

"She interests you?"

"She does. Decidedly. And I haven't even met her yet. Tell me about her."

"I don't know that there's much to tell you, is there? In what way, particularly?"

"Any way. I won't ask about her marriage, because you said that was a secret. Just tell me why you're afraid of her."

"Afraid of her?" Mrs. Lefroy echoed indignantly. "I'm not in the least afraid of her."

"Yes, you are," Roger said calmly. "Why?—or shall I ask Ronald?"

"No, don't ask Ronald," Mrs. Lefroy said quickly, and added, rather inconsequently: "Anyhow, he wouldn't tell you."

"Nor will you?" said Roger, half lightly and half seriously.

"You're really rather inquisitive, Mr. Sheringham, aren't you?"

"Intolerably. I can't help it. You see, I scent a mystery, and I can't bear mysteries."

"Oh," said Mrs. Lefroy slowly, "there's no *mystery* about Ena."

"And yet," Roger hazarded, "quite a number of people in this room cordially detest her."

"I can quite believe it," Mrs. Lefroy smiled. "She's really rather a dangerous woman."

"How can such a totally unimportant person be dangerous?" Roger asked, following the young woman in question round the room with his eyes. "And yet you're the second person within the last half-hour whom I've heard call her that. I suppose I ought not to ask you what she's been doing to Dr. Mitchell, and yet I wish I could."

"Oh, I'll tell you that. She's been spreading a ridiculous lie about his wife."

"Why?"

Mrs. Lefroy shrugged her shoulders. "She seems to enjoy doing that sort of thing."

"Which sort of thing? Lying for lying's sake, or doing an inoffensive person a bad turn?"

"Neither, exactly. I think it's really an opportunity to make herself appear important. That's her *idée fixe*. She must be the centre of things, the wonder of all beholders. Philip Chalmers—Ronald's great friend, you know—says she's a pronounced ego-maniac. No doubt that's as good a term for her as any."

"Williamson has a better one. He just says simply that she's mad."

Mrs. Lefroy laughed. "In a way, I suppose, she is. Anyhow, is that all you wanted to know?"

"Not quite. What's your own private trouble with her? Don't tell me, of course," Roger added kindly, "if you don't want to."

"I shouldn't dream of it. But I really don't mind, as it seems to worry you so much. I don't trust her, that's all."

"Don't trust her?"

"Ronald's been rather indiscreet in calling us engaged," Mrs. Lefroy explained. "It's all right, of course, in the family and so on, or should be, but, as I told you, I haven't got my absolute yet. Well, David warned Ronald this afternoon that Ena's been hinting that she could make trouble with the King's Proctor if she wanted to."

Roger whistled.

"Why should she want to?"

Mrs. Lefroy looked a little uncomfortable. "Oh, there are reasons, no doubt, from her point of view."

"Reasons for making trouble?"

"Reasons why she might be sorry to see Ronald marry again."

"Oh! Yes, I see."

It did not need very much perspicacity on Roger's part to guess something of what those reasons might be. Ronald and Margot Stratton had had no children. David and Ena had a small boy. As Roger knew, the boy was Ronald's godson. Ronald, who had a *flair* for business as well as for writing detective-stories, had made his money, not inherited it. It seemed likely that, as things had been, he might have made his godson his heir, with perhaps a life-interest for David. If he married again, another heir might present itself. It was decidedly in Ena Stratton's interests that her brother-in-law should not marry again.

"Yes, I see," Roger repeated. "Quite like a plot for one of Ronald's own detective-stories, isn't it?"

By Mrs. Lefroy's smile he knew that his guess had been

right. "So Ronald says himself. He looks on it as a joke," she added, "but it might be quite serious. An unscrupulous woman would do things that an equally unscrupulous man might boggle at."

"Yes, that's quite true. Is she unscrupulous?"

"Perfectly, I should think," said Mrs. Lefroy with resignation.

There was a short silence.

Then Roger looked puzzled. "I don't know much about these things, but would it really worry the King's Proctor to know that you were going to marry Ronald when you're free? I know the King's Proctor is very easily worried, but that does seem almost hypersensitive."

Mrs. Lefroy looked at the tip of her neat slipper. "Once he begins making special inquiries, who knows what might happen to him?" she said cryptically.

"Collusion, like a worm i' the bud, might feed on his damask cheek, as my friend, Lord Peter Wimsey, might say," Roger nodded, with sympathetic understanding. "Shall I strangle the woman for you?"

"I wish to heaven someone would," said Mrs. Lefroy, with sudden bitterness. "We all do."

Roger examined his finger-nails. "If I were Mistress Ena Stratton," he thought to himself, "I'd watch my step."

## III

In the end the introduction was effected with complete ease.

"Oh, Ena," said Ronald Stratton, "I don't think you've met Roger Sheringham yet, have you? Mr. Sheringham, my sister-in-law."

Ena Stratton looked at Roger with large eyes swimming with discipleship, *weltschmerz,* humble pride, and all the other things with which a high-souled young woman's eyes should swim when confronted with a successful author. Roger saw that these proper emotions were being registered for him almost automatically.

"How do you do?" he said, without any *weltschmerz* at all.

Ena Stratton was a young woman of about twenty-seven. She was moderately tall, of good, athletic-looking figure, with dark, almost black hair, which she wore cut in a straight fringe across her already rather low forehead; her hands and feet were on the large side. Her face was neither exactly ugly, nor exactly pretty. It was a hag-ridden face, Roger thought, with big grey eyes whose promise was counteracted by the wide, thin-lipped cruelty of her mouth. When she smiled, the corners of her mouth seemed in some curious way to be drawn downwards rather than up. There were innumerable wrinkles at the corners of her eyes, and two deeply graven lines running down from her nostrils. Her complexion was sallow.

Judging by appearances, Roger thought, not a nice person. He wondered why David Stratton had married her. Presumably she had looked nicer then. That neurotic type stamps its own face very early.

"Shall we dance?" said Roger.

"I'd rather have a drink. I haven't had one for at least half an hour." She spoke slowly, and her voice was not unpleasant, rather deep and with a particularly clear enunciation. She managed to convey that for a woman of her sophistication not to have had a drink for at least half an hour was quite too ridiculous.

Roger piloted her to the bar, and asked what she would have.

"A whisky, please. And don't drown it."

Roger gave her a stiff whisky-and-soda, and she tasted it.

"I think I'll have a little more whisky in this, please. I like it almost neat, you know."

"Ass of a woman!" thought Roger. "Why does she imagine it's clever to like her whisky neat, and a good deal too much of it at that?"

He handed her the amended drink.

"Thanks. Yes, that's better. I feel like getting drunk to-night."

"Do you?" said Roger lamely.

"Yes. I don't often feel like that, but I do to-night. Really, sometimes getting drunk seems the only thing worth while in life. Don't you ever feel like that?"

"Only in private," said Roger, rather prudishly. He noticed that she was repeating a set of remarks which he had overheard earlier, almost word for word. Evidently Mrs. Stratton was extremely proud of her own appreciation of intemperance.

"Oh," she expostulated, "there's no point in getting drunk in private."

In other words, thought Roger, she admits to being an exhibitionist. Well, that was probably exactly what she was: an exhibitionist. And rather a crude one at that.

Aloud he said:

"By the way, I really must congratulate you on your dress, Mrs. Stratton. It's extremely good. Just like Mrs. Pearcey's in Madame Tussaud's. I recognised her at once. How very brave of you to come as a charwoman, hat and all, against such competition."

"Competition? Oh, you mean Celia, and Mrs. Lefroy.

But you see, I'm a character-actress. Costume parts don't interest me at all. Anyone can do a costume part, don't you think?"

"Can they?"

"Oh, yes, I think so. Of course one of my best parts actually was a costume one. Did you see 'Sweet Nell of Old Drury'? No? It was a wonderful part; but of course it was character, not just being able to wear the dresses, that I got it on."

"I didn't know you'd been on the stage."

"Oh, yes," Mrs. Stratton sighed dramatically. "I was on the stage for a time."

"Before you were married, of course?"

"No, since. But I'd studied for it before. I didn't find," said Mrs. Stratton earnestly, "that marriage gave me the fulfilment I expected from it."

"And the stage did?"

"For a time. But even that didn't satisfy me altogether. But I managed to find fulfilment in the end. Can you imagine what it was that brought it? I expect *you* can, Mr. Sheringham."

"I can't think."

"Oh, and I did think you'd understand. The women in your books are always so very true. Why, having a baby. It's the only possible way really to fulfil oneself, Mr. Sheringham," said Mrs. Stratton with much intensity.

"Then I look like remaining unfulfilled," said Roger ribaldly.

Mrs. Stratton smiled tolerantly. "For a woman, of course, I meant. A man can fulfil himself in so many ways, of course; can't he?"

"Oh, yes," Roger agreed. He was wondering what people

like Mrs. Stratton really meant by that cant word, if indeed they meant anything at all. In any case, he had felt as yet no urge to be fulfilled in any of the many ways.

"Your writing, for instance," Mrs. Stratton added, rather helpfully.

"Yes, yes, of course. That fulfils me all right. Shall I put your glass down?"

"That would be rather wasting an opportunity, wouldn't it?" said Mrs. Stratton, with ponderous kittenishness.

As Roger poured out the drink he pondered on the determination with which Mrs. Stratton had dragged into the conversation, within three minutes, what were evidently the two most important achievements of her life: that she had been on the stage, and that she had had a baby. It was plain, too, that in Ena Stratton's opinion these two events reflected the greatest possible credit on Ena Stratton.

What Roger himself thought reflected credit on Ena Stratton was that in spite of the amount of whisky she had apparently absorbed during the evening, she showed no sign at all of approaching the only thing really worth while in life.

"Thank you," she said, as he gave her the replenished glass. "Let's go up on the roof, shall we? I feel stifled here, in this crowd. I want to look at the stars. Would you mind frightfully?"

"I should love to look at the stars," said Roger.

Carrying their glasses, they went up the little staircase that led to the big flat roof. In the middle of it the three straw figures still dangled from their heavy gallows. Mrs. Stratton gave them a tolerant smile.

"Ronald is really rather childish sometimes, isn't he, Mr. Sheringham?"

"It's a great thing to be able to be childish sometimes," Roger maintained.

"Oh, yes, I know. I can be absurdly childish when the fit takes me, of course."

The edge of the roof was bounded by a stout railing. The two leaned their elbows on it and gazed down into the blackness that shrouded the back kitchens below. Mrs. Stratton had apparently forgotten that she wanted to gaze upwards, at the stars.

The April night was mild and fine.

"Oh, dear," sighed Mrs. Stratton, "I'm an awful fool, I expect."

Roger deliberated between a polite "Oh, no," a blunt "Why?" or a not very tactful but encouraging "Yes?"

"I feel so terribly introspective to-night," pursued his companion, before he could decide on any of these choices.

"Do you?" he said feebly.

"Yes. Do you often feel introspective, Mr. Sheringham?"

"Not very often. At least, I try not to encourage it."

"It's terrible," said Mrs. Stratton, with gloomy relish.

"It must be."

There was a pause, for contemplation of the terribleness of Mrs. Stratton's introspection.

"One can't help asking oneself, is there really any use in life?"

"A dreadful question," said Roger, keeping his end up as well as he could.

"I've had a baby, I suppose I could say I've had some success on the stage, I've got a husband and a home—but is it *worth while*?"

"Ah!" said Roger sadly.

Mrs. Stratton moved a little nearer to him, so that their

elbows touched. "Sometimes I think," she said sombrely, "that the best thing to do would be to put an end to it all."

Roger did not reply that Mrs. Stratton would apparently find a number of persons in hearty agreement with this sentiment. He merely remarked, in a suitably hushed voice: "Oh, come."

"I do, really. If only one could find an easy way out..."

"Ah!" said Roger, repeating himself.

"You don't think it would be cowardly?"

"Come, come, Mrs. Stratton. You mustn't talk like this, you know. Of course you don't mean it."

"But I do! I assure you, Mr. Sheringham, I lie awake for hours sometimes, just wondering whether a gas-oven isn't after all the easiest solution."

"Solution of what?"

"Life!" exclaimed Mrs. Stratton with drama.

"Well, it certainly is a solution. One can't deny that."

"You don't *mind* me talking to you like this, do you?"

"Not in the least. On the contrary, I take it as a great compliment."

Mrs. Stratton moved an inch nearer. "I've been so much looking forward to meeting you, all the evening. I thought those silly charades would never come to an end. I knew I should be able to talk to you, and I've been feeling so introspective to-night. It's such a relief to talk it out."

"It must be," said Roger heartily.

"Do you believe in the soul?" asked Mrs. Stratton.

"Now she's really off," thought Roger. "The soul," he repeated in a meditative voice, as if weighing its value as an object of belief.

"I do. For some people. But I don't believe all of us have souls." Her voice throbbed on.

As the discourse proceeded, Roger began to perceive that the lady might be talking about souls, but she was undoubtedly preoccupied with bodies. She was pressing hard against him, her hand was on his sleeve, her whole attitude was one invitation to the waltz.

Very odd, thought Roger, and edged away.

Mrs. Stratton immediately pursued him.

As a rule Roger had no need to be pursued. If a lady happened to attract him, and herself was not averse, he saw no reason for wasting useful time. But Mrs. Stratton did not attract him. More, she definitely repelled him. Roger could at that moment imagine no woman in this world with whom he less wanted to dally.

He therefore decided to end the interview. He had no wish to hear more about Mrs. Stratton's soul, its presence or absence, or about her singular powers of self-analysis, or about her considered tendency towards self-immolation. Nor, on this last head, had he any good news to take down to such as would have welcomed an impending self-immolation. It is a truism that those who talk about suicide shrink from committing it, while those who do commit it never chatter about it in advance. There was no chance of Mrs. Stratton ever gratifying her relations-in-law with good news about a gas-oven.

For the rest, the lady bored him quite intolerably. She had not proved nearly so interesting as he had hoped; she was just a ridiculous mass of blind self-conceit—an ego-maniac, no doubt, as Dr. Chalmers had said. Any more time spent on her was time wasted, for even as a type she was too exaggerated to be of the least use to a writer of fiction who had to preserve the probabilities.

Roger waited until a sentence came to an end, and then asked abruptly if that were not the music?

Mrs. Stratton agreed perfunctorily that it might be the music.

"We must be getting down," said Roger, and led the way.

At the entrance to the ball-room he got rid of her, and sought the bar. He felt he needed a drink.

Chatting together there he found Williamson and Colin Nicolson, who with a paper frill stuck into his dress-waistcoat was calling himself William Palmer. Roger knew Nicolson tolerably well, a hefty young Scotchman who was a better rugger forward than an assistant editor, and a better fisherman than either.

"Ah, Sheringham, been taking the air?"

"Hullo, Colin, is that beer you're drinking? Can you find me a tankard?"

"Certainly I can. It's grand stuff too. Here's all the best. You know Williamson, don't you? Did you ever see anything more magnificent than his disguise? It's Crippen to the life. Upon my word, it is."

Williamson bestowed on Roger his slightly guilty, ruminative grin. "You were a long time on the roof, weren't you, Sheringham?"

"It seemed a long time," said Roger frankly.

"Did she tell you she was feeling terribly introspective to-night?"

"She did."

"Did she say that marriage hadn't given her enough fulfilment, or whatever it was?"

"She did."

"Did she tell you that she sometimes thought the best

thing to do would be to put an end to it all, if only one could find an easy way out?"

"She did."

"Did she talk like hell about her infernal soul?"

"Like hell she did."

"She's mad," said Mr. Williamson simply.

"She is," said Roger.

"What's all this?" asked Nicolson, bewildered. "Who's been talking about her infernal soul?"

"I name no names," said Mr. Williamson solemnly, "but it'll be your turn next."

"But what's it all about, man? Here, Ronald, ask these two what the deuce they're talking about, will you?"

Ronald Stratton was coming towards them, his face decorated with a large grin.

"Here, Sheringham," he said happily, "what have you been doing to my poor sister-in-law? Really, I'm surprised at you."

"What do you mean?"

"She's just told me that you lured her up on the roof and tried to flirt with her there, quite drastically. I gather it was all she could do to hold you off. She confided to me that you're the most disgusting man she's ever met."

"The devil she did!" said Roger, really annoyed.

# Chapter III
## SOMEONE OUGHT TO BE MURDERED

I

"Ronald, dance an Apache dance with me. Oh, Ronald, do dance an Apache dance with me. David, Ronald won't dance an Apache dance with me."

"Won't he, dear? Well, never mind."

"But I do mind. I want to dance an Apache dance. Ronald, you are a pig."

Everybody pretended not to notice Ena Stratton in the middle of the ball-room floor.

It was close on one o'clock. The local contingent, with the exception of the two doctors and their wives, had left nearly an hour ago. The party was warming up.

"Well, if you won't dance an Apache dance with me, Ronald, I'm going to climb up on the beam. David, give me a start."

Across the ball-room ran a big oak beam, about seven feet from the ground, part of the structure of the heavily timbered roof. It was Ronald's custom, when he felt so disposed, to take a flying leap at it, swing himself up, and then taunt his male guests into trying to join him there. This time his sister-in-law was bent on forestalling him.

"Aren't you going to applaud the athletic introvert?" Roger dryly asked Margot Stratton.

"No, I'm not. Ena's only making an exhibition of herself, as usual. Don't take any notice of her, Mr. Sheringham."

Mike Armstrong said nothing.

"There seems a conspiracy not to take any notice of her."

"I can't think why Ronald asked her. I never would. She's made an exhibition of herself at every single party here that I remember. I suppose he wanted David, and couldn't get him without her. Poor David!"

"He's very patient with her."

"Too patient. That's the trouble. Philip Chalmers says that what Ena needs is to be married to a great big he-man, who'd give her a sound thrashing every now and then. That's the only way to keep her in order. David's far too civilised for her."

Mike Armstrong said nothing.

"I hardly need to ask whether you like her," said Roger with a smile. Out of the corner of his eye he could see the lady in question struggling ungracefully to get abreast of the beam. Everywhere in the room people were talking in little knots, carefully not watching. Only her long-suffering husband stood by, to catch her if she fell.

Margot Stratton laughed. "I can't stand the sight of her. Luckily we're not on speaking terms, which saves a lot of trouble."

Mike Armstrong said nothing.

"It must have been very awkward for you, to refuse to have your own sister-in-law in the house?"

"She wasn't my sister-in-law; she was Ronald's. No, I don't think it was awkward. And in any case, she brought it on herself. She did her best once to do me a very bad turn, when I was perfectly friendly with her, and it was the sort of thing one just couldn't forgive."

Mike Armstrong broke his silence. "What was it?" he asked gruffly.

"Oh, far too bad to tell you, Mike," Margot said. She spoke lightly, but Roger had an idea that she was telling the truth.

Mike Armstrong bent a frowning glance on the clambering creature who had dared to do his lady-love a bad turn.

With a final spasm the creature succeeded in getting right way up on the beam. "Hullo, everyone!" she called.

From the other end of the room Ronald alone looked round. "Very clever, Ena," he said perfunctorily. "Now see if you can get down again."

Somebody put a record on the gramophone, and people began to dance again. As Margot Stratton and Mike Armstrong moved off, Roger strolled across the room to join Colin Nicolson who, like himself, did not find much pleasure in dancing.

"Well, Colin, going to accept the lady's challenge and have a try at the beam?"

Nicolson made a Scotch noise of disgust. "It's a sad thing to see a woman making such a fool of herself. Well, Sheringham, how's the criminology?"

"Ah!" said Roger, and they plunged happily into a discussion of the murder case of the moment. Among his other accomplishments Nicolson numbered a deep interest in criminology, with a minute knowledge of every murder of importance during the last hundred years. Roger had often been able to obtain from him details of almost forgotten crimes, which had been of considerable help to him in his work.

It was not long, however, before their attention was distracted by a repetition of Mrs. Stratton's importunities.

"Ronald, I insist on your dancing an Apache dance with me. I've an urge for it. Do dance an Apache dance with me, Ronald."

"I'm not your husband, Ena. Ask David."

"Oh, David couldn't do an Apache dance to save his life. Come on, Ronald. I shall probably run amok if you won't, and you wouldn't like that."

Roger and Nicolson exchanged looks.

"That's a very irritating woman," said Nicolson mildly. "What's the matter with her?"

"Exhibitionism," Roger explained. "The ordinary dancing doesn't give her a chance to show herself off. She must be the centre of the picture all the time. You notice she won't perform with her husband."

"Why not?"

"Too mild for her. She knows he wouldn't throw her about enough. And Ronald might. Besides, Ronald doesn't want to, and that in itself is enough for her."

"I've no patience with that sort. Hullo, Ronald's going to take her on."

Roger's prophecy was fulfilled. It appeared that Ronald knew quite well what was wanted of him, and he proceeded to give it in full measure.

"All right, Ena. I'll dance an Apache dance with you."

He caught his sister-in-law's hand, swung her round with all his strength, and let go. She shot across the wide floor, ended up on her hands and knees, and darted back for more. For a full three minutes Ronald threw her about, in and out of the other dancers, who refused to clear the floor for the pair. To Roger and Nicolson, looking on, it seemed that Ena Stratton must have suffered considerably in the process; but from the wailing outcry she raised when Ronald refused to maltreat her any more, it was clear that she had prodigiously enjoyed this singular amusement.

"And she the mother of a fine wee son," said Nicolson disgustedly.

Roger, the only person in the room who had watched the performance with any real interest, nodded gently. "It's typical, of course, and significant too."

"Significant of what?"

"Of everything that has happened to that young woman so far—and of anything that might happen to her in the future."

II

"Well, well," said Dr. Chalmers. "Time we were going home, I suppose?"

"You always want to go home as soon as I'm beginning to enjoy myself," said his wife bitterly.

"I've got to do a day's work to-morrow, my dear. It's nearly half-past one."

"Not just yet," Mrs. Chalmers pleaded. "Frank and Jean aren't going yet, are you, Frank?"

"Would you like to stay on a bit, darling?" Dr. Mitchell asked his wife.

"Yes, rather. I'm enjoying it."

"Sure you're not tired?" Dr. Mitchell asked anxiously.

"Not a bit."

"Well, we shall stay on for a bit, Lucy."

"There you are, Philip. Frank and Jean aren't going yet, and he's got to do a day's work to-morrow. We can stop for a bit too. You know Ronald's parties go on till about four."

"Sorry, dear," said Dr. Chalmers with the utmost heartiness. "Frank may be able to stand late hours, I can't. Run and get your cloak on, there's a good girl."

Roger turned away, marvelling. He did not know much about marriage, but he did know that such firmness in husbands is rare. Ena Stratton ought to have married Dr. Chalmers. He might have been able to keep her in order.

Ronald came running up the stairs. "Phil, you're wanted on the telephone."

"Hurray!" exclaimed Mrs. Chalmers callously, arresting her reluctant progress downstairs. "I hope it's a call, and I hope it keeps him out for *hours*."

"Loathsome woman," laughed Dr. Chalmers, unperturbed, and went downstairs.

As things turned out, it was a call.

"I shall be about an hour," said Dr. Chalmers.

"Good," said Mrs. Chalmers.

The party then resumed its course.

A little group was sitting at one end of the ball-room in amicable converse—Mrs. Lefroy, Ronald and David Stratton, Roger, and Nicolson. To them entered Ena Stratton.

"David, I'm bored. Let's go home." The David Strattons lived in a small house not five hundred yards away from the gates of Ronald's drive.

"Nonsense, Ena. You don't want to go home yet," said Ronald. "You'll spoil the party."

"I can't help that. I'm bored."

"Sit down, my dear, and don't be rude to your kind brother-in-law," said David.

"I won't sit down. And he isn't kind: he wouldn't do an Apache dance with me till I made him. Come on, David. Let's go."

"But I don't want to go yet."

"But I do. Well, give me the key, if you won't come. I tell you, I'm bored."

Roger wondered if everyone else was feeling as uncomfortable as this exchange was making him. He caught Mrs. Lefroy's eye and they smiled, surreptitiously and ruefully.

David Stratton could not recognise an opportunity when he saw one. Instead of handing the key over, thankfully, he attempted to persuade his wife to stay.

"Don't be an ass, David," said Ronald. "Give her the key if she really wants to go."

"I do," said Ena.

"All right, then, if you really want to. Here it is."

Ena took the key and balanced it on the palm of her hand.

"I don't think I will go after all. Let's do something amusing."

"Ena!" shouted Ronald.

"What?"

"Good night."

"But I'm not going."

"Yes, you are. You wanted to, and you shall. Besides, you're bored."

"Only because I'm tired of dancing. I shouldn't be if only we could do something amusing."

"Well, we're not going to do anything amusing, so off you go. I can't stand the sight of bored guests about the place. Good night."

Ena plumped herself down in a vacant chair, laughing triumphantly.

"Now she's got our attention, she's happy again," Roger confided to Mrs. Lefroy.

Ronald was happy, too, at the prospect of getting rid of Ena.

"Good night, Ena," he repeated.

"No, no, I'm not going. I've changed my mind. It's a woman's privilege to change her mind, you know."

"I don't care about that. You said you were going, and you are." Ronald spat ostentatiously on his hands. "Come on, David. You take her head, and I'll take her heels."

"Ronald doing the he-man stuff," said Roger to Mrs. Lefroy. "Take warning."

"They're only joking."

"Not altogether. Ronald's pretending to joke, but he's extremely annoyed; and I'm not surprised. What's the betting on him getting rid of her?"

"About a hundred to one against, I should think," said Mrs. Lefroy, not very hopefully.

With merry laughter the trio set about their tussle. Ronald caught his sister-in-law by the heels, David took her shoulders. On the surface it was just meaningless horse-play. At any rate, Ena herself seemed to be thoroughly enjoying it as such, while she pretended to struggle and resist.

The two men carried her, kicking and shrieking with laughter, across the floor.

Then, all of a sudden, by the door, Ena precipitated a change. She aimed a really vicious kick at Ronald, she struck up with her fists at her husband's face, and she screamed out:

"Let me go, you swine! Damn you, let me go."

They let her go, with a thud on the parquet floor.

Ena scrambled to her feet, rushed out of the room, and banged the door behind her with a crash that shook the house.

"Well, well, well," said Roger to Mrs. Lefroy.

## III

David Stratton stood looking uncertainly at the closed door.

"Oh, let her be," said Ronald.

David shrugged his shoulders. Then he walked back to the group where he had been sitting.

"Sorry, everyone," he said briefly, a flush on his usually rather pale face.

Everyone began to be as nice to him as they could, with the result that a perfectly unnatural atmosphere was created, and it was all rather embarrassing. Roger made what was probably a popular movement when he rose to his feet with the remark that a drink he must and would have, and carried David Stratton off with him to the bar, where he gave him a stiff whisky-and-soda and talked firmly to him about the exploits of the M.C.C. cricket team in Australia the previous winter—a topic in which, somewhat to his surprise, he discovered Stratton to be passionately interested.

In the meantime the party, relieved of Ena Stratton's blighting presence, went on with renewed vigour; dancing was resumed, those who wanted to do so stood in little groups and discussed, with the academic ferocity appropriate to two A.M., such questions as interested them, and everything in the ball-room was harmony.

At a quarter-past two David Stratton joined his brother and Roger, who happened to be together at the bar, and announced that he thought he must be pushing off.

"Don't go yet, David. Everyone will think they ought to go too, if they see you slinking away."

"I think I'd better."

"If you're thinking of Ena, much better leave her alone for a bit longer. She'll take it out on you as usual if you get back before she's safely asleep."

"Still," said David, with a rueful smile, "I think I'd better, if you don't mind."

"All right, if you really mean it. Anyhow, good luck."

"Thanks. I'll probably need it. Good night, Sheringham."

When he had gone, Ronald sighed.

"I'm afraid the poor lad's in for a nasty quarter of an hour."

"But he didn't do anything."

"Oh, that doesn't matter. He's always the scapegoat, when that maniac of a woman doesn't think she's had enough admiration. David's such a good chap, and she leads him an absolute dog's life. Oh, well, thank heaven I'm a bachelor."

"Very temporarily, though?"

"Oh, very," said Ronald with a laugh.

"Once a married man, always a married man, I'm afraid," Roger said compassionately. "Both you and your brother are marrying types, aren't you?"

"Yes, I suppose so," Ronald agreed, and swallowed a sip of

his whisky-and-soda. "Poor David, though. A first marriage should never be binding."

Roger, who had heard something like this already during the evening, knew what line to take. "One develops," he said tactfully.

"Yes, of course. But apart from that one hasn't the knowledge of the other sex. An experienced man might have seen through Ena during the engagement, and been able to save his soul; David was far too green. And now that he has..."

"Seen through her?"

"No, met the girl who would be exactly right for him. Yes, it's very tough luck."

"There's no chance of a friendly divorce?"

"None. Ena would certainly never agree. She's got her bird in its cage, and it wouldn't be she who'd ever open the door. So David hasn't approached her on the topic at all. She'd only be more impossible than ever if she knew he was in love with someone else. I don't know why I'm telling you all this, Sheringham?"

"You should drink beer instead of whisky," Roger suggested.

"Perhaps that's it. Anyhow, I apologise for inflicting all this family history on you. It can't possibly interest you."

"On the contrary, all human relationships interest me, especially tangles. But I really am very sorry for your brother. Isn't it possible for anything to be done?"

"Nothing short of murder," said Ronald gloomily.

"And that," said Roger, "always does seem to me a little drastic. Well, here's luck to you, Ronald, at any rate."

"Thanks," said Ronald, brightening. "Yes, my goodness, Sheringham, I've struck it lucky. Agatha really is..." His conversation threatened to become maudlin. Ronald should have stuck to beer.

"Yes, rather," said Roger hastily. "Look here, hadn't we better be getting back to the ball-room?"

# Chapter IV

## SOMEONE IS MURDERED

### I

Dr. Philip Chalmers ran his car into the garage-yard, which had once been the stable-yard. His radiator had nearly boiled on the way back, and he wanted to fill it up now and not keep Lucy waiting when they came down. He had had to drive past, but not across, the big semicircle of gravel in front of the house to reach the yard, and in the moonlight had seen three cars still standing there, so evidently the party had not broken up yet. Without bothering to work it out, Dr. Chalmers knew that one of these cars must be the Mitchells', one the David Strattons', and the other the one which had brought Margot Stratton and Mike Armstrong from London, whither they were returning that night. The party therefore remained exactly as he had left it three-quarters of an hour ago.

Dr. Chalmers was a little sorry, because that meant that it would be he who would break up the gathering. Lucy would be annoyed, too, because the visit had not taken so long as he had expected; he had been only three-quarters of an hour over it instead of the hour he had promised her. But that could not be helped. Dr. Chalmers was tired, and he intended to get to bed as soon as he possibly could, party or no party, Lucy or no Lucy. Late hours did not suit him any longer. Dr. Chalmers mildly envied Ronald, who, in spite of being three years older, seemed to thrive on late hours.

While he was filling his radiator he heard one of the cars starting up and, a moment later, saw its tail-light disappearing down the drive. That was rather a relief. He and Lucy would not now be the first to leave. As, a minute later, he passed the two remaining cars on his way to the front door, Dr. Chalmers had the curiosity to see which one it was that had gone. He noticed that it was David's. Poor David! Dr. Chalmers sighed. That damnable Ena had spoiled the evening again. Dr. Chalmers wished for the thousandth time that he could somehow wangle a certificate and get her put into an asylum; but that, of course, was impossible.

The latch was still up on the front door, and Dr. Chalmers walked in.

As he climbed the stairs he could hear the radio-gramophone in the ball-room. So they were still dancing. Turning the last angle of the staircase, Dr. Chalmers saw a back disappearing through the ball-room door which looked like Ronald's. He called out a greeting, but the owner of the back evidently had not heard it, for the door was closed the next instant behind him. As his head came level with the floor of the bar-room Dr. Chalmers looked in there, but the room was empty. A last, very small drink would be pleasant, after his cold drive. He took a step or two into the room, and then remembered that he was still without his pipe, which he had missed badly on the journey back. He was dying for a smoke; the drink could wait. He had an idea that he had left his pipe in the sun-parlour, after he had been sitting up there with Margot.

Dr. Chalmers went up on to the roof. Any noise his footsteps might have made on the landing carpet was drowned in the music from the big gramophone, but Dr. Chalmers did not appreciate that.

The sun-parlour was apparently empty, for the lights were out. Dr. Chalmers switched them on, and glanced round for his pipe. He saw, not the pipe, but Ena Stratton, lying in a basket-chair and frowning at him.

"Why, hullo, Ena," he said, in the pleasant, hearty tones with which he was accustomed to greet everyone, whether he happened to love or detest them. As a matter of fact, Dr. Chalmers, although mildly disliking one or two people, detested only two—Ena Stratton, and an aunt of his wife's. He was a tolerant man.

"Hullo, Phil," said Ena flatly.

Dr. Chalmers gave his useless arm a twitch so as to lodge the hand in his dinner-jacket pocket, and smiled in a friendly way. The more he disliked a person, the more careful he was to smile at her in a friendly way.

"I thought you and David had gone. Wasn't it David's car that drove away just now?"

"Was it? I dare say."

"Anything the matter?" asked Dr. Chalmers, smiling more amicably than ever.

"Oh, David and Ronald between them threw me out of

the ball-room just after you'd gone. I don't know whether you call that anything," said Ena, in a martyr's voice.

"Threw you out? Oh, come, Ena; that can't be quite accurate, surely."

Ena's scanty bosom heaved. "That's right. Now you begin, Phil. Go on, call me a liar."

"My dear girl, I have no intention of calling you a liar. But I can't believe that you're not exaggerating a little when you say Ronald and David threw you out of the ball-room."

"Then ask anyone else who was there. They did. They picked me up by the head and the heels and carried me across the room. My God, I tell you, I've had about enough. I'm not going to stand it much longer, Phil."

"But if they did carry you across the room, it must have been only in fun?"

"Oh no, it wasn't. They may have pretended it was, but it wasn't. They wanted to get rid of me. Ronald especially. He's been publicly insulting me all the evening. Even you must have noticed that. I tell you, Phil, I'm not going to stand that kind of treatment. Ronald needn't think he's going to get away with that kind of thing from me. In front of all those grinning apes..."

Dr. Chalmers may have meant well, but his tact was not always very tactful. "I expect we've all had a little too much to drink this evening," said Dr. Chalmers, smiling pleasantly. "You'll feel different about it in the morning, Ena."

"If you mean I'm drunk," Ena said indignantly, "I'm not. I only wish I were. Heaven knows I've tried hard enough this evening, but it just seems as if my head were cast-iron. I simply can't get drunk; so it's no good saying that, Phil."

"But why on earth did you want to get drunk?"

"Because getting drunk," explained Mrs. Stratton with dignity, "is the only thing worth while. In a life such as I have to lead, getting drunk is the only thing that's *real*."

"Oh, rubbish," said Dr. Chalmers, far too robustly.

Mrs. Stratton rolled her eyes. "You can say that, of course. You just don't happen to know me, that's all—not the real me."

Dr. Chalmers dropped into a chair. He knocked out the pipe he had retrieved, and refilled it.

"Now look here, Ena, aren't you talking a little wildly? I'm quite sure Ronald hadn't the slightest wish to get rid of you, nor David. If they really did pick you up, then it must have been just horse-play. You mustn't take that sort of thing seriously, you know." Dr. Chalmers's voice was quite treacly with soothing syrup.

"Ronald will find he's got to take me seriously," said Ena, setting her mouth like a rat-trap.

"How do you mean?"

"I could make things very awkward for Ronald. *Very* awkward. And that's just what I intend to do."

"But how?"

"I don't like that woman he thinks he's going to marry. Mrs. Lefroy."

"Oh, don't you? I think she's particularly charming."

"Yes, no doubt. It takes a woman to see through her type. *I* call her a bad lot."

"Really, Ena, you mustn't say that kind of thing, you know."

Ena began to breathe more quickly. "I shall say exactly what I like. I shall say what I think. Mrs. Lefroy isn't the kind of woman whom *I* intend to have as a sister-in-law."

"But why?"

"She's been extremely rude to me this evening."

"Oh, come, Ena, I'm sure she didn't mean to be."

"Oh, yes, she did. Do you think I don't know?"

"But what has she done?"

"Nothing! That's just the point. She just nodded to me, in the most off-hand way, when we arrived, and hasn't spoken a word to me all the evening. If she thinks she can treat me like that, she's quite mistaken."

"Ena, you're exaggerating again."

"I tell you I'm not, Phil. I *know*. Margot was bad enough, but this woman's worse. But I can get my own back on them. They'll soon see that."

"What are you thinking of doing, Ena?" Dr. Chalmers asked, re-lighting his pipe.

"It's not what I'm thinking of doing, it's what I'm jolly well going to do. I'm going to write to the King's Proctor about the two of them."

"Oh, nonsense, Ena. You can't do a thing like that."

"Can't I? They'll very soon see whether I can or not. No, it's no good you saying anything, Phil. I've been thinking about it, up here, and I've made up my mind. It's simply horrible the way they go on. Somebody ought to stop it in any case."

"But, my dear girl, you've nothing to go on. This is only guesswork. You've no evidence."

Ena uttered a hard little bray of a laugh. "Oh, yes, I have. I'm afraid they'll be surprised, but I have. And evidence that they won't be able to explain away, either."

"But how could you possibly have got it?"

"Never mind that, Phil; I've got it. And I'm going to use it. You can tell Ronald so, if you like. I don't care. If he thinks he can treat me like that in public, he'll find he's very much mistaken."

Dr. Chalmers sighed. The emollient did not seem to have acted. "You'll feel quite different in the morning, Ena. Believe me, you will."

"Then I don't believe you, Phil," said Mrs. Stratton shortly.

Dr. Chalmers sighed again. He did not believe himself either.

Mrs. Stratton's bosom began to heave once more. "And as for David..."

"Yes?" asked Dr. Chalmers, disguising with difficulty his apprehension.

Mrs. Stratton sat for a moment or two in silence, while the heaving of her bosom grew more and more tumultuous. Then she almost threw herself round in her chair and burst out:

"What do *you* know about David and that Griffiths creature?"

"Elsie Griffiths? Why, nothing. What is there to know?"

"But you know all right which of the Griffiths girls it is, don't you?" cried Ena with bitter triumph.

"My dear Ena, I simply don't know what you're talking about."

"Oh, yes, you do, Phil, so you needn't put on that damned smooth voice any longer. Everyone's known about it, I expect, except me. That's always the way, isn't it? The wife hears last of all." Ena began to laugh shrilly.

"Ena," said Dr. Chalmers most impressively, "if you're suggesting that there's anything at all between David and Elsie Griffiths, I can assure you you're absolutely mistaken."

"Oh, you can, can you? And how do you happen to know there isn't, Phil?"

"I'm quite certain there isn't."

"Then you're wrong, because there is. My God, when I think of all I've done for David… But if that little cat thinks she's going to get him… Oh, really, Phil, it's terribly funny, when one comes to think of it, isn't it? Terribly funny!"

"Ena, you're getting hysterical," Dr. Chalmers said, with professional sharpness.

"I don't care. Why shouldn't I? I've had enough to make me. I've had a terrible evening, Phil. You must have seen how rude Ronald's been to me all the time. And horrible men trying to make love to me." She looked expectantly at Dr. Chalmers.

"Oh?" said that gentleman, warily.

"Yes. My God, Phil, why can't men leave a woman alone? Really, you're the only decent one of the lot. It's simply disgusting."

"Who's been trying to make love to you, Ena?"

"Oh, everyone. They always do. I suppose there must be something about me… Good heavens, I wish there wasn't. That horrible Mr. Williamson…"

"Oh, yes?" said Dr. Chalmers with great heartiness. "What did he do?"

"He tried to make me sit on his knee. In here. It was frightfully awkward. And Mr. Sheringham was worse. Really, Phil, I can't think how Ronald could have invited him. He's the most disgusting man I've ever met. I simply had to *fight* him, to get away."

"You do have a tough time with the lads, don't you, Ena?" said Dr. Chalmers.

"With all except you," said Mrs. Stratton seriously. "You've never tried to make love to me, Phil. I wonder why you haven't."

This time Dr. Chalmers was a little more tactful. "David happens to be a friend of mine, Ena."

"Yes," agreed Mrs. Stratton mournfully. "You're terribly fond of David, aren't you, Phil?"

"He's always been my best friend," said Dr. Chalmers, with hearty lack of emotion.

"It must be wonderful, to be a man and be able to have a real friend," regretted Mrs. Stratton.

"Yes, I expect it is."

The conversation then paused, apparently for contemplation by Mrs. Stratton of her feminine handicap.

Then she leaned a little towards her companion. "I don't think David would mind in the least, you know, Phil. Not *now*."

"Mind what?"

"Your making love to me," said Ena, in a small but hopeful voice.

Dr. Chalmers realised that he had already been labelled as suffering from a hopeless passion for his companion, which only masculine loyalty withheld him from voicing. He was in something of a difficulty. Ena was usually ready to pay attention to him, he knew; so far as she could respect anyone besides herself, she respected him. He had not yet given up all hope of persuading her to take no steps in the two matters in which her emotions were involved. But to do so, he must reduce her to softer mood. That Ronald had wanted to get rid of her, and had let her see it quite plainly, he was perfectly ready to believe; Ronald was not tactful. Ena's *amour-propre,* that tender plant, had been badly damaged. He was being offered the chance of administering a little nourishment to it in the obvious and traditional way.

Dr. Chalmers, however, was a cautious man. He never acted on impulse. Before taking action, he would weigh the fors and againsts not once but several times. It is possible that had he been a little less deliberate, he might have shut his eyes, taken a deep breath, and proceeded to administer the more practical rehabilitation for which he was being asked. As it was, consideration showed him that to embrace Ena Stratton would probably make him physically ill. He therefore contented himself, but not her, with reaching out his sound hand, patting her paternally on the shoulder, and saying with bluff joviality:

"Nonsense, Ena. Of course David would mind. Besides, you know you wouldn't like me to do anything of the sort. Would you? It would spoil—h'm!—everything."

Ena paused for a moment. Then she nodded solemnly.

"Yes, Phil. You're quite right. I shouldn't like it at all. Oh dear, how I wish all men were like you."

"You mustn't say that," said Dr. Chalmers, much encouraged. "I don't expect they're so bad really, you know. Anyhow, Ena, I want you to do me a favour. Will you?"

"What, Phil?"

Dr. Chalmers laid his pipe on the table beside him, and spoke with deliberation.

"I want you to give up this idea of writing to the King's Proctor about Ronald, and I want you to put quite out of your head this idea about David and Elsie Griffiths, and not say a word to him about it. You'll only upset him very much, you know, without any cause at all."

Ena shook her head. "No, I'm sorry, Phil. I can't do that. I feel it's really my duty to write to the King's Proctor. After all, what are laws for unless we all help to enforce them?"

"Well, well, we can talk about that again to-morrow. There's no hurry, and you mustn't do anything without thinking it over very carefully first. And as for David..."

Ena's thin lips set in an ugly line. "As for David," she said sharply, "you must leave that to me. No, I'm sorry, Phil. It was decent of you to try to shield him, but I must have that out with him myself."

"Not to-night, at any rate," Dr. Chalmers pleaded.

"Yes, to-night. There's no point in losing time. I only heard about it this evening."

Dr. Chalmers wondered savagely which of the local busy-bodies had laid up this trouble for David.

"But listen, Ena. You—"

"It's stifling in here," Ena said abruptly. "I want some air." She jumped up, and almost ran up on to the roof.

Dr. Chalmers followed gloomily. He had thought she was landed, and she had wriggled away once more. He knew it was no good appealing to her again. For months now, possibly for years, she would be throwing Elsie Griffiths up at David, till she had succeeded in driving him almost as insane as herself.

"Oh, curse the woman!" muttered Dr. Chalmers, who never swore.

He followed her to where she was leaning over the railing.

"You'll catch cold, Ena," he said mechanically.

"I don't care if I do. I wish I could catch pneumonia, and die. Could I catch pneumonia, if I stayed up here long enough, Phil? David would be glad. He could have Elsie all right then."

"Don't talk such nonsense, Ena."

"It isn't nonsense. You know it isn't. David would be glad. Oh, Phil, aren't men brutes? I've given David everything.

Everything a woman can! And now he's got it all, he doesn't want it any longer. Oh, what's the good of going on living, Phil?"

"Now, Ena, you know you don't mean that."

"Yes, I do. I often think how wonderful it would be to end it all, if only one could find an easy way out. Nobody's really fond of me—no, Phil, not even you, really. I'm sick of life. I've a good mind to jump over this railing here and now. Shall I?" She looked round at Dr. Chalmers wildly.

"That wouldn't be a very easy way out," said Dr. Chalmers with bluff common sense.

"Oh, I wouldn't mind a little pain. It would be worth it. It's terribly appropriate, isn't it," said Mrs. Stratton, with a hollow laugh, "to be standing under a gallows, while we talk about life and death?"

"A gallows from which, I perceive, one of the felons has fallen, if you can draw a moral from that," said Dr. Chalmers, and aimed a vicious kick at the felon's severed head. It soared up in the air, and out of sight. Somewhat relieved, Dr. Chalmers dealt in a similar manner with the trunk.

"Yes, there ought to be a moral in that, oughtn't there?" said Mrs. Stratton, with mournful relish. "Do you think it's an invitation, Phil? An invitation from fate for me to take its place?"

"I shouldn't think so," returned Dr. Chalmers. "Well, are you ready to go downstairs, Ena? It's a bit too cold out here. Besides, David will be wondering what's happened to you."

"Let him wonder. He doesn't care. Phil, don't you really think it's an invitation from fate? I think that's such a nice idea. Look—it would be so easy."

Mrs. Stratton pulled a chair up underneath the swinging rope, mounted on it, and put the stiff noose round her neck.

"Where do they have the knot, Phil? Let's get the details right, at any rate. I know they have a special place for the knot."

"Under the left ear, I believe," said Dr. Chalmers, bored with this play-acting, and kicked moodily at one of the uprights of the gallows.

Mrs. Stratton adjusted the knot under her left ear, and tightened the noose a little round her throat.

"Look, Phil. It would be terribly easy, wouldn't it? I've only got to jump off the seat of this chair. Shall I? Nobody would mind. David and Ronald wouldn't. I don't believe even you'd mind much. Shall I?"

Dr. Chalmers leant with his sound hand on the back of the chair. "Come on, Ena. I'm cold."

"No, but shall I jump off this chair, Phil? Shall I? Tell me. I will if you say so. Shall I?"

"Yes!" said Dr. Chalmers suddenly, and walked away: with the chair. For the only time in his life Dr. Chalmers had acted on impulse.

## II

Dr. Chalmers did not hear the faint thud and the gurgle behind him. He did not even look round, and so was able to pretend to himself, in some curious way, that nothing had happened. Without pausing, he dumped the chair down on the roof somewhere near the door, where it promptly fell over, and with his hands in his pockets continued on his way, whistling under his breath a little out of tune.

He could hardly believe that, technically, he had committed a murder; yet presumably he had.

Inside the door to the house he remembered that he must take precautions. He was perfectly safe, of course, so long as no one saw him coming in from the roof. Suicide would be taken for granted, and there was nothing to disprove it. Everyone knew that one of Ena's favourite topics of conversation was suicide.

Still whistling softly under his breath, Dr. Chalmers closed the door very quietly behind him and stood stock-still, listening. There was no sound of voices. He ventured a peep round the concealing angle of the ceiling into the bar-room. It was empty. The sound of music still came from the ball-room.

On quiet feet Dr. Chalmers ran down two flights of stairs. There he turned and, whistling loudly now, mounted once more, slowly and trampingly. He glanced at the watch on his wrist. To his surprise it was only a quarter of an hour since he had come in. All that had happened in fifteen minutes. And that made exactly Lucy's hour.

Dr. Chalmers's luck held. Just as he arrived at the top landing the door of the ball-room opened and Margot Stratton came out, passing him on the landing on her way upstairs.

"Hullo, Phil," she called out. "I'm looking for Mike. Have you seen him anywhere?"

"No," said Dr. Chalmers, "I've only just got back."

# Chapter V
## SEARCH PARTY

I

It was a minute or so before half-past two when Dr. Chalmers presented himself again in the ball-room.

"Oh, hang!" observed Mrs. Chalmers, with even less tact than she knew. "I'm going to finish this dance, anyhow," she called across the room.

Dr. Chalmers nodded pleasantly as he shut the ball-room door behind him.

Roger, alone at the moment, strolled across the room and joined him.

"Had a drink, Chalmers? You look as if you could do with one."

"I could," admitted Dr. Chalmers with a smile. "It was quite cold driving. But I think I'll wait till my wife's gone to put her things on. Otherwise we'll never get off. You know what women are."

They waited till the dance was over.

"Now, Lucy," said Dr. Chalmers, with good-humoured firmness.

"Oh, no, Phil," pleaded Mrs. Chalmers.

"Now come along, my dear," said Dr. Chalmers.

"But Margot isn't here. I must say good night to her."

"Off with you, woman! Margot will be back by the time you've got your things on."

Mrs. Chalmers, who had known it was hopeless all the time, consented to go.

"Now, Sheringham, what about that drink?" said Dr. Chalmers.

They strolled into the other room, to the bar.

Dr. and Mrs. Mitchell decided that it was high time for them to go too, and husband and wife divided in the same directions as the Chalmers.

The other dancers, realising that the party was breaking up, drifted automatically towards the bar.

"Oh, there you are, Mike," said Margot Stratton. "I was looking for you. We'd better go, too, I suppose?"

"Had a good party, Margot?" asked her late husband.

"A marvellous party, Ronald, thank you."

"It's been a grand party," Colin Nicolson chimed in. "Have another drink before you go, Margot."

"Well, it is getting cold out now," Margot agreed.

Mike Armstrong said nothing.

"Wonderful, our Margot, isn't she?" Dr. Chalmers appealed to Roger. "Getting on for three in the morning, and not a hair out of place. I believe if Margot was in a liner that sunk, she'd be found sitting on a life-belt, perfectly powdered and waved, and looking as if she'd stepped straight out of a band-box."

"Thank you, Phil," said Margot affably.

"Ha, ha!" said Mike Armstrong suddenly, and blushed.

"What was that you said just now, Colin?" asked Mr. Williamson thoughtfully. "Another drink, eh? Was that it? Well, that's not a bad idea. Eh? That isn't a bad idea at all, is it?"

"It's a magnificent idea, Osbert."

"It is," affirmed Mr. Williamson, much struck. "It *is* a munificent idea, Colin. Mine's whisky."

"Oh, Osbert," said Mrs. Williamson tentatively, "do you really think you'd better?"

"I said, mine's a whisky," repeated Mr. Williamson firmly. "Yes, and make it a double one. Thanks, Colin. Well, cheerio, Margot!"

"Cheerio, Osbert."

"Osbert, you are awful," said Mr. Williamson's wife, and removed herself, somewhat huffily.

The women took their usual time to get their things on, delayed in this case longer than usual by the arrival of Margot Stratton in the bedroom just as they were ready to leave. At last, however, they presented themselves, cloaked and befurred, and the chorus of farewells arose.

"Well, good night, Ronald... It's been a lovely party... Good night, Mr. Sheringham... Good night, I'll ring you up to-morrow... Perhaps you and Ronald would dine with us one night, Mrs. Lefroy?... Say good night to Mrs. Williamson for me... Don't forget that book you promised me, Mr. Nicolson... Well, good night, Sheringham... Good night... It's been a marvellous party, Ronald, darling... Well, good night..."

At last and at last only the house-party remained.

"We are seven," said Ronald, looking round the circle of faces. "Or should be, I think. Do we go to bed, or not? I think not. Then help yourselves to more drinks, everyone, and be merry. Seven has always struck me as absolutely the ideal number for a party."

The party complied.

"I don't want to dance any more," announced Mr. Williamson, suddenly and weightily.

"No," agreed Mrs. Lefroy. "Let's turn out the lights and sit round the fire, while Mr. Sheringham tells us about his murders."

"Oh, yes, Roger!" said Celia with enthusiasm.

"That's a good idea," Ronald backed them up. "In the strictest confidence, Roger, of course."

"I really ought not," said Roger happily.

"Oh, *do*, Mr. Sheringham!" begged Mrs. Lefroy.

"Come along, Roger, be a man," added Colin Nicolson. "It won't go any farther."

"Oh, very well," said Roger.

Mr. Williamson went to the landing and roared like a bull.

"*Lilian!*"

"Hullo?" came a faint and distant voice.

"You're wanted!"

"What for?"

"*Murder!*" howled Mr. Williamson, and left it at that. Certainly it brought him his Lilian, hot foot; but then he had all the bother of explaining.

In the meantime chairs were being pulled into a semicircle round the fire which still glowed on the big open Jacobean hearth, and the party settled down to enjoy itself.

"Sheringham!" said Mr. Williamson, in a confidential tone.

"Hullo?"

"Before you begin, will you promise me one thing?"

"What?"

"That if I murder Lilian, you won't give me away. You won't, will you? Eh?"

"That," said Roger, "depends entirely on the amount of provocation you've had."

"Oh, I've had plenty. You see," said Mr. Williamson, still more confidentially, "I can't bear her wearing my trousers." And having delivered himself of this complaint, Mr. Williamson leaned back in his chair and instantly went to sleep.

"Carry on, Sheringham," Ronald Stratton ordered comfortably.

Roger was clearing his throat while he wondered on which case to begin, when a voice from the doorway checked him.

It was David Stratton, changed and in a lounge suit.

"Sorry to interrupt," he said, "but can I speak to you a minute, Ronald?"

II

Ronald was only out of the room for a couple of minutes, before he returned with his brother.

"David says Ena doesn't seem to have gone home. He thinks she may still be here. We're just going to have a look round."

"Magnificent!" said Nicolson, jumping up. "We'll help you."

"Oh, it doesn't matter," David demurred. "Don't you bother. Ronald and I can manage."

"Not a bit of it; of course we'll give you a hand. Come along, Osbert, you lazy devil."

"Eh? What? What's up?"

"Hide-and-seek," said Nicolson. "You're seeking. Get up and do it."

Under his rousing energy the whole party was stirred into action.

Roger noticed that, after a first few moments of uncertainty, everyone seemed to be taking the search as a huge joke. Even David's deprecatory air did not check the growing hilarity. No doubt it was the best way to treat the situation, and really, for David's own sake, the most tactful. It was no good going about with long faces, silently sympathising with the unfortunate Stratton in his possession of an almost insane wife. Ena was after all a joke, if rather a bad one. Come out in the open and laugh with David, instead of weeping with him.

In twos and threes the search-party worked through the various rooms.

Ronald Stratton's house was Jacobean and spacious. It had belonged to the Stratton family for nearly three hundred years, almost ever since its erection as the dower-house of a mansion nearly six miles away. Ronald had inherited it, but not the land and the farms which had once belonged to it, or the money to keep it up properly. He had made the latter, and bought back the former.

Since it had come into his hands Ronald had spent a great deal on it. In a thoroughly dilapidated condition, it had been actually in danger of collapsing altogether. Ronald had reroofed it, replanned it, and almost rebuilt it. The top of the three stories, where the party had been held, had been completely reorganised by him. Originally this had consisted of almost a dozen small bedrooms; Ronald had ruthlessly knocked more than half of these into one huge room, running from front to back of the house, and one other almost as big; the former, with a parquet floor added, had become the ball-room; the other, with one of its walls knocked completely out to open on to the lovely well-staircase, was anything from a studio to a music-room. To-night it had done duty as a bar-parlour. The rest of the top floor, served by another staircase, constituted the servants' quarters.

Ronald had been as ruthless with the roof as with the top story. He had kept only the main gables in the front of the house. The rest he had levelled and put in a concrete roof with an asphalt surface, which was just large enough for a badminton court. The game was a little windy at such a height, but Ronald played it with zest. This evening the net and posts had been stowed away, and the rather gruesome triple gallows erected in their place. Over a subsidiary roof, a few feet lower than the main roof and reached from it by a short flight of steps, had been erected a fair-sized hot-house, where Stratton amused himself with growing certain exotic plants, or it might be more accurate to say, trying to grow them. It was called the sun-parlour and furnished with wicker chairs and tables, and was usually in considerable use at dances.

As for the rest of the house, the main bedrooms and bath-rooms occupied the first floor; while the library and a small morning-room opened off one side of the big hall on the ground floor, the drawing-room off the other. The kitchens were stowed away somewhere at the back, with access to the hall and through a service-door, to the dining-room.

To search such a house thoroughly was no small task. At first the party confined itself to the top floor and the roof, in spite of the extreme unlikelihood of the lady being stowed away in either. Roger himself felt a little perfunctory in his seeking. He had no expectation that Mrs. Stratton really was on the premises. Most probably she had gone off to knock up some unfortunate friend and explain, with sobs and heroic gestures, and complete untruth, that her husband had practically barred her own door against her.

Nevertheless, slightly annoyed as he was at having been cut short so abruptly in his storytelling, his sense of the picturesque appreciated the appropriateness of its setting for such a search. The heavy oak beams which formed the fire-place opening and studded the unevenly-plastered walls, gleamed with age and generations of elbow-grease as they threw back the red glow of the log fire; and the carefully-placed electric lights left the quaint angles of the ceiling, which Ronald had thrown up from its original seven feet to a dozen or more to show off the roof-timbers, dim and mysterious. On the outside walls long casement windows, with the original tiny diamond panes of greenish, much-scratched glass, heavily leaded, looked out over the blackness which covered that part of the grounds lying between the house and the main road a hundred yards away. Roger opened one and leaned out. Everything was still and remote and obscure. It was odd to remember that London was within eighteen miles.

"Now then, Roger. She's not out there, you know. Why, man, this ought to be a job after your own heart."

Roger drew back guiltily and looked round.

"Well, you see, Colin, I don't believe she's here at all."

"What does that matter?" demanded Nicolson robustly. "A

game of hide-and-seek's a game of hide-and-seek, wherever the person's hiding. Off with you, and search like a man."

"Has anyone tried the sun-parlour?" Roger asked languidly.

"I expect so, but no one of your skill. Who knows? She may have dug into the big bed and be disguised as a sweet-pea by now."

"More probably a cactus," said Roger sourly, and went up to look.

Electric light was laid on to the sun-parlour, but the place was in darkness when Roger reached it. He was about to turn on the switch, when a slight movement on the farther side of the room made him jump violently. There is nothing more disconcerting than a human movement in the darkness when one has been quite sure there is nothing human there. The next instant he smiled.

"I've got her!" he said to himself.

He could see now the figure whose movement had startled him. It was leaning out of an opened window, just as he had been leaning out of the room below two minutes ago, and evidently it had not heard his approach. It was small and slight, and quite obviously feminine.

"I've a jolly good mind to smack her hard, as she stands," thought Roger vindictively. "She deserves a fright."

It was Roger, however, who got the fright; for the figure shifted its position slightly, and Roger saw that it was not a woman at all. The faint moonlight gave just enough illumination to throw up the whitewashed wall underneath the windows, and Roger could now see white wall between the figure's legs. Moreover, those legs were clothed in unmistakable trousers.

Roger stared at it with something like alarm. No man in

the party was nearly so small or so slight as that. Who on earth could it be?

He solved the problem by switching on the light—and the rather witch-like face of Mrs. Williamson shot round over her shoulder with a little exclamation.

"Oh, how you frightened me!"

"Not before you'd already frightened me. I thought you must be an elf or a hobgoblin or something, brooding out of that window."

Mrs. Williamson laughed. "The night was so perfect. I simply had to get away from everyone and drink a little of it in."

Funny, thought Roger; she can say that sort of thing and one accepts it, because she's natural, whereas exactly the same words from Ena Stratton would sound just nauseating.

"I'm sorry I disturbed you," he said. "I was sent up, by Colin, to search this place."

"She's not here. I looked round before I turned the light out. All I could find here was someone's pipe." She nodded towards one of the wicker tables, on which lay a briar pipe.

Roger picked it up. "I expect someone's missing this. I'd better take it to Ronald."

"They haven't found her yet, then?"

"No. I suppose I must go and help look. Shall I turn out the light again and leave you and the night together?"

"No, I feel better now. Do people ever make you feel like that—that you simply must get away from everybody, to get the bad taste out of your mouth?"

"I can quite believe that Ena Stratton would leave a bad taste in anyone's mouth," said Roger, as he stood aside for Mrs. Williamson to precede him up the steps.

## III

In the house the search had now spread to the lower floors.

Roger could hear Colin Nicolson, in one of the bedrooms, protesting his fears to his hostess.

"It's no good, Celia, I won't be able to get a wink of sleep to-night, and that's the truth. Each time I shut an eye I'll imagine the pestilential woman ready to pop out at me from every nook and cranny." He pulled open the bottom drawer of a chest of drawers and peered hopefully inside.

"Well, I don't suppose she's in there," said Celia, somewhat literally.

"Who knows what she may not have squeezed herself into?" Colin lifted the lid of a powder-box on the dressing-table, which happened to be that of Mrs. Lefroy, and then opened the door of an extremely small cupboard in the wall into which one could with difficulty have squeezed a top-hat. "Hey, I see you! Come oot now, will you? Come away oot! Ach, who knows where she is?"

"Curse the woman," said Celia with feeling. "I want to go to bed. I'm simply dropping."

"It's a bit thick. It is really. Besides, Roger's sure she isn't here. Can't we call it off, and all get to our beds?"

"David really is rather worried," Celia said doubtfully.

"Why is he worried? He ought to be glad to be rid of her for a bit."

"He doesn't know what she might do, you see."

"And isn't that just playing her own game? Why do you think she's hiding like this at all, and giving us all this bother looking for her? Just to make herself important, of course. She just wants us to be bothered about her, and here we are, playing her game. It's sickening, that's what it is."

"Colin, Colin, what's this?" said Roger, walking into the room. "You, who were hounding us all on, to be fainting by the roadside like this."

"Ah, a joke's a joke, but this is too much. Here's poor Celia dropping with fatigue, and all of us wanting our beds. No, it's too much. Besides, we're just playing the woman's own game."

"Yes, that's her idea, of course; you're perfectly right. She must be the centre of the picture, even when she isn't in it. I agree, we'd much better go to bed."

"Well, then, where's wee Ronald?"

"Wee Ronald's downstairs, I think, with wee David, having a look round there," said Celia.

"Very well, let's go down and tell him we've struck. Come along and back me up, Roger."

"But don't be too hard on David," said Celia, as the two men went out of the room. "It isn't the poor lad's fault, and it's a rotten position for him."

"It's certainly a rotten position for David," Roger agreed to Colin outside, "having to admit tacitly to a lot of strangers that he's got an imbecile for a wife. Very rotten."

"Ach, why doesn't he give the woman a sound thrashing? That's what she needs. A jolly good hiding."

"I'd like to have the administering of it," wistfully said Roger, who also would have liked to get to bed.

Ronald and David were discovered in the morning-room. They looked at the two inquiringly.

"No luck," said Roger. "Honestly, Ronald, I don't think she's here. Better call the search off, don't you think?"

"Yes, I think so. I'm sure we've looked everywhere now, David."

"All right," David nodded. "Can I use your telephone before I go?"

"Whom on earth do you want to telephone to at this time of night?"

"The police."

"Oh, come, Stratton," Roger said, with a slight smile. "That's hardly necessary, is it?"

"You don't know my wife, Sheringham," David Stratton said ruefully. "In these moods of hers she simply isn't responsible. I wouldn't put anything past her."

"You mean, she might walk into the pond at Westerford and pretend to drown herself?" said Ronald.

"For all one knows, she might actually drown herself."

"Then for heaven's sake, man," said Ronald fervently, "let her. Don't raise one little finger to stop her from such a blessed action."

"I won't," David Stratton said candidly. "But I've got to cover myself."

"How?"

"By warning the police that there's a woman loose who isn't responsible for her actions. Don't you agree that I should, Sheringham?"

"Yes," said Roger. "I don't for one moment think that she's in the least likely to do any such thing, but it certainly won't do any harm to warn the police; and if you tell your wife later that you felt you had to do so, and why, it may give her the fright which, if you'll allow me to say so, she very badly needs."

"Yes," said David briefly. "I'd thought of that."

"All right," Ronald nodded. "Well, you know where the telephone is, David."

David disappeared in the direction of the morning-room, and the others loitered in the hall, waiting for him.

"We'll give the poor lad a stiff night-cap before he goes off into the jaws of his doom," Ronald remarked.

"Yes, it's ten to one that he'll find her there when he gets home this time. And I hope he deals with her faithfully. Oh, by the way, Mrs. Williamson found this pipe on the table in the sun-parlour. Someone left it there, I suppose. You'd better take charge of it, Ronald."

Ronald glanced at it before he dropped it into his pocket. "Oh, yes, I know whose this is. It's Phil Chalmers's."

IV

"Just a final night-cap, everyone," said Ronald, as he went towards the bar. "No dissentients, I hope?"

There appeared to be no dissentients.

"Do you really think you'd better, Osbert?" doubtfully suggested Mrs. Williamson.

Mr. Williamson gazed at her with owlish disapproval. "Are you *trying* to drive me to drink, Lilian? Don't you know that's absolutely the surest way of making a man drink when he doesn't want to, practically hinting that... Isn't it, Sheringham?"

"Absolutely," said Roger.

"Then give me a double," said Mr. Williamson.

V

Mr. Williamson lurched slightly as he trod on a last step that wasn't there, before emerging on the roof. The others were still finishing their night-caps, but a sudden craving for fresh air had invaded Mr. Williamson. Fresh air and plenty of it, and space for a man to sway in, was what Mr. Williamson wanted.

He stood just outside the doorway that gave egress to the roof, his back propped against the lintel, and contemplated with some disapproval the gallows in the middle. The lantern which had crowned it had gone out long since, but the gallows itself, and its three grisly occupants, stood out clearly against the moonlit sky.

"Dam' silly idea," commented Mr. Williamson sternly. "*Dam'* silly. Some people wouldn't like it at all. Some people would dislike it very much. Morbid. Thass word. Morbid. And damsilly."

He set out towards the railing on the other side of the roof, the same railing over which Roger and Ena Stratton had leaned earlier in the evening. It was a railing which seemed to invite leaning. To lean over it now seemed to Mr. Williamson the height of admirable ideas. Leaning is so much less trouble than standing.

It was not really necessary for Mr. Williamson to walk right through the gallows in order to reach the railing. He could quite easily have gone round it. But Mr. Williamson was full of ideas just at present, and to walk right under the middle of the triple gallows seemed a positively brilliant idea. By that gesture he would be able to express all sorts of things; what sort of things did not matter; Mr. Williamson would be able to express them.

He steered carefully round a chair that was lying in his path to self-expressionism.

In the same way, it seemed to Mr. Williamson an equally clever idea to halt, right in the middle of the gallows, and hiccough his contempt of them; so halt he did, not without a bit of a lurch. Recovering himself from the lurch, Mr. Williamson happened to knock, quite gently, into one of the dangling figures. The figure, swinging back, promptly dealt him a shrewd buffet in the side.

"Hey!" said Mr. Williamson resentfully.

Mr. Williamson was not drunk. Or, if he had been drunk, he very quickly became almost sober. It was less than half a minute before he realised that it was a very shrewd buffet indeed to have been delivered by a straw figure.

He stared up at the figure in question.

Even then Mr. Williamson did not lose his head. He turned round and walked, with some care and extreme dignity, down into the bar-room. There he grasped Roger Sheringham by the elbow, and drew him firmly aside.

"I say, Sheringham, just come with me a minute, will you? Eh? Just come with me a minute."

"Where to?" Roger asked good-humouredly.

"Just with me. Just in here. Eh? Just come with me."

With great deliberation Mr. Williamson led him into the exact middle of the ball-room floor.

"I say, Sheringham."

"Well?"

"I've found her," said Mr. Williamson.

# Chapter VI
## ODOUR OF A RAT

I

Ena Stratton was quite dead. There was no doubt about that.

With a hurried injunction to Williamson not to alarm the company for the moment, Roger had called Ronald Stratton out as normally as he could, and rushed up to the roof with him, breaking the news as he went. There Ronald had held the dangling body up to take its weight off the rope round its neck, while Roger had quickly felt its hands. They were icy cold.

"I'm afraid she's dead," he said, "but we must make quite sure. Run and get a sharp knife, Ronald, and we'll cut her down. And bring Colin back with you; he knows something about first aid. I'll hold her up."

Ronald went and returned with the knife and Colin Nicolson, and Williamson too for safety. Between them they cut the cord, which was too thick and stiff to have buried itself in the dead woman's neck, and laid her flat on the roof a little way from the gallows. Nicolson at once set about trying artificial respiration.

Mr. Williamson took one horrified look at the distorted face, and then retired to the railing and was sick. Mrs. Stratton was not a soothing sight for a queasy stomach.

After five minutes strenuous work, Nicolson sat back on his heels.

"I'm afraid it's no good. She's gone."

Roger nodded. "I was sure. But we had to try. No one's telephoned for the police, Ronald? You'd better do that at once."

"Yes," Ronald said soberly.

"And your brother hasn't gone yet. Tell him."

"And hadn't we better get her into the house?" Ronald asked doubtfully. "I know one isn't supposed to disturb things, but we had to cut her down, so it can't matter. I don't think we ought to leave her out here. Just in case, you know..."

"Well..." said Roger.

"It can't matter moving her, in such an obvious case of suicide, man," urged Nicolson. "Ronald's right."

"No," Roger acquiesced. "It can't matter. Well, will you go along, Colin, and get the women somehow into the ballroom? They'd better not see her. Then we'll get her down as soon as Ronald's telephoned."

"We'll get her down before I telephone," said Ronald. "I'll go and fetch David." He made for the door into the house.

Roger raised his eyebrows slightly at Colin. "By rights the police ought to be told the very first thing."

"Ach, what does that matter? Ronald's right. Let's get the poor body comfortable first. It's too cold out here altogether."

"Well, I don't suppose it matters, in this case. And Ronald will have to break the news to the women."

"I'll go down and get them out of the way," said Colin.

Left alone, Roger walked over to comfort Mr. Williamson.

"She's quite gone?" asked that gentleman, now somewhat restored and impeccably sober.

"I'm afraid so. But we're going to get her downstairs into the warmth, just in case there's any hope."

"Ah!" said Mr. Williamson profoundly.

Roger looked at him. "What?"

"I was just wondering how many people would thank you if you did bring her to life again; that's all."

"After the first shock," said Roger, "probably not very many."

"No, that's what I was thinking. Eh? Well, it's no good pretending, is it? Eh? Don't you agree?"

"I think," Roger said gently, "that those same people will have to put up a decent pretence to the police, however thankful they may feel privately."

"Eh? Oh, yes, of course. Yes, they will, won't they? Well, I," said Mr. Williamson nobly, "won't drop any hints."

"Any hints about what?" Roger asked, a little sharply.

"Why, that they aren't as sorry as they make out. If you like, that they're jolly thankful she strung herself up. Suicide during temporary insanity, eh? Well, I remember asking Ronald if she were mad, hours ago. I thought she was, then. You agree, eh? She was mad, wasn't she? Eh?"

"Perfectly mad," Roger agreed. "The police will have to be told that, of course. It will help them."

"Will it? Oh, I see what you mean. Yes, it will, won't it? Yes."

The arrival of Ronald Stratton and his brother put an end to this somewhat laboured conversation.

In the moonlight David's face showed no change of colour, and it was almost without expression that he stood for a few moments staring down at the body of his wife. It was impossible to say what emotion he was feeling, or even whether he were feeling any at all.

Finally Ronald touched him gently on the arm. "All right, David. Don't look at her any more. Roger and I will take her downstairs."

As if he had become an automaton, David stood obediently aside. Nor did he attempt to help in any way as his brother and Roger between them picked the body up and carried it, past the closed door of the ball-room, down to the floor below, leaving Mr. Williamson to look after the roof alone.

"Have to put her in my room," Ronald muttered. "There isn't an empty one."

They laid her on the bed, and Ronald, with a shudder he could not suppress, spread a little towel across her face. From the doorway David watched them lifelessly.

Ronald turned to Roger.

"Look here, once I telephone the police things are taken out of our hands. They'll be here in less than a quarter of an hour, I should think. Are we quite sure there's nothing we want to do first?"

Roger hid a slight start. "What kind of thing?"

"Well," Ronald hesitated. "I mean, about the party. It's bound to look rather bad, isn't it? Well-known murderers and victims, and here's one of the party hangs herself. The coroner could make himself quite unpleasant about it."

"I don't see how you can very well hide it up. The women are all in fancy dress; and so are you."

"We could change."

"Much too risky," said Roger decidedly. "It would only look as if you were trying to keep something back."

Ronald glanced down at his own velvet suit. "Well, I'm going to change, anyhow, whatever it looks like. I don't feel like facing the police like this. David's changed, too, you see. And you and Williamson are in your dinner-jackets. Colin's only got to take his paper-frill out. As for the women, why not just say they were in fancy dress, and leave it at that?"

"I suppose you could, if you really think it's important."

"I do, rather. Otherwise the newspapers will probably get hold of us, and heaven knows what."

"Yes, that's true enough. And Mrs. Stratton herself?"

"Ena? Well, she was in fancy dress, too, wasn't she? As a charwoman."

"Yes, and that's an important point. It's just because she was in that nondescript, shapeless black dress, that no one found her earlier. If she'd been in an ordinary evening frock, Mrs. Williamson and I, and anyone else who went on the roof, could hardly have failed to notice her. So there's point in the fancy dress situation."

"Yes, I see that. Well, I'll go up and tell the women, and warn them that we're not saying anything about murderers and victims. They can easily find historical characters to fit their costumes, if necessary."

"And don't forget the doctors. I don't think it matters much about the people who left early, but both Chalmers and Mitchell were on the premises after Mrs. Stratton left the ball-room, so the police are bound to interview them. In fact, the best thing you can do is to ring one or both of them up at once and ask them to come round here, even before you ring up the police. A doctor ought to examine her immediately, you see. And really, you'd better hurry, Ronald."

"Yes, I will. But do you know it's only eight minutes since you called me up on the roof?" said Ronald, glancing at his wrist-watch. "So we can't be said to have lost any time. In the meantime, take David upstairs and give him a stiff drink, will you?" he added in an undertone.

Roger nodded.

David Stratton could hardly have had much affection left for his wife, and when the sudden shock of her death was over, he could hardly have any regrets; but at the moment he seemed quite dazed.

"Coming upstairs, Stratton?" Roger said to him.

David did not answer.

Ronald, passing him in the doorway, gave his arm a brotherly squeeze. "Buck up, David, old lad."

"Come upstairs and let me get you a drink," Roger repeated.

David looked at him. "Yes, I could do with a drink," he said in a perfectly normal voice.

He followed Roger upstairs like a child.

II

"And so," said Roger thoughtfully, "she really did do it, after all."

"Why 'after all'?" asked Mrs. Lefroy.

They were standing alone in the bar-room, in front of

the fire. After breaking the news to the women, Ronald had telephoned to the two doctors and the police, and was now downstairs, changing his clothes. Celia Stratton had taken charge of her younger brother, whom even the stiff drink administered by Roger did not seem to have shaken quite out of his trance of amazement, or incredulity, or concealed relief, or whatever it was that had temporarily numbed him. Colin Nicolson and the Williamsons were in the ball-room, debating whether Lilian Williamson should change out of her husband's trousers, or whether this action would look suspicious to the local police force.

"Why 'after all'?" Roger repeated. "Because she was telling me herself earlier in the evening how much she would have liked to commit suicide, if only she could find 'an easy way out.'"

"I believe she said as much to Osbert too," nodded Mrs. Lefroy.

"She did. He told me so."

There was a little pause.

"That," said Mrs. Lefroy, as if speaking rather carefully, "will be a useful piece of information for the police."

"Yes. And yet," Roger meditated, with a vivid remembrance of that distorted face, "I shouldn't have said that hanging was a very easy way out, would you?"

"I suppose it depends," said Mrs. Lefroy vaguely. Her hands smoothed over the white satin on her waist in a series of nervous little jerks. Roger noticed that she had very pretty hands, white and small.

"As a matter of fact," he pursued, "I never thought for single moment that she meant a word of what she was saying. Of course I didn't. I imagined she was just talking for silly effect, as usual. Well, that seems to dispose of the good old cliché, doesn't it?"

"What good old cliché?"

"That people who talk about committing suicide never do it. And yet," Roger ruminated, "I could have sworn that it applied in her case more forcibly than it could in any other. The more I think of it, the more certain I'd have been that she was just talking poppycock. I suppose it couldn't possibly have been an accident?"

"Is this the celebrated detective's brain working for our benefit?" asked Mrs. Lefroy, with a laugh that sounded a little forced.

"Hardly," Roger smiled. "But if you'd like to hear the celebrated novelist's opinion, it is that such a situation simply couldn't be entrusted to fiction. One has to go to real life for such boldness."

"What do you mean?"

"The coincidence of it all. Here is a woman whose existence is a source of annoyance, and perhaps a good deal more than annoyance, to several different people, and that for several different reasons. And just at the moment when those people are resenting it perhaps more intensely than ever before, she very obligingly, and most unexpectedly, kills herself. You must admit that the coincidence is far too violent to be stomached in fiction."

"Is it?" Mrs. Lefroy asked reluctantly. "I don't think really it's as strong as all that."

"Don't you?"

"Well—it *is* just a coincidence, of course, and nothing else."

"Oh, of course," said Roger.

They looked into the fire for a few moments.

Mrs. Lefroy leaned her bare arm on the beam that formed the rough mantelpiece and fidgeted with the toe of her white satin slipper among the dead ashes on the edge of the fire.

"I wish the police would hurry up and come," she burst out suddenly.

"I thought you said just now you were dreading them?"

"Did I? How foolish of me. Of course I'm not," said Mrs. Lefroy, with an unnatural little laugh.

Roger said nothing.

Apparently Mrs. Lefroy read into his silence a mild expostulation, for she added:

"Yes, you're quite right. I am dreading them. It was ridiculous to pretend that I'm not."

"Why are you dreading them?"

Mrs. Lefroy looked at him bravely. "Because there isn't a single person connected with this family who won't be absolutely delighted to hear that Ena's dead. It's no good beating about the bush: there won't be. And I'm so afraid that the police may guess it."

"Is there any particular reason why they shouldn't guess it? I mean, as you say, Mrs. Stratton wasn't a very pleasant person: and, not to beat about the bush myself, I should say that she's a lot more use to the community dead than alive. But does it matter that the police should know that too?"

"Well, it's not very—nice, is it?" Mrs. Lefroy hedged.

"Sudden death never is very nice," Roger said solemnly.

Mrs. Lefroy moved impatiently. "Oh, don't talk platitudes."

"Weren't you rather talking platitudes yourself, Mrs. Lefroy?"

"Well, you know perfectly well what's in my mind. It's in your own, too. If you want me to put it into plain words, I'm terribly afraid that if the police do guess that, they may suspect something absolutely preposterous."

"Yes," Roger agreed, with a little sigh, "you're right; that was in my own mind too."

## III

Dr. Chalmers arrived before the police. He came up the stairs alone. Roger looked round from where he was standing by the fire-place and saw him ascending the last short flight of the well-staircase.

"Ah, Chalmers. You've been very quick."

"I hadn't got to bed. This is a terrible business, Sheringham."

"Yes. Have you seen Ronald?"

"No, I came straight in; the front door's still unlocked. Where is he?"

"In his bathroom, I think, changing."

"And—Mrs. Stratton?"

"On Ronald's bed. Shall I tell him you've come?"

"Oh, it's all right, thanks. I'll find him myself."

Dr. Chalmers turned and went down the stairs again.

"Did you notice?" Roger said conversationally to Mrs. Lefroy. "Did you notice how his manner had changed? Meeting him before, one couldn't possibly have told that he was a doctor, except for the very faint smell of ether that always hangs about a doctor. But just then he couldn't have been anything else. Even his voice was a bedside voice."

"Yes," said Mrs. Lefroy.

Colin Nicolson appeared in the ball-room door.

"Was that the police?" he asked.

"No—Chalmers."

"Lilian's decided to change at last. Cut along, Lilian. It wasn't the police. Agatha, you haven't forgotten who you are now, have you?"

Mrs. Lefroy looked at him vacantly for a moment, before her face resumed its normal expression. "Oh! Yes, of course, Henrietta of France, wasn't it? I don't think it matters much, in any case."

Lilian Williamson hurried off to change, and her husband followed her out of the ball-room to join the group in the other room. Nicolson began to forecast the questions which the police would probably ask.

Roger stood for a moment uncertainly among them. Then he edged towards the stairs. A sudden wish had come to him to have another, and a closer look at the roof before the police arrived.

## IV

And yet there seemed very little to be seen on the roof.

Literally very little. The heavy beams of the gallows, a chair or two here and there for those willing to brave the temperature of an April night, and a little arbour of trellis-work set in wooden troughs of earth, with the bare stems of Virginia creepers and *polygonum baldschuanicum* writhing in and out of it—there was nothing else at all.

Yet Roger felt that there ought to be something else.

He did not know what, but he was not satisfied. It was too

neat, too tidy altogether, too convenient that Ena Stratton should have committed suicide just at this juncture, when so many people desired it.

Did Mrs. Lefroy suspect that perhaps her future sister-in-law had not committed suicide? Mrs. Lefroy was a shrewd woman, as well as an intelligent one. She was worried about something. Was it only what she had voiced, or had she a deeper, untellable fear?

Yet, of course, Ena Stratton must have committed suicide. There was absolutely no evidence of anything else, not the smallest sign of it. And Roger very sincerely hoped that she had committed suicide. He would have been extremely sorry to see a decent person hang for such a worthless excrescence on humanity's surface.

And yet…

He stood in the middle of the gallows triangle, peering up at the cross-beams. They were high. There were three good feet of cord showing above the heads of the two life-size figures that remained, and the toes of their shoes were at least eighteen inches off the ground. Those cross-beams were ten foot high and more.

But that did not appear to have the least significance.

Roger fetched a chair which was standing somewhere between the gallows and the door into the house, set it beside one of the dangling figures, and mounted upon it. His body stood almost level with that of the figure, neck and neck practically on the same plane. Standing there, he could have unfastened the noose from the figure's neck and draped it around his own. It would have sagged a little on his shoulders, but not much when the noose was enlarged.

Unquestionably Ena Stratton could have stood there and done the same.

He jumped down on to the roof again. The chair, spurned by his retreating foot, tumbled over with a crash, and Roger cursed. His nerves were upset, and that added to his sense of frustration.

Yet he did not know why he should be feeling frustrated at all. If there was nothing there to discover, he could discover nothing. And he wanted nothing there to be discovered. Why, then, feel frustrated if nothing presented itself for discovery?

He walked down into the sun-parlour, switched on the light, and looked moodily round, found nothing, and walked back to the roof again.

A thought pulled him up with a jerk. Where, after all, was the third straw dummy?

It took him twenty-five seconds to find it, in the shadow of the little arbour.

It lay there, huddled grotesquely. The path from it to the gallows was unobstructed, so that it might have been carelessly tossed or kicked there. Roger knelt down to examine it, and found that it was headless. It was a minute or two before he found the ball of plaited straw which had served as the head, lying in a gulley on the way down to the sun-parlour. He wondered how it had got there.

But chiefly he was wondering whether the figure had fallen down, or had been torn down. The answer to that question might be quite significant; but Roger did not see how an answer could possibly be obtained. The few wisps at the top of the trunk were no indication either way.

Well, what did it matter? He was only wasting time, playing

at being a detective till the real police should arrive, trying to be cleverer with the facts than the facts themselves would allow. Coincidences, and far worse coincidences too, had occurred in the history of crime before now. Undoubtedly Ena Stratton had committed suicide—and a very good thing for all concerned, that hag-ridden lady herself included. And that was that, and he would go downstairs again and behave like a reasonable being and have another tankard of beer before the police came.

He walked quickly over to the house-door.

Nevertheless something caused him to stop there and turn back for a last look across the roof: some remnant that had refused to be stifled of that extra sense of his which automatically rejected the improbable in human nature, however plausibly probable argument might make it. His hands in his pockets, he stood still and let his eyes move very slowly over the whole space before him, as if to give them one last chance to pick out any detail to which they had been blind before.

It was then that Roger decided, with an incredulous shock, that his powers were waning. For the detail on which his eyes alighted was no insignificant one, but a glaring, enormous, whitewashed elephant of a detail. It was no less than the fallen chair off which he himself had stepped.

Not till then did he realise that where that chair now was, no chair had been before. And quite certainly Mrs. Stratton had not taken a flying and accurate leap upwards, straight into the noose. To hang oneself, it is necessary first to adjust the noose about one's neck and then step off an eminence into vacancy: and there had been no eminence.

The phantom pricking of Roger's mental thumbs had been justified.

Murder had been committed.

# Chapter VII

## FACTS AND FANCIES

I

RIGHT UNDER THE VERY NOSE OF ROGER SHERINGHAM himself murder had been committed.

In spite of the tragedy, Roger could hardly suppress a smile at the audacity of it. He was not unaware of his reputation among the laity; at times, indeed, he was almost childishly pleased about it. Somebody evidently thought it undeserved—somebody, too, who could make such a colossal blunder of his own as to leave that hanging body without the overturned chair which should have been its natural corollary. And Roger had to admit that the unknown might not have made such a mistake in his estimate of Roger Sheringham's stupidity. It was only by the smallest chance that he had turned round, right in the doorway, for that last look.

Roger smiled again.

Then he turned round, passed through the doorway, and walked downstairs. It was the murderer's own huge luck which had placed an overturned chair just where an overturned chair ought to be, and Roger was not going to interfere with it. Let the police make anything of it if they could.

Roger was accustomed to look facts in the eye. It was a fact, if a regrettable one, that Mrs. Ena Stratton meant nothing at all to him as a person, dead or alive. It was no less a fact that as a human being she had herself thrown away any sympathy in her fate; more, she had pulled that fate upon her with both hands. Roger could not feel any drivings of conscience to help the police towards avenging her.

But he could, and did feel that a challenge had been thrown down to him personally, and a rush of exhilaration drove the fatigue out of him. No, he would not take that chair away again, any more than he would tell the authorities exactly what he knew. Not yet. This was going to be played out first as a perfectly private battle of brains.

He hurried downstairs. In view of what he had learnt, he must have another look at the body, alone, before the police arrived.

II

Dr. Chalmers had not quite finished his examination. The stethoscope hanging round his neck, he was bending over the bed when Roger looked in at the doorway.

"No hope, I'm afraid?" Roger asked tentatively.

Dr. Chalmers glanced round, and then straightened up. "None. A dreadful business. What can have possessed her to take her life like that?"

"You think it was suicide, then?"

Dr. Chalmers stared at him, his pleasant face showing his surprise. "Why, what else could it be?"

"Oh, nothing, I suppose," Roger said airily. "I just wondered if there was any possibility of accident, that's all. I shouldn't have said she was a suicidal type at all, you see; at least, on the little I saw of her."

Dr. Chalmers drew the coverlet carefully over the body before he replied. "Wouldn't you?" he said slowly. "Well, of course that's more in your line than mine, but I should certainly have said that Ena's neurotic, ego-centrical type has a predisposition to suicide. I may be wrong, of course. Morbid psychology doesn't enter very much into a general practitioner's work. But though I was very shocked when Ronald told me what had happened, I can't say I felt much surprise."

"You'll be prepared to give evidence at the inquest, then, that in your professional opinion Mrs. Stratton was a suicidal subject?" Roger asked, wishing that Chalmers would go.

"I think so. Unless," said Dr. Chalmers with interest, "you can convert me to the opposite view?" He looked as if he would like to embark upon such a discussion at once.

"Oh, no," Roger said firmly. "For all I know, you're right." The stage seemed to be setting itself without hesitation for a verdict of suicide, and Roger had no intention of interfering with it at this juncture.

"Well," he added, "I expect you want to see Ronald. Is he still changing?"

"No, he looked in a minute ago to say he was going upstairs."

"I think someone ought to stay with the body," Roger said cunningly. "I'll take charge if you like, while you go upstairs."

Dr. Chalmers looked for a moment a little doubtful as to the propriety of this suggestion. Then he nodded:

"Thanks. I don't suppose it will be for more than a minute or two in any case. The police ought to be here any minute now."

"You live nearer here than Dr. Mitchell does, I suppose?" Roger asked casually, as the other moved over to the doorway.

"Yes. We both live in Westerford, but Frank's at the farther end."

Roger waited until the door was safely closed. Then he hurried over to the bed.

Turning back the coverlet, he stood for a moment looking down at Ena Stratton's body. She was still dressed exactly as she had been, even to the misshapen hat on her head, and Roger could not see that her dress had been torn or damaged in any way. If violence had been used, it must have been a tidy violence. He would have liked very much to know whether there were any marks or bruises on the trunk, but that was impossible; forcing himself to look calmly at her face, he could detect none there. With careful fingers he felt gingerly round the back of her head, sliding his hand underneath the hat, but no lump or swelling rewarded his search.

He lifted her hands, and scrutinised in turn the space beneath each nail.

So far as he could make out without a magnifying-glass, nothing was to be seen there except a few tiny strands belonging obviously to the cord that had hanged her, and some fragments of skin. On either side of her neck, as Roger had expected, was a number of long, deep scratches. Before losing consciousness, Ena Stratton must have scrabbled desperately at the cord that was choking her. The palms of her hands, too, showed distinct signs of excoriation.

But that did not of necessity say that all of the little lumps of skin under her nails came from her own neck. Had the murderer succeeded in removing himself quickly enough out of the range of those clawing hands? Or was there anyone in the party who carried a brand-new scratch on his or her own hands or face?

Roger could not go and look for the answer to that interesting question until the police arrived to set him free from his vigil.

## III

Ronald Stratton's house, Sedge Park, lay three miles or so outside the fair-sized town of Westerford. The constable who had been on duty in Westerford police-station had to cover them on his push-cycle. He arrived just thirteen minutes after Ronald had telephoned, which in view of the number of things the man himself had had to do before he could leave the station, was not too bad. Ronald, who was perfectly well known to all the members of the Westerford police and himself knew most of them, brought him up to the bedroom, where he at once began asking his routine questions.

Perfectly unnecessary, thought Roger, as he left them to it, because the inspector will ask exactly the same ones all over again as soon as he arrives; but they always do it.

He went upstairs once more.

Most of the party were collected now in the big room with the side open to the head of the well-staircase, where the bar had been set up. Nearly everyone was extremely tired and conversation was only spasmodic, but bed was out of the question. Ronald had already warned them that the police would almost certainly want to question each person. Standing about, or thrown into the big leather arm-chairs, they stared moodily into the still-glowing fire.

At Roger's arrival, a flicker of interest went round; and Dr. Chalmers asked whether Frank Mitchell had yet arrived.

"No," Roger explained, "but the police have. A constable. He says the inspector will be here in five or ten minutes."

He looked round the room. There was no scratch visible on any face. He had hardly expected that there would be.

He joined Dr. Chalmers by the fire-place, and opened a low-toned conversation.

"Did you arrive at any conclusion as to how long she'd been dead?" he asked.

Dr. Chalmers looked at him inquiringly. "How long?" he repeated.

"Yes. I was just wondering whether she did it immediately after she rushed out of the ball-room, or whether she brooded about it first."

"Oh, I see. Well, it's difficult to say to a few minutes, you know. I took the temperature of the body, and from that, and certain other indications, I should say that, allowing for the temperature of the outside air, she must have been dead at least two hours."

"Two hours," Roger said thoughtfully. "Then she probably did it at once."

"Oh, I think so, undoubtedly. She made the scene, my wife told me, just after I was called out?"

"Yes?" said Roger inattentively. "Yes. By the way, what's the local police-inspector like?"

"A very good fellow. Not a fusser, but quite thorough. He'll go into all details of course, but in such a straightforward case there's not very much he can do, is there?"

"No," said Roger. "I suppose there isn't."

His eyes were on the top of the staircase, perfectly visible through the low balustrade which had replaced the wall on that side of the room. The staircase ended in a small landing, off which the ball-room opened. The landing ran on for a few yards past the ball-room door, and at the end on the left there rose the short flight of stairs which led up on to the roof. This flight pierced through one of the remaining gables, so that its upper half was concealed from the bar-room; but the lower half, and the whole of the landing, was perfectly visible. Anyone mounting to the roof would therefore be under the observation of anyone standing at the bar.

The conversation with Dr. Chalmers petered out as Roger pondered over his very meagre two and two, and tried to make them into a robust four.

Anyone going up on to the roof could be seen by anyone in the bar-room. But nobody knew where Ena Stratton had gone; therefore nobody had been in the bar-room just then, because the most absorbed toper could not have remained oblivious of her exit and passage. Therefore, if her murderer followed her almost at once on to the roof, again nobody was in the bar-room, or in all probability nobody, to mark his passage either. But, of course, one must not forget that the murderer might have been on the roof already, and met her there.

Anyhow, the obvious question was: who was in the ball-room just then, and stayed there? It was possible at any rate to eliminate, if one could not construct.

Quite unconscious of the fact that to Dr. Chalmers his conduct might appear extremely rude, Roger pushed his hands in his pockets, turned his back on the other man, and wandered, absorbed in his thoughts, on to the landing, where he propped his back against the stalwart pillar which ended the balustrade, and frowned ferociously as he tried to throw his memory back over the last two hours.

First of all Dr. Chalmers himself was eliminated, as he had not been on the premises at all. Then, Ronald, Mrs. Lefroy, Celia Stratton, and Mrs. Williamson had been with himself in the group which had tried to be kind to David Stratton. Yes, and Margot Stratton and Mike Armstrong. So they were all cleared. Whom did that leave? Williamson, Colin Nicolson, Mrs. Chalmers, Dr. and Mrs. Mitchell—but the last two had been the first to begin the dancing again (Roger distinctly remembered that), just before he himself had led David Stratton—why, dash it all, he himself had been at the bar within a few minutes of Mrs. Stratton's disappearance! He himself had been mounting guard over the only way of access to the roof. And had anyone passed along the landing and gone up there? Roger smiled to himself with exasperation. For the life of him he could not say. Of so much value is the evidence of the man on the spot. Roger Sheringham himself simply had not the faintest idea whether anyone had slipped out of the ball-room or not.

Nevertheless, this line of inquiry had not been quite fruitless. One thing at any rate was certain. David Stratton, who after all might be said to have a greater motive than anyone else, could not possibly have murdered his wife. During the really critical period he had been in Roger's own company.

Well, that was one step, and a big one.

Roger looked up, to find Colin Nicolson talking to him.

"...thought about?" said Colin.

"Do you mind saying that again, Colin?" said Roger politely.

"I said, well, what's the great man plunged in thought about? Not very well put, perhaps, but that's what I said." Nicolson lifted a hand and felt, in the eternal gesture of the dinner-jacketed male, the sit of his tie.

Roger looked at the hand with interest. Just above the knuckles ran a long new scratch.

IV

It was impossible, of course, that Colin Nicolson could be the murderer of Mrs. Stratton. Absolutely and entirely out of the question. For one thing Colin would no more commit a murder than rob a blind widow, and for another he scarcely knew Mrs. Stratton at all—possibly had not spoken to her the whole evening. It was quite out of the question that Colin could have done such an incredible thing.

Nevertheless, Roger had been looking for someone who bore a nice new scratch somewhere visible, and here was a nice new scratch on Colin. Colin, at any rate, must account for the scratch.

"What was I thinking about?" Roger repeated vaguely. "Ah!"

"Very interesting, no doubt. Well, this is a nice business, I must say. How long do you think the police are going to keep us hanging about?"

"Oh, most of the night, I expect. You seem to have scratched your hand, Colin," Roger said mildly.

"Ach, yes. A nasty jab."

"Yes. Come up on the roof."

"On the roof?"

"I want a mouthful of fresh air."

"It'll be deuced parky fresh air. Besides, we've only just come down. No, no. If you want more fresh air, you can go up there alone."

"As a matter of fact, I want to speak to you rather particularly, Colin. Away from these people."

"Ach, you're a nuisance, Roger. All right, I suppose you'll give me no peace till I do."

Roger led an unwilling Colin out on the roof.

"Ah, that's better. You ought to do something about that scratch, Colin. How did you get it?"

"Oh, it's nothing. Do you expect me to faint at every wee scratch I get? Well, what do you want to say, now you've got me here?" asked Colin, turning up the collar of his coat. "For pity's sake, hurry up and get it over."

Roger took the other's hand and examined the scratch. It was broad, but not deep.

"How did you get it, Colin?" he repeated.

"Och, man, what's it matter?"

"I'd just like to know."

Colin stared at him. "You're very suspicious. What's the idea?"

Roger laughed soothingly. "Just exercising my well-known powers. Whatever caused that scratch, my dear Colin, it wasn't, for instance, a pin. Look at it for yourself."

"Does it matter a tuppenny damn what caused it?"

"Not even a three-ha'penny one. It's just my regrettable curiosity. Don't tell me if it's anything terribly private."

"Why should it be private, you old rascal?"

"Well, it looks to me like a scratch from someone's fingernail. In fact, if I didn't know you so well, Colin, I should say you had been making a nuisance of yourself to a lady, and got very properly scratched for your pains."

Roger's fly-fishing was rewarded.

"Well, it was nothing of the sort," Colin said crossly, "and no one but a mind like yours would have thought it was. If you're really so curious, I got it on a bit of broken glass."

"And where have you been playing with broken glass?"

Colin grudgingly gave the commonplace particulars. He had broken a glass at the bar, and hidden the pieces under the table.

# Chapter VIII

## THE CASE AGAINST ROGER SHERINGHAM

### I

"I ACCEPT YOUR EXPLANATION, COLIN," ROGER SAID judicially, leaning back against the railing that bordered the roof.

"The deuce you do, Roger. That's very kind of you."

"Don't get heated. I was only thinking that men have been hanged before now, because their explanations weren't accepted. Many, many men, Colin."

"Have you brought me up here in the cold just to tell me that?"

"We'll go into the sun-parlour, if you prefer it," Roger said kindly.

"I do prefer it. I've reached the age when I appreciate comfort." Colin Nicolson was an elderly and disillusioned twenty-eight.

They went down the steps to the sun-parlour, switched on the light, and found two chairs.

"Well, now, what's on your mind, Roger?" Colin asked when they were settled.

"Why should you think anything's on my mind?"

"I know the signs. You're like an old warhorse that smells the powder. Surely you're not trying to twist this business into anything serious?"

"I should have thought," Roger said mildly, "that it was quite serious enough already."

"Huh!" Colin made a Scotch noise, expressive of any interpretation which its hearer might care to put on it.

Roger was minded to try a little experiment.

"No, of course not. I was just thinking on what small points these cases depend. One single piece of evidence is enough to turn an apparently obvious case of suicide into a still more obvious case of murder, or an accident into a suicide, or what you will. As a student of crime yourself, Colin, can you pick out the vital piece of evidence in this case?"

"Vital, you mean, for suicide?"

"Yes."

Colin thought. "That she'd been talking about killing herself half the evening?"

"No, no, no. That's evidence the other way, if anything. No, I mean material evidence."

Colin pondered. "No, I'm blessed if I can."

"Well, everyone just takes it for granted that it was suicide. Why? No, I'll tell you. Because there *is* a piece of evidence which does actually prove it was suicide, but which in all probability no one has consciously realised. They've seen it, and they've absorbed it, but because it was part of the general picture of suicide they just take it for granted. Like you, not one of them could put a name to it. Can't you, Colin? It's something perfectly obvious."

"Do you mean the absence of any signs of violence?"

"No, but of course that is a point, too," Roger had to concede.

"Well, what is it, then?"

"Why, that chair on the ground below her, of course. You remember there was a chair lying on its side under the gallows?"

"Yes."

"Well, the presence of that chair proves that she wasn't lifted up into the noose, and it proves, too, that she did voluntarily put her own head in. Doesn't it?"

"Yes, I see what you mean. Very interesting, Roger. Yes, that's the important piece of evidence, without a doubt."

Roger nodded, and lit a cigarette.

His experiment had been successful. The human mind is apt to accept what it thinks ought to exist with such decision that it will even construct and imprint on the memory perfectly detailed pictures the originals of which never, in fact, did exist at all. Colin without doubt had looked several times when they were on the roof just now at the gallows. Underneath the gallows was a fallen chair. That fallen chair was a necessary detail in a stage set for suicide. Colin therefore perfectly remembered it being there while he was administering first-aid to Mrs. Stratton twenty minutes ago. The picture was firmly printed on his brain: a gallows with only two figures instead of three, and a fallen chair on the ground beneath the third cross-beam. It was impossible that the chair could not have been there twenty minutes ago. Colin remembered its presence perfectly. He would swear, with complete sincerity, not merely that he thought the chair was there when he first came out on the roof, but that it actually was there.

And so would everyone else in the party.

Roger never had been troubled by the smallest doubt that the addition of the chair to the picture would be noticed by a single person.

"And you think," Colin pursued, "that if the chair hadn't been there, the case would have smelt of murder?"

"I'd put it a little more strongly than that. I should say that murder would have been perfectly obvious." Roger was enjoying the irony of discussing fact as if it was wild hypothesis. It was a pity Colin could not appreciate the irony.

"Because she couldn't possibly have got her neck into the noose without either being lifted up, or standing on something high enough?"

"Exactly. Do you agree?"

"Yes, I certainly do. This is very interesting, Roger."

"It's good exercise, to appreciate the importance of trifles," Roger said cautiously.

"And that's why you were so interested in my scratch?"

Roger laughed. If Colin only knew how near the wind he was sailing…

"Well, we can say that it amused me, by way of exercise, to pretend to myself that the chair never had been there at all, and therefore it was a case of murder; and there were you with a nice scratch on your hand, just such as I might have been looking for on one of the party in that event."

"Well, well. But what motive could I have had for making away with the unfortunate woman? There's motive enough going about, I'll grant you, but not in my case. I'd never met her before this evening."

"But don't you see, that's precisely what would make the perfect murder," Roger said with enthusiasm. "It's motive, in ninety-nine cases out of a hundred, that really pins a murder on a certain individual. Without a motive, suspicion might never be directed towards him at all."

"Without a motive there'd be no murder." Colin was entering into the discussion with nearly as much interest as Roger himself, although to him it must have seemed almost preposterously academic.

"When I say without a motive, of course I mean without an apparent motive. But take this very instance. You apparently had no motive at all for Mrs. Stratton's death. That is to say, no material motive. But need a motive always be material? What about a spiritual one?"

"Well, what about a spiritual one?" said Colin, rather aggressively.

"*De mortuis nil nisi verum.* I see no reason why one shouldn't speak the truth about the dead. The woman was a pest. She was making a nuisance of herself to almost everyone she came in contact with, she was a real menace to the happiness of at least two people here to-night, and she was making her husband's life a misery to him. There were only two things that could be done to stop her: shut her up in a mad-house, or polish her off. Unfortunately she wasn't quite insane enough to be certifiable; therefore only the second alternative remains. But not one of the people who had a material motive for her removal had the moral guts to effect it.

"Along comes Colin Nicolson, judicial, sympathetic, strong-minded, clear-sighted enough to see right through shibboleths, and courageous enough to act on his own judgment. He knows that laws were made for man, but he knows too that some people put themselves outside those laws. He is socialistic enough to believe that the security of the majority demands the sacrifice of the individual. He is intelligent enough to realise that it is hardly possible that suspicion can ever fall on him, and that he is taking very little risk. He is sorry, of course, that what he conceives to be his duty should require of him anything so drastic, and he is sorry too for Mrs. Stratton; but he is a great deal more sorry for the people whose lives might be ruined if Mrs. Stratton is allowed to go on living. And so..."

"Well, well," said Colin calmly. "But I'm not sure you've got my character so well. I'm afraid I'm not so noble as all that, Roger. It all sounded to me much more like you."

"It did rather, didn't it?" said Roger, not without surprise. "Anyhow, you see what I mean?"

"Oh, yes," said Colin slowly. "I see that."

He sat for a moment in thoughtful silence, and then lifted his stocky bulk to its feet.

"Going down again?" Roger asked.

"No, back in a minute."

Colin went out of the sun-parlour and up on to the roof. Through the glass wall Roger saw him walk across the roof and come to a halt under the gallows. With his hands in his pockets, he seemed to be staring at the chair which had been the cause of all the talk. Then Roger saw him take a large white silk handkerchief out of his breast-pocket and thoroughly wipe over the back, rails, and seat of the chair. After that he walked, in his unhurried way, back to the sun-parlour.

"What on earth…?" said Roger, in bewilderment not unmixed with apprehension.

Colin looked at him with some severity. "The trouble with you, Roger," he said, "is that you talk a jolly sight too much."

"Talk?"

"Yes. In the circumstances, I should keep my mouth shut, if I were you. How on earth did you know I was safe? I might not have been."

"My dear Colin, what on earth are you talking about? And what were you doing with that chair?"

"Wiping your finger-prints off," Colin said calmly, "just in case you'd forgotten to do so yourself."

"Wiping my…"

"Yes. You see, I happen to know that chair wasn't under the gallows at all when we first came up on the roof. It was in the middle somewhere. I know, because I almost fell over it, and barked my shin rather nastily. If I were you, I wouldn't tell anyone else you moved it. It might look fishy."

"But I didn't…"

"Yes, you did, in so many words. I tell you, Roger, you talk too much. If I were you, I wouldn't sound anyone else about suicide or murder. In fact, I wouldn't say a word about the case at all. It's too dangerous, man. Of course, I know you've probably got an urge to talk about it, but you must just shut it down. I won't give you away, of course, and I suppose really it was a pretty good thing for you to have done; but you can't bank on everyone else, you know."

"I don't think there was any risk, really," Roger said feebly, somewhat taken aback by this severity and cursing himself for having under-estimated Colin's shrewdness.

"No risk!" Colin snorted. "It's all very well to talk of spiritual motives and no suspicion and all that, but if you think you can get away with murder without any risk, and then go boasting about it, you'll soon find your own neck in the same place as you put Mrs. Stratton's."

## II

"Is it the least good," Roger said desperately, "for me to go on telling you that I did *not* murder Mrs. Stratton?"

"I'll believe you, of course," Colin said, without the least trace of credulity in his voice.

"Thank you, Colin," Roger said bitterly.

"And in any case," Colin added, "I told you I wouldn't give you away."

Roger began all over again.

"Well, anyhow," Colin said judicially, "someone murdered her."

"I know someone did! My goodness, I wish I'd never moved that blessed chair. This is what comes of trying to do someone a good turn."

"Even in that case," said Colin smugly, "it's a pretty serious thing, you know, monkeying about with evidence."

"But, dash it all, man, the woman deserved murdering! I know that in theory it's a shocking thing to shield a murderer. But this case is exceptional. Who ever did such a good deed deserves shielding. You'd have done the same yourself."

"I would not," said Colin with decision. "I've told you I'll hold my tongue, but that's as far as I'd go. I wouldn't fake the evidence. The game wouldn't be worth the candle. I wouldn't risk my neck to get other people out of their own troubles."

"Risk your neck?"

"It would make me an accessory after the fact, wouldn't it? And the legal penalty for that is the same as for murder. I suppose, by the way," Colin added uneasily, "that I'm an accessory after some sort of fact now. Why on earth couldn't you hold your tongue, Roger? I should never have guessed if you hadn't given yourself away. I was a fool though, too, to let you know I had guessed."

"But I keep on telling you I didn't murder the woman!"

"I know you do," said Colin. "And I keep on telling you that I won't give you away."

"Oh, hell!" said Roger.

There was an unhappy little silence.

"My dear Colin, you can't possibly pretend there's a *case* against me," Roger said, almost plaintively.

"Do you want me to show you the case against you?"

"I'd love you to," Roger said bitterly.

"Well, man, you told me the motive yourself. It was silly to pretend it was a motive for me, because it isn't. I'm not nearly high-minded enough to take a risk like that for someone I hardly know. And I might add that I'm not officious enough, either, to meddle in other people's affairs to such an extent as that. But you are, Roger, if you want me to be candid. You're the most officious person I know, and the most self-confident. If anyone in this world could commit an entirely spiritual, altruistic, infernally officious murder, it's you."

"Thank you, Colin," said Roger, without gratitude.

"Well, I'm just applying your own methods."

"And all you've proved is that I might possibly be said to have a motive, out of having no motive at all. What sort of proof do you call that? The small fact that I had no opportunity at all just doesn't concern you, I suppose."

"Opportunity!" Colin exclaimed. "Well, if you hadn't the opportunity, I don't know who had."

"When did I have an opportunity?" Roger demanded, astonished.

"Mrs. Stratton was found on the roof, wasn't she? So it's a reasonable inference that she was on the roof, or in here, all the time after she left the ball-room. In fact, as no one saw her again, it's more than a reasonable inference that she was up here. It's almost a dead certainty. You'll agree with that, I suppose."

"Yes, I do," Roger said defiantly. "Well?"

"Well, so far as I know, you were the only person, during the time she was missing, who was up here too."

*"What!"*

"After you'd been consoling poor wee David at the bar, didn't you come straight up here when I joined the two of you?" asked Colin calmly.

"Good—good *lord*!" exclaimed Roger, thunderstruck.

It was perfectly true. The advent of Colin had given Roger the excuse to slip away. The conversation with David had, in the circumstances, been somewhat forced; and Roger felt that the enormous log-fire was making the room not only uncomfortably hot but much too smoky. He had gone up on to the roof and stood for a few minutes just outside the door, smoking a cigarette, and allowing the smoke from the room below to pour out through the open doorway. He had forgotten all about it, but Colin was perfectly right.

He had seen no one on the roof, but he must have been there at least four or five minutes; and during that time there could be no doubt now that Ena Stratton must have been in the sun-parlour, alone—or with her murderer.

This was infernally awkward.

"And of course," Colin pursued, "after that poor David had been telling you all his troubles, you'd have been feeling nasty and worked-up."

Roger turned a distressed face on his accuser.

"David didn't tell me all his troubles," he could only say feebly. "He didn't even mention his wife at all. We talked about the Test-matches, and the leg-theory. You can ask him."

"I wouldn't think of it," said Colin primly.

Roger said nothing.

"It was you who asked me for the case," said Colin.

"And you think," Roger said with emotion, "that during those few minutes I was up here, I carried Mrs. Stratton to the gallows and hanged her there?"

"Someone did. If it wasn't you, Roger, who was it?"

"You might at least give me the credit of not being such a bungler as to have forgotten the essential chair."

"Someone forgot it. It was a bad mistake, of course. But the murderer who's found out always has made a bad mistake. I suppose," said Colin, regarding the end of his cigarette, "that having been mixed up with murder so much, you didn't regard it quite so seriously as some of us do; and that may have made you a bit careless about the details."

Roger choked.

"And, of course, it was your talking about the chair that gave the whole thing away," Colin went on, with complete imperturbability. "I wondered what you were driving at. Then I understood. You were worried about that chair. You knew you'd forgotten to put it there at the time; and though you'd seen your mistake and put it right afterwards, you were a bit frightened that somebody might have noticed it wasn't there before. So you tried to suggest it on me, in order to have a witness that it had been there all the time, just in case of trouble. That was jolly clever of you, Roger."

"But it didn't come off, did it?"

"No, you overdid it," said Colin frankly. "Still, it was a bright idea, after you'd given yourself away, to pretend you'd moved it to shield someone else. Very bright. But unfortunately, not very probable."

"It just happens to be the truth, that's all."

"And as you'd made so many bloomers already," Colin went on, just as if Roger had not spoken at all, "I thought you might quite well have been ass enough to have left your finger-prints on it too, and I'd better wipe them off first and hear what you'd got to say afterwards. Did you leave your prints on it, by the way?" Colin asked with interest.

"Yes," said Roger wrathfully.

"I thought you would have done," said Colin, with insufferable complacence.

"I do seem to have been a clumsy murderer, don't I?"

"I expect it takes practice," Colin soothed him.

Again there was a little pause. "Well, any more?"

"Isn't that enough?" asked Colin.

"And are you going to the police with this fool of a story?"

"I told you, *I* won't give you away. But you'd better watch out that you don't give yourself away, again."

"I wish you would go to the police," Roger yammered.

"Thanks, I don't want to be mixed up in it at all."

"Then I'll go to them myself, and tell them exactly what you've said!"

"You're a fool if you do," Colin said coolly.

In spite of his indignation Roger still had enough sense left to see that he would, indeed, be a very great fool if he did.

Once more there was a raging silence.

Then there was the sound of footsteps outside, and Ronald Stratton appeared in the doorway.

"Oh, here you are, Roger. I've been looking for you everywhere. The inspector's here and wants to see you. In the dining-room."

Roger rose, not unthankful to escape.

He caught Colin's eye.

Colin nodded reassuringly.

# Chapter IX

## THE CASE AGAINST DR. CHALMERS

### I

Inspector Crane, of the Westerford police, was a tall, loosely-built man, not in the least like the usual drill-sergeant type of police-inspector. He had a pleasant face and, in this house at any rate, almost an apologetic manner; certainly there was none of the snapping self-importance about him which some police officials adopt. Ronald Stratton already knew him fairly well, and so had been able to explain the circumstances to him without the uneasy constraint which the presence of a stranger might have induced.

On learning that Roger Sheringham had been among the guests, the inspector had named that gentleman as the first of the party whom he would like to interview.

"Very pleased to meet you, sir," he greeted Roger. "Heard about you before now, of course. A terrible business this, sir, though fortunately not in your line, we hope."

"No," said Roger firmly. "Of course not."

"No. Well, sir, if you'll sit down, I should very much like to hear from you anything which you think may throw light on the tragedy, or assist the coroner."

It was the dining-room which had been offered to the inspector for the conduct of his interviews, and both men seated themselves at one end of the long table, the inspector with his notebook expectantly open before him. Roger saw at once that the proceedings were not going to be unduly formal, for both the Stratton brothers were present, too, Ronald perched on the edge of the table with his foot on a chair's seat, and David leaning silently back against the mantelpiece.

"You must understand, inspector, that I scarcely knew Mrs. Stratton," Roger began, and went on to give an account of his own dealings with her that evening.

"Ah!" The inspector pricked up his ears and licked his pencil hopefully. "Mrs. Stratton actually mentioned to you her intention of taking her own life?"

"The possibility, rather than the intention," Roger corrected. "Still, yes, she did."

"But in spite of that, you did nothing?" said the inspector, somewhat apologetically.

"What could I have done? She merely referred to the possibility in the future. She said nothing about carrying out any such intention to-night."

"So you took no steps, sir?"

"None."

"I ought to ask you," said the inspector still more apologetically, "why you did not consider it necessary to take steps?"

"Because I didn't believe a word of what she'd been saying. I'm bound to tell you that I thought she was talking just for effect."

"'I did not consider her intentions serious,'" said the inspector, writing, busily. "Does that express what you felt, Mr. Sheringham?"

"I think so," Roger agreed, avoiding Ronald Stratton's eye.

"You didn't mention her words to anyone else? To Mr. Stratton, for instance?"

"No; as you say, I didn't take them seriously enough. But somebody else mentioned them to me."

"Sir?"

"Someone else asked me if she had spoken to me about doing away with herself. I gather," Roger said dryly, "that she had touched on this possibility to other people besides myself."

"Is that the case? That's very interesting. Will you be good enough to tell me who asked you that?"

"Certainly. It was Mr. Williamson."

"'Mr. Williamson asked me at one period whether...'"

"Mr. Williamson had already asked me, in Mr. Sheringham's hearing," put in Ronald Stratton, "whether my sister-in-law were mad. You remember, Sheringham? Quite early."

"Yes," Roger nodded. "I remember quite well. It made me wonder at the time."

"What did it make you wonder, sir?"

"Whether Mrs. Stratton might be a little unbalanced."

"And am I right in thinking that your subsequent conversation with Mrs. Stratton did lead you to that conclusion?" asked the inspector, with an uneasy glance at David Stratton.

"It did. I think Mrs. Stratton was undoubtedly a little unbalanced. But not, I thought then, to the point of suicide." Roger did not add that he did not think that now, either.

The inspector turned with awkward sympathy to David Stratton. "That did not coincide with your own opinion, Mr. Stratton?"

"No," David said shortly. "That's why I rang you people up. I considered my wife totally irresponsible for her actions."

"Yes, yes." The inspector was a little flustered. "I have our man's report. Very curious that should have happened on the very same evening, when… The coroner's bound to ask something about that."

"But it all fits in, Inspector, doesn't it?" Ronald put in smoothly. "I mean, it's a rather remarkable piece of corroborative evidence about Mrs. Stratton's state of mind. Why should the coroner ask about it particularly?"

"Well, you see, Mr. Stratton hadn't ever rung us up like that before; had you, Mr. Stratton?"

"No."

"There'd never been any occasion to do so," Ronald amplified.

"It struck you this evening that Mrs. Stratton was behaving—how shall I put it?—in a more irresponsible way than usual?" the inspector asked David.

"Yes, I think she was." David Stratton had spoken all the time in a curiously sharp voice, as if he wanted to get his words out and be done with them.

"After all," Ronald put in again, "my brother didn't ring up until Mrs. Stratton had been missing from her home for some time, and not until we'd looked everywhere here first, as I told you. He was naturally alarmed; and I don't suppose Mrs. Stratton had ever behaved in that way before. Had she, David?"

"Never."

"So in view of the irresponsibility she had shown during the evening, and which other people had noticed besides ourselves, he thought that you people ought to be warned, just in case; though I don't think he anticipated anything really serious. Did you, David?"

"Not really. I thought it better to be on the safe side, that's all."

"You didn't anticipate that Mrs. Stratton might do away with herself, sir?"

"No; I said, not really. My wife had often talked about suicide. She had moods of great depression. But like Mr. Sheringham, I'm afraid I didn't take it very seriously."

"I see. What was it that Mrs. Stratton was depressed about?"

"Nothing."

"Mrs. Stratton suffered from melancholia to some extent," Ronald supplied, as smoothly as before. "She had nothing to worry about, really; her life should have been a very happy one; but you know how that kind of person magnifies trifles, and twists the smallest things into big ones. It was all part of her complaint. It's no good trying to hide the fact, Inspector," said Ronald, with an air of frankness. "My sister-in-law was really not quite normal. I think the doctors will be able to give you some useful information on that point, if they haven't done so already."

"No, sir, we haven't got on to that yet, but no doubt they will. Now, Mr. Sheringham, let me see, you were telling me..."

Roger resumed his story.

He had been listening with considerable interest to

the three-cornered conversation which had just taken place. It was the attitude of David Stratton which had been puzzling him. That of Ronald was plain enough; he had been trying to take as much of the burden off David's thinner shoulders as he possibly could, even to the risk of getting rapped over the knuckles for answering David's questions for him.

But why this sharp, almost aggressive manner of David's when he did speak? And why did he answer sometimes just as if he were repeating a lesson, and a lesson not too intelligently learned at that? He did not seem to Roger to be suffering still from shock. But he did seem to be concealing by this attitude some emotion which he did not care to show; though whether that emotion were joy or sorrow, fear or relief, it was impossible to guess.

## II

The laborious interrogatory was resumed.

Roger corroborated the account Ronald Stratton had already given of the scene in the ball-room and Mrs. Stratton's exit, and provided his own version of the return of David and the subsequent search. Everything was written down by the careful inspector, and though Roger made his story as brief as possible, it seemed as if the thing never would be finished.

"Yes, Mr. Sheringham? And after Mr. Williamson made his communication to you?"

"I called Mr. Stratton, and we ran up on the roof. Mr. Stratton held Mrs. Stratton up," Roger dictated slowly, "while I made a quick examination which convinced me that she was already dead. I then held her up while Mr. Stratton went to fetch a knife, on my instructions. When he returned, I told him to cut the cord, and I would take full responsibility for the fact that she was cut down."

"It would, in fact, not be an exaggeration to say that you took charge immediately you suspected that Mrs. Stratton was dead?"

"Yes, in view of the experience I've had in similar circumstances, I felt justified in taking charge."

"Quite so, Mr. Sheringham; and a very fortunate thing for Mr. Stratton, no doubt, that he had you on the premises. Now did you form any opinion when you examined Mrs. Stratton as to the length of time she had been dead?"

"No, that would be impossible for me; I haven't the knowledge. All I can say is that I thought she must have been dead some time, an hour at least and probably more, because her hands were quite cold."

"I understand the doctors thought she must have been dead not less than two hours, when they examined her just now. Would you agree with that?"

"Oh, yes; but that's a matter for them, you know, not me. Mitchell's arrived, then?" Roger added to Ronald Stratton.

"Yes; he came just after the inspector, and Chalmers brought him in to see the body at once."

"He agrees with Chalmers's estimate of the length of time she had been dead?"

"Yes."

Roger nodded to the inspector to go on with his questions.

It was all very informal and pleasingly unofficial, but it was all very tedious, too.

## III

Twenty minutes later, after the inspector had dealt with and dwelt on every conceivably relevant point and a great many irrelevant ones, Roger was allowed to escape and send Williamson in his place. The inspector was a thorough man and obviously intended to earn his superintendent's praise for taking pains; but it was clear that no thought of anything but suicide had ever seriously entered his mind. Not a question had Roger been asked, among all the welter of questions, which might have caused him to depart from the strict truth concerning any such matters as chairs or finger-prints.

And yet Colin Nicolson was convinced that he, Roger Sheringham of all people, had murdered Ena Stratton.

Colin was being quite nice about it; but that he was so convinced, Roger was sure. And Roger was worried. The crime of evidence-faking had come home to roost on him with a vengeance. He cursed the self-satisfied, smug impulse which had prompted him to alter the position of that chair. That, and the fact that he was known to have been up on the roof during the crucial period, gave Colin an unpleasantly strong case against him. Not that Roger was afraid that Colin would inform on him; he was quite sure that nothing of that kind would enter Colin's head. But nevertheless to be suspected so strongly of a murder which one has not committed, does give one a nasty, haunted feeling. In justice to himself now, as well as in mere acceptance of a challenge, it was up to Roger to discover the real murderer.

And Colin should jolly well help him!

He went upstairs in search of Colin.

Roger had always respected Colin, in rather a tolerant way. Now he found himself respecting Colin in great sincerity. One does respect a person who could land one quite easily in a singularly unpleasant prison-cell.

IV

He found Williamson and sent him downstairs, now unassailably sober, to be interrogated.

In the bar-room Colin was alone, dozing in front of the fire just as Williamson had been dozing alone in the ball-room. When shaken into consciousness, the latter had informed Roger that the women had retired, worn-out, to get a little sleep before the inspector wanted to see them. The time was now close on half-past four in the morning.

With ruthless hand Roger roused Colin into complete wakefulness.

"There's going to be no sleep for you this night, my lad; nor for me either. Come into the ball-room. I want to talk to you, seriously."

"Ach, let me alone, man. I told you, I'd forget it." At four-thirty in the morning sleep becomes almost more important than murder.

"Come along," said Roger sternly.

Grumbling, Colin went.

"Where are the doctors?" Roger asked, as they shut themselves in and sat down.

"Gone, while you were downstairs. They came up for a wee night-cap and then went off. Poor chaps, they looked whacked, both of them."

"I wonder they were able to get away so early?" Roger said heartlessly.

"They'd made their report, and the inspector said he wouldn't want them any more. They've got to see the superintendent some time to-day. You were a very long time downstairs, Roger. Put you through it, did they?"

"Oh, they were quite kind," Roger said bitterly. "I told them how I'd committed the murder, and they just told me to run away and be a good boy and not do that sort of thing again."

"Ah!" said Colin. Evidently he did not consider this a suitable topic for jest.

"Blast you, Colin, I've *got* to find out who did it now. I'm not going to have you looking at me for the rest of my life as if I was a murderer. It's going to keep me up all night, and it's going to keep you up, too; so that for your infernal interference."

"Why me?"

"Because you're going to help me. So we'd better get down to it."

But they did not get down to it at once. For some minutes they sat in silence, busy with their thoughts.

Then Colin looked up.

"You know, Roger, say what you like, this is damned interesting. It really was murder, was it? You're convinced of that?"

"Absolutely. It must have been. The hypothetical case I put to you in the sun-parlour, like a damned fool, was the real one. That chair wasn't there at all. I put it there."

"But why? That's what I can't understand. Why?"

Roger tried to explain why.

"And have you blabbed it out to anyone else besides me?" asked Colin.

"No," said Roger, wincing.

"Well, what's your idea? I'll help you. Why, man, this is great stuff. I hope it wasn't wee Ronald, because I like him."

"No," Roger said slowly. "I have an idea it wasn't wee Ronald."

"But you have an idea it might have been someone else? Come on, Roger, out with it. This is grand."

"Yes, I have got an idea. Do you remember what I was saying to you in the sun-parlour, about a man being actuated not by a material motive but a spiritual one?"

"Sure I do. What's in your mind?"

"Well, I was trying out a theory on you, to see how it sounded."

"It sounded all right to me. Or the way you put it, it did."

"And to me, too. Colin, I'm pretty sure I know who did string up Ena Stratton."

"The dickens, you do! Who?"

"Dr. Philip Chalmers," said Roger.

V

"Phil Chalmers?" Colin echoed incredulously. "Oh, come now, Roger. He's a grand fellow."

"It's just because he's a grand fellow that I suspect him," Roger retorted. "Or partially. You see, he hasn't any other motive."

"This is going a bit too deep for me. I don't see this at all."

"Well, look at it this way," Roger explained with energy. "Chalmers is a very old friend of the Strattons. And he's a doctor. That means that he's in a better situation than anyone else to know exactly the position with regard to Ena Stratton: that she'd make the life of any man living with her a burden and a misery to him, and that there's no hope at all of her ever getting any better. He knows, in fact, that Mrs. Stratton ought to be behind locked doors, but that she just can't be.

"Now, Chalmers's particularly close friend among the Strattons is not Ronald, but David. And Chalmers, as you say, is a grand fellow. It's impossible that Chalmers shouldn't have been very worried and very upset by the fact that his great friend David is being led the hell of a life by a worthless woman. Obviously he must have been. You're with me so far, I suppose?"

"Yes, I'll grant you all that. But what next?"

"Well, briefly, that he saw an opportunity to-night of getting rid of her, and just took it."

"Ach!"

"Wait a minute. I said, he saw an opportunity. I don't for a moment suggest that Chalmers planned to get rid of Ena Stratton. He isn't that type at all. He couldn't plan a crime; certainly not a murder. But on the other hand, he's a man of character. If the opportunity presented itself, I can quite see him seizing it. And you must remember that he'd seen enough this evening to stir him up to a considerable pitch of indignation on David's behalf. Mrs. Stratton did make an exhibition of herself, didn't she? And as David's friend, Chalmers was probably quite as embarrassed, altruistically, as David was on his own behalf. Perhaps a little more so. David seems to have become rather dulled to his wife's performances in public. You needn't look at me like that, Colin. It's quite conceivable."

"Well, say it was. What was the opportunity, then? How did he do it?"

"I imagine they must have been on the roof together. Perhaps they were leaning over the railing, and she was inflicting her remarkable introspections on him, as she seems to have done on most people this evening. She may even have been trying to get him to make love to her."

"Ah, come; steady now, Roger. Talk sense."

"Women have been known to do such a thing," Roger said dryly. "Anyhow, let's say she goaded him just beyond that limit of endurance which we call sanity. They were somewhere near the gallows. Chalmers sees that the figure of the woman has fallen on to the roof; the straw neck wasn't strong enough to last. Instantly the idea jumps into his mind: put a woman where a woman was! He looks round. It's all perfectly safe. No one else is likely to come up; it's too cold. And once she's safely strung up, it's odds against anyone finding her for hours. Let him get out of the house on that call of his, and he's safe. She's been talking of suicide; it's bound to be put down to suicide. And then David can live a life of his own again, and half a dozen other people will be able to sleep more easily at night. And no one will regret her. It will be the best minute's work he ever did in his life."

"By the time he'd thought all that out, she'd have been down at the bar again, lapping up more double whiskies without soda."

"Idiot! All those things flash through his mind in ten seconds. There was no time to *think*, or he'd never have done it. Well, he inveigles her to the gallows, just underneath the noose. And then… For a strong man, just one second would do it, before she even realised what he was after or had time to scream out. Well?"

"Well, it's a case, I suppose," Colin said judicially.

"But not so strong as the case against me?"

"I told you, I'd forgotten that. But come now, Roger, you know well enough that's all guesswork. You haven't a mite of evidence. Besides, you said 'once he got out of the house on that call of his.' But he'd gone. He wasn't here at all. We saw him go."

"And then we went into the ball-room. All of us. Chalmers could have come up again, couldn't he?"

"But man, you're talking at random. He could have come up again, yes. But where's even a wee bit of evidence that he did?"

"As a matter of fact, Colin, there is a tiny bit of evidence. I don't say that it proves Chalmers did come up again after we'd all gone into the ball-room; but it does prove that he was on the roof some time this evening. Mrs. Williamson found his pipe in the sun-parlour. Ronald identified it."

"Ach! He could have left it there any time."

"He could, yes. And he did. That's the point. I'm not suggesting that he left it there then, and the talk with Mrs. Stratton was conducted in the sun-parlour. I'm suggesting that he had left it there earlier; and when he got outside the house on the way to his call, perhaps not until he was actually in his car, he felt for his pipe in the way one does and remembered that he had left it there. So he ran up for it. We know the front door was left unlatched all the evening, so there was no difficulty in getting in again. And in the sun-parlour he found not only his pipe, but Mrs. Stratton, too, sulking. Perhaps they did talk there, before moving up to the main roof. Anyhow, Mrs. Stratton was intense enough to make him forget his pipe all over again.

"But considering it was Mrs. Stratton," Roger added

shrewdly, "I shouldn't be surprised if she wasn't in the sun-parlour at all. It would have been far more typical for her to have been out on the cold, cold roof, pretending to commit suicide by pneumonia, and praying for someone to come up and catch her at it, for a little more glorification."

"Now, you're at your guesswork again."

"Oh, admittedly. But if you're going to call every theory guesswork, even when I can argue it from observed facts and reasonable inferences, we're not going to get much further."

"No, no. I won't do that. But I would like to hear a little more evidence to support your theories. I don't deny that you've put up quite a possible case against Chalmers, but it all depends on one thing, doesn't it? And that is that he did it before he went out on that call."

Roger considered. "Yes, that's right. The time of death shows that she must have died within half an hour at most of leaving the ball-room, and Chalmers was away an hour. Yes, if he did it, it must have been before he went."

Colin heaved himself up in his chair, stretched, and grinned.

"Well, I didn't say anything before, because I didn't want to spoil your fun; but I'm afraid your case falls to the ground, Roger. I'm willing to bet you five pounds to a sixpence that Chalmers went out on that call before Mrs. Stratton ever left the ball-room at all. What do you say to that?"

Roger's face fell. "Oh! My goodness, yes, I believe you're right, Colin. You would be, of course. Yes, I remember distinctly. She only began saying she wanted to go home after Chalmers had gone out, and that was what led up to the scene. Dash you, Colin, that seems to have scuppered it."

"Ah!" said Colin complacently.

"Does it, though? Wait a minute. It was only because of the time of death that I said Chalmers must have done it before he went out. Supposing the presumed time of death isn't correct. It's Chalmers's own word we've got for that, you see, and if it suited him he could have pronounced a false time of death quite easily."

"No, you're wrong again, Roger. Mitchell supported him."

"He did?"

"Yes, they were talking about it up here while you were downstairs with the inspector."

"Oh!" Roger considered.

"But that might have been a case of unconscious suasion, Colin," he went on eagerly. "I should think that a second doctor is always prejudiced in favour of the opinion of the one who made the examination first. Mitchell knows Chalmers is a sound man; he'd be perfectly ready to accept Chalmers's opinion, especially in a matter like this, where there's a certain amount of latitude.

"Yes, the more I think of it, the more it fits in. The point may be a small one, but Chalmers has been gently rubbing his alibi into all of us, hasn't he? I remember now, he took the very first opportunity of mentioning to me that the ball-room scene occurred after he'd been called out. It may have been quite a natural thing to say; but it may equally have been rather gratuitous.

"And look," Roger continued quite excitedly, "how quickly he got here after Ronald telephoned. He does live nearer than Mitchell, it's true. But why hadn't he gone to bed? He must have been home very nearly an hour—three-quarters, at any rate. Three-quarters of an hour, at that time in the morning, and he hasn't even gone to bed. Or, apparently, undressed. Doesn't that look as if he might have been waiting for the telephone call which he knew very well would come?

Obviously he wanted to get here first, before any other doctor or the police, to have a good look at the body in the light, and remove any possibly suspicious or incriminating traces. Well? Isn't that all perfectly reasonable?"

"Ach, come now, Roger," Colin shook his head. "Your case against Chalmers won't hold water, and you can't twist it into doing so."

"Perhaps you still believe I'm the man?" Roger asked unpleasantly.

"I wouldn't be surprised. Though if you say not, I'll help you look for another. But Chalmers won't do. He won't do at all."

"I still think he's got a lot to explain away," Roger said obstinately. "Yes, I'd very much like to ask friend Chalmers a few questions. No, it's no good shaking your head like a mantelpiece mandarin; there is a case against Chalmers. If he is the man, we can assume that he could cook the time of death to make it appear that Mrs. Stratton was dead half an hour before he got back to the house, can't we? Can't we, Colin?"

"Yes; but wait a minute, Roger. I..."

"No, you wait a minute. Well, if we can assume that, there's a very big hole in his defence. In that case the theory is that he came back from his visit, and instead of coming into the ballroom to the rest of us, went straight up to the sun-parlour to get his pipe. Then everything else as before. He knows he's pretty safe, because not a soul has seen him go up on the roof. Well, all he's got to do then is to wait till the coast is clear, run downstairs again, and then walk up, singing loudly, and announce himself. And he could know when the coast was clear because the roof-door can't be seen from the bar-room or the landing. He'd only have to slip inside it and wait. How's that?"

"Oh, very neat, no doubt; but listen to me. I—"

"No, you listen to me. Therefore, the objection you made just now has no point, and the case against Chalmers remains as strong as ever it did. Stronger, if anything. And what's more, it may be quite easy to test it. All we've got to do is to find out where that call of his came from, and then very gently and subtly get to know at what exact time Chalmers left there to come back here. Of course they may not—"

"Will you listen to me, Roger!" Colin shouted. "I've just thought of something."

"Well done, Colin," Roger said kindly.

"It's your theory that whoever killed Mrs. Stratton held her up with one arm and pulled the noose round her neck with the other. That's right, isn't it?"

"Certainly. For a strong man..."

"Never mind about your strong men. That's how you say Chalmers did it, and he couldn't have done it any other way?"

"Yes. Well?"

"He couldn't, for instance, have done it without using both arms?"

"No. What about it?—Oh..." said Roger in a dying kind of voice.

"Exactly," Colin cried, with tactless triumph. "Why, Roger, man, where were your eyes? You know as well as I do that Chalmers has a dud arm. He couldn't have held a fly with it that didn't want a noose round its neck, let alone a great strapping wench like Mrs. Stratton. Now perhaps you'll have the sense to admit that whoever did it, Chalmers couldn't? Will you?"

"Dash you, Colin," said Roger, annoyed, "must you rub it in?"

He tried to look on the bright side. At any rate, the

discussion had not been totally useless. Chalmers, as well as David Stratton, was now eliminated.

But at this rate it looked like being a long job.

Colin was lighting a fresh cigarette.

"Well, Roger," he said, "you've got to show me."

"Show you what?"

"That it wasn't you who strung up Mrs. Stratton," Colin said calmly.

# Chapter X
## THE CASE AGAINST DAVID STRATTON

I

In spite of Roger's prophecy, he and Colin did get to bed that night, some time after five o'clock. When Roger got down the same morning, Colin had already breakfasted. The women and Williamson had not yet appeared. Roger was rather annoyed that he had got up so early.

Ronald Stratton found him in the dining-room, toying in a somewhat disaffected way with a tired-looking egg and some bacon.

"Look here, Roger, I don't know if you were thinking you ought to hurry away this morning, but I don't want anyone to go unless they really prefer. I don't think there's the least need, and though the police haven't definitely said so, I think they'd rather that the party remained here intact till to-morrow."

"I'll stay, with pleasure," Roger agreed. "But isn't it a little awkward, with...?"

"The body was taken away this morning, to my brother's house," Ronald explained. "The inspector gave permission."

"Oh, I see. That was very quick, wasn't it, for a Sunday morning?"

"Very. David made the arrangements himself. I offered to let her stay here till the funeral, considering the boy and everything, but David thought better not."

"And the inquest?"

"Eleven o'clock to-morrow morning, here. I rather think the police will want you to give evidence."

"Yes. The inquest's to be here, is it? Then wouldn't it have been more convenient in that case for...?"

"For Ena to stop here? Yes, I should have thought so, but David imagined it might upset my arrangements for you people."

"I see. That was very thoughtful of him. Is he...?" Roger appeared to himself to be putting most of his questions in the form of dots.

"Is he all right? Oh, yes, perfectly. It's an open secret between ourselves that Ena's death is just nothing but a huge relief—to him more than to anyone else. But, of course, we don't want to advertise the fact at the inquest."

"No, of course not. The police hadn't gone, by the way, when I went to bed this morning. I suppose they're perfectly satisfied?" said Roger in a casual voice, helping himself to another cup of coffee.

"Oh, quite. Here, let me do that. After all, why shouldn't they be?"

"Why, indeed? But you seemed a little worried last night about the nature of the party."

Ronald smiled. "Yes, I'm afraid I kept quiet about that. I just said that some of the guests were in fancy dress. I don't think it's likely to come out before the inquest; but if it does, I really can't help it. After all, we're not children. One can't be expected to take precautions against the word 'murderer,' or the sight of a gallows suggesting someone into suicide, can one?"

"Not really, but you must anticipate a possible howl from the sensational Press if it does come. It sounds like jam for them. 'Morbid Amusements at House-Party' 'Ghoulish Jests Lead to Tragedy.'"

Ronald made a grimace. "Yes, I know. It all rather depends on the coroner. Luckily, I know him pretty well, and he's quite a decent fellow."

"Then you ought to be fairly safe. But you'll have to explain away the gallows, in any case. How are you going to do that?"

"The gallows," said Ronald with a grin, "were a subtle compliment to the presence among us of the Great Detective."

"In dam' bad taste, I've no doubt. Were the police shocked?"

"Not so much as I expected. In fact, the inspector was really rather amused, I think, if anything, though, of course, he had to hide it. He's a good chap."

"Well, well."

"Hullo," said Ronald. "Wasn't that the telephone? Excuse me a minute."

He was away for some minutes.

"Margot," he explained briefly, "wanted to know how we all were this morning, so I broke the news."

"I shouldn't imagine she was very distressed to hear it?"

"No," Ronald smiled. "She seemed a little more agitated than I'd have expected, but I suppose that was the surprise."

"And your sister?" asked Roger. "How's she this morning?"

"I haven't had her disturbed. The poor girl was quite whacked. She practically collapsed while the inspector was interviewing her, and I had to call down Agatha to help me get her to bed. She hadn't anything of the least importance to tell the police, of course, so it didn't really matter. I shall keep her in bed till lunch."

"Yes, I should," said Roger mechanically, and took another piece of toast.

II

Roger found Colin smoking his morning pipe in the rose garden.

"Ah, Roger," Colin greeted him; and added, a little pointedly, "How did you sleep?"

"My guilty slumbers were perfectly sound, thank you," Roger replied coldly. "I hope your position as accessory after the fact didn't interfere with yours?"

"Nothing could have interfered with them last night," Colin said simply. "I wonder why Ronald built his rose garden just like a ruined Roman temple?"

Roger looked round. The sunken oval of lawn in the centre, surrounded by a wide, raised bed within little walls of red brick and enclosed by tall brick columns beyond to carry the ramblers, did look like a ruined Roman temple. At the moment, however, Roger was not interested in Roman temples.

"I couldn't tell you, Colin." He seated himself in the sun on the brick parapet. "Look here, when I left you and David last night by the bar, to go up on the roof (a thing I wish most sincerely now that I'd never done), what happened to the two of you? When I came down you weren't there. In fact, that room was empty. Had you gone back to the ball-room?"

Colin made the face of one trying to chase an elusive memory. "I'm not sure. Why? Are you still on the trail, Roger?"

"I am," Roger said grimly. "And that's your fault. So kindly rack those things of yours you call brains, and answer my question."

Colin thoughtfully scratched the top of his slightly bald head. "Deuce take it, I don't know. Does it matter?"

"Of course it matters. I want to trace the movements of every single person with a motive for Mrs. Stratton's death, from the time the woman left the ball-room till the time David came back to say she hadn't gone home."

"The devil you do. That's not an easy job. Well, I'll do my best for you. Wait now, and let me think again."

Roger waited, fiddling with a wireworm which had been illegally investigating the roots of one of the rose-bushes.

"If you kept still," said Colin, "I might have a chance to think."

Roger kept still.

"I believe I've got it! I went back to the ball-room—yes, that's how it was, because I remember Lilian asking me how wee David was, and I said I thought the drink had done him good. Yes, I went back to the ball-room, and David didn't."

"Where did David go?"

"How on earth should I know?"

"But we must know. Can't you see how important it is?" Roger said excitedly. "Did he go up on the roof?"

"Why should he do that?"

"Look here, Colin," Roger said patiently, "is it lack of sleep that's made you this way this morning, or are you deliberately trying to be obstructive? Can't you see that after I came down, *someone* went up on the roof, and that someone killed Ena Stratton?"

"After you came down. Yes. Well? Who was it?"

"That's what I'm asking you. Because can't you see, too, that of all the people who had motives for putting Mrs. Stratton out of the way, her husband had the biggest? So far as motive goes, David Stratton is it."

III

"No, no, no. You'll not persuade me. It's no good, Roger. No good at all. You'll never persuade me that wee David strung his wife up on that gallows."

"Colin, will you talk sense," said Roger, exasperated.

"I'm not trying to 'persuade' you. I'm only asking you to consider the possibility, and then see if there's any evidence to support it. We must keep open minds if we're to get anywhere in this job at all. You're just one lump of prejudices."

"David wouldn't have the heart to squash a slug."

"I can quite believe that several people who hadn't the heart to squash slugs have found they had the heart to commit murder."

"Ach, come now, Roger. Do you mean to tell me you consider that wee David a potential murderer?"

"Most certainly I do, and all criminological history supports me—as you ought very well to know. David Stratton's just exactly the type that *does* commit murder."

"I thought you were saying last night that Chalmers was? They're as different as—as—"

"Chalk from cheese. Yes, of course they are. Don't be so *dense*, Colin!" Roger thumped the brick parapet beside him, and hurt his hand. "Can't you see the difference in what I'm suggesting for them? Chalmers could never possibly commit a murder on his own behalf; David Stratton couldn't conceivably commit one for somebody else. But Philip Chalmers can be imagined as doing for his David what he wouldn't do for himself; and David, as I said, is own brother to hundreds of excellent, long-suffering husbands married to domestic pests, who just couldn't stand it any longer and reached for the meat-chopper."

"Well, I'll be fair with you," Colin conceded. "I'll grant you that. Crippen."

"Crippen, precisely. A charming little man, driven completely off his balance by that terrible wife of his. Though in his case of course there was the extra motive in—*Colin!*" Roger stared at the other with sparkling eyes.

"What's the matter now?"

"I happen to *know* that David's in love with another woman. My goodness, and he had motive enough without that."

"How do you know?"

"I was told, last night. As a matter of fact someone let it out, I needn't say who. But I'd stake my income on its truth."

"Now see here, Roger," Colin said, not without heat, "I'm not going on with this. If you're going to try to fasten it on that poor chap, I'm not going on with it, and that's flat."

"You didn't in the least mind it being fastened on me, though," Roger said bitterly.

"You fastened it on yourself. But if you're going to prove that David did it, then let's not do anything of the kind. I don't want to know if he did or he didn't; but if he did, in heaven's name let's leave him in peace. He must have been goaded pretty far."

"Ah, so you're beginning to admit the possibility?"

"I just don't want to have anything more to do with it."

"And be at liberty to drop hints for the rest of your life, I suppose, that *I* did it? No, Colin, I'm afraid that's not good enough for me. And in any case, I can't quite see what your trouble is. Are you afraid of knowing that a friend of yours has committed murder, just like the ostrich husband who'd much rather not know that his wife has kicked over the traces? Where ignorance is bliss. Is that your idea? And yet it didn't seem to shatter you when you jumped to the conclusion that I had."

"That was different," Colin growled. "You can look after yourself. David can't."

"Oh, stop being an old hen," Roger said impatiently, "and discuss it reasonably. I didn't say we were bound to act on anything we discovered. In any case I doubt very much whether we could prove it, as the police consider proof, since I moved that chair. You needn't be so frightened on behalf of your poor wee David. I'm quite prepared to shield him, if it does turn out that he made away with her. I'll even shake his hand and congratulate him, if you like. But I must *know*."

"Why must you know?" Colin asked plaintively.

"Because, dash it," Roger shouted, "you've accused me, and I didn't do it. You've nibbled at the roots of my self-respect, you—you wireworm, and I've got to restore them."

"Oh, well," Colin grumbled. "All right, then. Get on with it."

IV

Roger moved himself along to another patch of sun-warmed brickwork and, thus comforted, took up his rede.

"It's quite plain, Colin, that you're going to disagree with every single thing I say this morning, so you'd better take up the position of counsel for the defence at once, and I'll prosecute. First of all, then, I'd like to hear from you why you thought David behaved in that very strange manner last night, after we'd found the body? Or didn't you consider his manner strange?"

"It was a terrible shock to the man, naturally. What do you expect?"

"Not quite what I saw, I think," Roger said meditatively. "It would have been a shock, of course. On the other hand David must have detested his wife; and it can't be such a shock to lose a wife you detest as to lose a wife you love. Though I'll grant you that the first reaction, for an innocent man of course, would probably be horror. After all, a wife is a wife, even if you do detest her; and there must be times and moments to which one instinctively looks back with emotion. Even with Ena Stratton there must have been such times, or David would never have married her. And why the deuce he ever wanted to do so, is more than I can say. Nevertheless, he evidently did.

"But David's manner last night didn't strike me quite as a result of that natural and innocent feeling. There was shock, but somehow I shouldn't have said that it was the shock of loss. Am I unconsciously influencing myself now if I think that it was much more like the shock of fear?" demanded Roger oratorically. "Quite possibly. But there was no doubt about

Ronald. He was clucking round David just like an old hen. What, I wonder, is there about David that causes perfectly strong men to cluck like hens? I don't know. Ronald, anyhow, was much concerned about David. Why, Colin?"

"I don't know."

"Nor do I. But would you jump down my throat if I suggested that it was because Ronald knew what David had done, and was frightened out of his wits that David might give himself away to the police? Would you be extremely angry if I put that forward as the reason why Ronald should have nipped in and answered the questions addressed by the inspector to David almost before his brother could open his own mouth? Would you, Colin?"

"Oh, so we've got a brand-new accessory after the fact, as well as a new murderer, have we?" Colin asked sarcastically.

"It looks as if we might have," Roger admitted. "I hope so, for David's sake. Well, there's the question of David's reactions, as expressed in his manner. As a matter of fact, David might be said to have had two manners, an early and a late. In his early manner he appeared to be dazed, no doubt by shock; possibly by the shock of loss, possibly not. His late manner was exactly the opposite. When he was allowed by Ronald to answer the inspector's questions, he almost barked out his replies. They were curt to the point of rudeness.

"Now I actually did have during that interview two rather interesting thoughts. It seemed to me that David had been rehearsed in what he was to say to the inspector, and perhaps hurriedly and sketchily rehearsed at that; and it seemed too that he was concealing an emotion of some kind. Both these suppositions fit in very well with David's guilt."

"But great snakes, man, it's all so vague. It's only possibly this, and perhaps that. Not a fact in the lot of it," vigorously complained Colin.

"Yes, I know. We haven't got on to the facts yet. I'm just dealing first with the tiny straws. We'll come on to the trusses in a minute.

"So far, then, we've established that David had an overwhelming motive beforehand, and an uneasy manner afterwards. And now, if you want facts, here's a very big fact indeed, and I'd like to hear you explain it away if you can. Why did David ring up the police about his wife before it was ever known that anything had happened to her at all?"

"Ach, come now, Roger. You know why he did that."

"I know what he gives as his reason for doing it."

"To warn them that an irresponsible woman was loose in the country-side."

"Yes, that's what he said at the time: *in case of suicide.* And yet David Stratton, as an intelligent man, must have known that the chances of his wife committing suicide were extremely remote. He must know as well as I do that the people who chat impressively about committing suicide aren't the people who do it. That was the very first thing that made me really suspicious about the death. But doesn't it strike you as a very cunning move, if Mrs. Stratton were (as indeed she was) actually dead and the stage set for suicide, to suggest to the police the fear of suicide in advance?"

"I'm not sure that it does. Wouldn't it be just as likely to make the police more suspicious?"

"I don't think so, with all the evidence for suicide that was waiting for them to collect. The police, you see, don't bother about psychological probabilities. Like you, it's facts they want. And the fact is that Mrs. Stratton had been braying her intention of committing suicide all the evening. Very nice."

"It seems to me," said Colin, "that for David to go and do a thing like that when all the time he'd really murdered her, would be just like those detective stories where the murderer himself goes rushing off for the Great Detective and begs him to take up the case, which only proves that he was daft as well as a murderer."

"That's a point," Roger said thoughtfully. "But not, I think, in this instance, a sound one. The police are bound to investigate in any case, you see; the Great Detective isn't. Though you're right to the extent that the inspector himself did appear a little curious as to why David should have rung up the police station on this particular occasion, and never before. Ronald jumped in and explained it all away, by the way. Another confirmation of collusion between those two." Roger had spoken a little mechanically. He was thinking of someone else who had voiced to him a fear that the police might suspect "something absolutely preposterous." And that was before he himself had proved murder at all. But he had suspected it and probably he had shown that he suspected it. Had this remark been by way of a feeler? Was there, by any chance, a second accessory after the fact? Roger would have to secure a few tactful words with Mrs. Lefroy some time during the day.

"What? Say that again, Colin. Sorry, I was thinking."

"I don't believe a word of it," Colin repeated robustly. "There was no reason why David shouldn't have rung up the police as an innocent man, with a daft woman about the place like that. No reason at all. And every reason why he should."

"Well, I disagree, that's all. I think, with the inspector, that it was, to say the least, curious. Now, what else have we got against David?"

"Ach!"

"Supposing him innocent, was it really quite natural for him to come back to the house and search?" Roger asked argumentatively. "Could he really have thought that she actually was hiding there? I don't know. It seems a little odd. Much more likely that she'd have rushed off to the house of some friend, or hidden herself outside—anywhere rather than in the house of the hated Ronald, wouldn't you think?"

"You're just twisting things."

"No, I'm not. That's a perfectly sound point. And so is its corollary. In fact, more interesting still."

"What?"

"Why, don't you see, if David *knew* she was dead—and Ronald too, we might say, knew she was dead, either then or later—then they'd have to organise that search just exactly as they did in fact organise it; because neither of them must find the body, or it would look better if neither did, and so we had to be kept at it till one of us did. Don't you think that's rather interesting, Colin?"

"But these are nothings, man—just nothings."

"No, they're not nothings. I grant you they're not very big somethings, but they are somethings: just tiny little pointers, which all seem to me to indicate guilt more than innocence. Not much separately, of course, but in the mass just a bit formidable, don't you think? And another one is David's anxiety to have the body in his own keeping at the first possible moment. Quite natural, no doubt, if he's innocent; but still more explicable, I should have said, if he's not."

Colin made a Scotch noise of exasperation, which Roger ignored.

"That's interesting, by the way," he resumed. "It shows that the police have no suspicion at all. Otherwise, of course, they'd have taken the body off to the mortuary. Well, I can't say I'm sorry."

"I believe you," said Colin meaningly.

Roger laughed. "So I'm still under suspicion, am I?"

"More than that wee David, at any rate," Colin muttered. "Why, man, you said yourself last night that he and Chalmers were the only two who were definitely cleared."

"Yes, but that was before I'd fully realised that the time of death might not be so accurate as Chalmers suggested."

"You can't have it both ways, Roger," Colin pointed out. "It wasn't till you were trying to prove that Chalmers was the man that you decided the time of death might be half an hour later than he fixed it, because he might have been deliberately misleading us. It's only if Chalmers is guilty that the time of death might be late enough for David to have done it; and if Chalmers were guilty, David couldn't be. If Chalmers isn't guilty, then the time of death must be as he said; and that lets wee David out again. You've no case at all."

"Time of death is never so rigid as that," Roger retorted. "Within two hours, as this was, and in the cold outside air to complicate things, the doctors may well have made a perfectly genuine error of half an hour. Anyhow, you don't agree that I'm building up against David a case quite worth answering?"

"No, I don't," Colin maintained stoutly. "I think you've

exaggerated all the points against him out of all proportion, and not even considered the ones in his favour."

"That's quite true; I haven't. I'm not concerned with them. I just wanted to see whether there was a case for him to answer. And there is."

"Ach, you could make out as good a case as that against any of us."

"Well, it's as good at least as the case you made out against me," Roger retorted. "Would you like to lay both of them before the inspector? I'm quite willing."

"You're not really thinking of stirring up the mud like that, Roger, are you?" Colin asked, in some alarm.

"No, I'm not. But your answer shows what you won't admit: that there is a case against David." Roger rose and stretched himself. "Well, I'm quite willing to leave it at that, if you are."

"Great guns, yes. I don't want to have anything more to do with the business at all."

"Then that's all right." Roger bent over his pipe, which had been unable to stand up to this oratory.

"What are you going to do now?" Colin asked.

"Me? Oh, I think I shall stroll back to the house, to see if there's anything doing. I rather liked that inspector fellow. I think I'll have a chat with him. By the way, I suppose you're staying till to-morrow? Ronald seems to want us to."

"No," said Colin. "I don't care about the idea at all. I've told him I'll be pushing off after lunch."

"Oh. Well, I think I shall stay. But what about the inquest?"

"Ach," said Colin confidently, "they won't want me for that. Why should they?"

Roger walked back to the house.

If he had not succeeded in convincing Colin, he had convinced himself. He was quite sure now that either David Stratton or Ronald had been responsible for Ena's death, with the other brother as accomplice either before or after. In any case, they were both in it.

On the whole Roger fancied Ronald as the more probable candidate for the actual deed. Ronald was a man of more decision than David, and he was a man, Roger fancied, who could be fairly ruthless if he had decided that ruthlessness was necessary. Besides, he had the double motive; solicitude for his brother, of whom he was obviously very fond, and the silencing of Ena on his own behalf.

For that matter, however, David had a double motive, too, as a husband and as a lover.

"I should like to know where David went when Colin left him," Roger thought to himself. "Did he go up on to the roof then, or didn't he? The time of death does give us that amount of latitude, whatever the doctors say. Now I wonder how I can possibly find that out?"

The more closely he looked at his new solution, the more certain Roger became that it was the right one. He had been led away before, by the pretty will-of-the-wisp of Chalmers. But examining the situation with an unprejudiced eye, he saw now that a simple elimination left no one at all but one of the Stratton brothers as the guilty man. Colin, Williamson, and himself were out of the question; Dr. Mitchell, he was sure, had not left the ball-room or his wife's side during that hour; Mike Armstrong equally had been constant in his attendance on Margot; the women were all ruled out as not possessing the necessary physical strength; Chalmers was cleared for the same reason—only David and Ronald remained. And still further against these two, David's alibi was not sound, and Ronald's had not even been examined.

Well, good luck to both of them.

By the time he reached the house Roger had decided that he no longer wanted to find out where David had gone when Colin left him. Whether it were he or Ronald who had done the actual deed, Roger had not the least intention of interfering. Murder could seldom be justified, but it was difficult to look on the elimination of a piece of blight like Ena Stratton as murder. And the best thing for Roger was simply not to know who had done it, or anything about it.

But as he passed through the front door Roger could not help smiling.

Did any lingering suspicion still really remain with Colin that he of all people, Roger Sheringham, had taken it upon himself to string up Ena Stratton? Or was that merely a retort on the part of that obstinate young man to Roger's charges against David?

In either case, Roger could not help feeling amused at the idea of Roger Sheringham being suspected of murder.

# Chapter XI

## A HIVE IN THE HELMETS

I

Roger found Inspector Crane on the roof, talking to Ronald Stratton. A uniformed constable hovered in the background.

"Good morning, Inspector," Roger said cheerfully.

"Good morning, sir. Funny, I was just saying to Mr. Stratton, could I have a word with you up here."

"Were you? A lucky arrival then."

Roger glanced round with interest. He had not seen the roof in daylight before, and it did not look quite as he had imagined it in the dark. Much smaller, for one thing, and the arbour was almost at the end instead of nearly in the middle, as he had thought. The gallows were exactly in the middle, and from them still hung the two remaining straw effigies. In the sunlight these looked merely ludicrous, and no longer in the least grisly.

The inspector and Ronald were standing close to the gallows, and Roger intercepted a surreptitious wink from the latter which puzzled him slightly.

"It's about this chair, Mr. Sheringham," the inspector explained, in a somewhat apologetic voice, and pointed at the chair lying on its side underneath the gallows.

A tiny stab of alarm pierced Roger's chest, but he answered easily enough.

"Oh, yes? What about it?"

"Well, sir, you see how it's lying, right underneath the rope. Now, I've taken measurements, and it appears that the poor lady would have been able to stand on it quite easily if it had been like that. These rungs support me, as I've tried, so they would quite easily have supported her."

"Yes, I see what you mean. But perhaps it's been moved."

"That's just what I wanted to ask you, Mr. Sheringham. Was it, to your knowledge, moved last night, while you and Mr. Stratton were cutting the poor lady down?"

Roger looked, as meaningly as he dared, at Ronald. He did not want his reply to clash with any story that Ronald might have told.

"Well, that's rather difficult to say," he answered cautiously. "Do you remember if it got moved, Ronald?" To Roger's horror, Ronald said brightly:

"No, I can't say. As a matter of fact, I was just telling the inspector that I don't remember it being there at all when we were cutting her down."

After a moment's stupefaction before this stupidity, Roger regained control of himself. "Don't you? Oh, I think I do. It was rather in the way. Yes, I expect someone must have kicked it aside, Inspector."

"Yes, I can understand that, sir," agreed the inspector, in a worried voice, "but why was it put back again?"

"Oh, well—probably someone just kicked it back. In any case, I don't think it's a point of any importance, is it?"

"No. Mr. Sheringham. Probably not. I just didn't quite understand about it, and I thought you might have been able to give me some information."

"Yes, well, you see, Inspector, it isn't the kind of thing about which one can be very accurate. I dare say I ought to have noticed exactly the position of the chair when Mr. Stratton and I got up here, but I'm afraid I was much more concerned in finding out if she was really dead, and trying to save her life if she wasn't."

"Yes, sir, of course. Yes, I quite understand that. No doubt it's of no importance at all."

"And there was a certain amount of confusion up here, you must remember. Mr. Stratton and I, and Mr. Williamson and Mr. Nicolson, too. And it was quite dark. No, I think it's only surprising that the chair didn't end up in the garden below, instead of more or less where it started from."

"Yes, no doubt you're quite right, Mr. Sheringham," agreed the inspector, and made a note in his little book.

But he did not sound quite so convinced as Roger would have liked.

Ronald Stratton, who had been viewing this exchange apparently with tolerant amusement, said:

"Well, that was all you wanted to ask Mr. Sheringham, Inspector?"

It's all very well, my dear Ronald, thought Roger, but there is such a thing as over-confidence. He was astonished that Ronald should have made such a blunder over the chair, for the second time. Apparently he still did not realise its vital importance.

"Yes, I think so, Mr. Stratton, thank you," the inspector replied, perhaps a little uncertainly.

"And you've finished up here?"

"For the time being, sir, yes."

"Then come down into the house and let me give you a glass of beer. It's getting on for twelve o'clock."

"Thank you, Mr. Stratton. I wish I could say yes, but I have to see the superintendent. I'll just say a word to my man, and then I must be off."

The inspector walked aside and said a few words to his constable in a low voice. Neither Roger nor Stratton could overhear them, nor tried.

"You'll have a spot of beer, Roger?" Ronald remarked, more in the manner of one making a statement than asking a question.

"Thanks," Roger agreed. "I will."

"I'll come upstairs again, when I've seen the inspector off."

"No," said Roger, "I'll come down." He wanted a closed door between them and the rest of the world while he said a few firm words to Ronald on the topic of his imbecility, and the late bar-room was altogether too public.

They escorted the inspector politely to the front door, chatting about the weather, and Stratton took Roger into his study.

"I keep a cask in here," he said happily. "It's handier. This cupboard might have been specially built for a cask, mightn't it?"

"Yes," said Roger. "Look here, Ronald..."

Ronald looked round from the tankard he was filling. "Yes?"

"I want to speak to you, in words of one syllable. Don't,

you inconceivable bonehead, say anything more about not remembering that chair being there when we were taking down the body last night."

Ronald turned off the tap, put the other tankard under it, and turned it on again.

"What's that? Why not?"

"Because," Roger explained, with suppressed fury, "the presence of that chair, nincompoop, means suicide, and its absence means—*murder*. Think it out, and you'll see."

Ronald Stratton turned a suddenly white face over his shoulder and stared at Roger, while the beer ran unheeded over the top of the tankard.

"Good lord!" he muttered. "That had simply never occurred to me."

He turned back, mechanically stopped the flow from the cask, and got to his feet.

"I say, Roger—"

"No," Roger interrupted quickly. "Much better not."

Ronald didn't.

II

They drank their beer, looking surreptitiously at each other.

Then Roger said, in quite a casual voice:

"Want any help in getting things down from the roof, Ronald? There are still some things up there—chairs and things. It's nice and sunny now, but who knows whether it mayn't rain later, in April?"

Ronald grinned. "That's quite a sound idea, Roger. Yes, I'd like your help."

They finished off their tankards and went solemnly up to the roof.

With a nod to the constable, who was still loitering there, Ronald walked over to the nearest pair of chairs, near the steps that led down to the sun-parlour. Before he could touch them, however, the constable had lifted his voice.

"Sorry, Mr. Stratton, sir, were you wanting anything?"

"Yes, we're going to take these chairs and things into the house, in case it rains later. It's April, you know."

"I'm sorry, sir," said the constable portentously, "but the inspector said for me to see that nothing wasn't moved up here."

"He did?" Roger could not tell whether Stratton was really surprised, or was only acting surprised; in either case he sounded highly surprised. "But why?"

"Couldn't tell you, sir. But that's what he said. Nothing to be moved, nor touched. He left me here for the purpose."

"What on earth…?" said Stratton, and lifted his eyebrows at Roger.

"But surely Inspector Crane didn't mean that nothing was to be touched on the whole roof, constable?" Roger came to the rescue.

"Sorry, sir, those are my orders. Nothing to be moved on this roof, nor yet touched."

"Oh, well!" Roger shrugged his shoulders. "There must be some mistake, I think, but you'll have to wait for the inspector to put it right, Ronald. Inspector Crane will be coming back soon, I take it, as he's left you here?" he added to the constable.

"'Bout half an hour, he said, sir."

"I see. Well, Ronald, we must just wait, that's all. Shall we go in?"

As they went down the stairs Ronald said:

"Surely that's rather queer, Sheringham, isn't it?"

"Oh, no, I don't think so," Roger replied. "Probably the superintendent has told Crane he'd like to have a look at the scene before things are moved, and Crane's gone off to get him."

"But Crane didn't say anything last night about things not being moved on the roof, when I took him up there."

"Well, he hadn't seen the superintendent then, had he?" Roger said smoothly. But he felt a little uneasy. It certainly was rather queer.

Downstairs they found Colin, reading the *Sunday Times* in front of the hall fire.

"Hullo, Colin, all alone?" said Ronald. "None of the women down yet?"

"No, nor Osbert either, the lazy hound. Oh, by the way, Ronald, I told you I'd be pushing off after lunch. Sorry, I've got to change my plans. I'll be staying to-night."

"Well, we shall be very glad to have you, Colin. Decided your appointment wasn't so urgent after all?"

"Not a bit of it. I met that inspector chap as I was coming in just now, and he asked me was it a fact that I was going off after lunch? I said it was; and he told me there was nothing doing, or words to that effect."

"Told you you couldn't go?" Ronald said incredulously.

"Well, not quite like that. He said I should probably be wanted at the inquest to-morrow, and it would be a great convenience to him if I stayed; so of course I said I would. But if I'd said I couldn't, I wouldn't put it past him to have told me I'd jolly well got to. He had that sort of look in his eye."

"The devil he had!" said Ronald.

## III

The half-hour passed slowly, and as it passed Roger's uneasiness grew.

He knew the signs, and he knew the ways of the police. The inspector was not satisfied: that was quite obvious. But what on earth could have managed to rouse his dissatisfaction? If it was just the position of the chair, then that really was the most thundering bad luck; for had everything been as innocent as it could be, it was inevitable that the chair should have been kicked about a bit, with four men scrimmaging round it. The inspector could hardly have expected that it could have been left quite untouched.

No, in spite of his deferential manner, Inspector Crane must be a busybody. With a death at such a house as Sedge Park, he saw his chance of making himself important. If he could find a few niggling points over which to raise queries, he could get his name put forward as a keen man. And the devil of it was that, without knowing it, Inspector Crane might be carrying a match towards a powder-magazine. If he really did begin to uncover the surface, heaven knew what train he might not fire. Roger hoped most sincerely, and with all the fervour of a guilty conscience, that Inspector Crane's match might prove a damp one.

The same constraint seemed to be resting on the others as on himself. They sat, in gloomy silence, round the big open fire-place and rustled their newspapers; but it was doubtful if any of the three read very much. As the time passed Roger began to feel more and more like a school-boy before a house-match; that nasty sensation of sick emptiness. And if he felt like that, what must Ronald Stratton be feeling?

For Ronald's reception of the warning about the chair had gone all the way to confirm Roger's conclusion. There had been real fear on the face that Ronald had shown him: and in these circumstances fear could surely be caused only by a knowledge of guilt, either on his own behalf or David's. Well, Roger would do all he possibly could for him, but there might be some awkward times ahead, with this infernal inspector raking over the dung-heap. It would look bad, uncommonly bad, if the man brought to light the feelings with which the Stratton family in general had regarded Ena; and precious little raking would be needed to do that.

A few minutes after twelve o'clock Mr. Williamson appeared, looking perhaps a trifle yellow round the eyes, and, with a perfunctory remark or two, added himself to the silent circle. Again the rustling of newspapers was the only sound in the hall.

Once Ronald Stratton betrayed his anxiety by a muttered remark.

"I thought the constable said Crane would be back in half an hour? It's forty minutes already since he went."

At twenty-five minutes past twelve Ronald's parlourmaid presented herself at Williamson's side and said, in a flat voice which must have masked much interior fluttering:

"I beg your pardon, sir, but Inspector Crane would like to speak to you for a moment, on the roof."

"What? To me, did you say? He wants to speak to me?"

"If you please, sir."

"Inspector Crane?" Stratton repeated. "I didn't know he was here, Edith."

"Yes, sir. He came about a quarter of an hour ago, with Superintendent Jamieson and another gentleman."

"But—I never saw them come, and I've been in here all the time."

"They came to the back door, sir."

"But why didn't you tell me?"

"They said they were just going up to the roof for a minute or two, sir, and it wasn't necessary to disturb you, so I didn't think to tell you."

"I see. Well, if they come—if anyone comes like that another time, Edith, I think you'd better let me know."

"Very good, sir."

"What's up?" asked Williamson, as the parlourmaid disappeared. "Eh? What's it all about? What's he want to see me for? I saw him last night, and told him everything I knew. What's he want to see me again for?"

"I don't know, Osbert, but presumably you'd better go."

"Yes, I suppose I had. Well, I wonder what the devil he wants to see me for."

Williamson began to climb the staircase which led up from one end of the big hall.

Roger watched his back in an agonised way. He was quite sure there was some terribly important thing he must say to Williamson before the interview, some warning hint he must give him which would smooth everything out. There was such a thing, but his mind seemed paralysed. He could think of nothing at all. In a kind of hopeless despair he watched Williamson out of sight.

"Well," Ronald muttered, "and what the deuce do you make of that?"

Colin looked at them over the huge horn-rimmed spectacles he used for reading. "Dirty work in the camp?" he asked tentatively.

"Don't know yet," Roger answered, in a tone to discourage further questions in front of Ronald.

Ronald made a movement as if to rise. "Shall I go up?" he asked.

"Better not," Roger said. "They obviously don't want you."

"The superintendent has come, then?"

"Yes. I thought that's what it might be."

"Yes. I wonder who the other one is?"

"Oh, some plain-clothes man, I expect."

"I expect so. But why on earth should they want Williamson?"

"Well, he found the body, didn't he?"

"Oh, yes, so he did. Yes, that's why the superintendent wants to see him, of course. Just routine, I suppose?"

"That's it, no doubt. Just routine."

But Roger did not think it was routine at all.

Williamson was away for twenty minutes, and they were the longest twenty minutes that Roger had ever known.

Williamson was wearing his guilty grin.

"Third degree's nothing to it," he said, as he dropped into his chair.

"Nothing to what, Osbert?" asked Colin.

"To what they've been putting me through up there. Eh? This is a nice party of yours, Ronald. Haven't you even got a drink to offer me? Eh? Haven't you?"

"Damn drinks. Are the police still up there?"

"You bet they are. The superintendent, the inspector, two constables, and—"

"What did they want to see you for?"

"Oh, a lot of damn nonsense. Wanted me to tell the superintendent everything I told the inspector last night, and a hell of a lot more. How I found the body, which way it was facing, how far I thought the feet were off the ground, where some chair or other was, how—"

Roger uttered an exclamation. He had remembered at last what the thing was about which he should have warned Williamson—the chair. He ought to have inserted into Williamson's consciousness, just as he had tried last night to insert it into Colin's, the idea that the chair had been there from the beginning. Now it was too late.

"Eh, Sheringham? What did you say?"

"Nothing. Oh, yes. What did you tell them about the chair?" Roger avoided Colin's eye.

"Told them I couldn't remember, of course. How could I possibly remember a thing like that?"

"And what did they say to that?"

"Told me to try and remember. Told me to try and throw my mind back to the moment I found the body, and see if I couldn't picture the scene and all that, and where was the chair? Well, I did remember as a matter of fact that it couldn't have been in the middle of the gallows, because I walked clean through them. So I said it must have been under the body."

"Yes?"

"And then they said it couldn't have been under the body or Mrs. Stratton would have been able to stand on it. So I said it must have been beyond the body, then, mustn't it? Well, it must, mustn't it? So then they asked me if I remembered now that it was beyond the body, and so I was getting a bit fed up and said I did, and would I swear to it, and I said no, I wouldn't swear to it, because I wasn't prepared to swear to it, but that's where it must have been, and now for heaven's sake, Ronald, let me have a drink. I've been through the third degree, man. Eh? You don't seem to understand. What with the police and then Lilian, and now you people—"

"Lilian?" said Colin idly.

"I met her on the stairs, and of course she had to know all about everything, too." Mr. Williamson sighed deeply, as a husband will.

Roger was considering Mr. Williamson's story. Williamson had given him better luck than might have been expected. At any rate he had not denied the presence of the chair altogether, as he very well might have done. But according to Williamson's account, the police had framed their questions in a rather odd way; they had seemed much more concerned with the exact position of the chair than with the possibility of its total absence. Did that mean that they really were worrying only over Inspector Crane's ridiculously insignificant point and the other alternative had never occurred to them at all? If so, they were more foolish than Roger would have expected; but he would be very grateful to them for their foolishness.

Williamson sipped the glass of sherry with which he had now been provided, and continued his story.

"Well, I don't know what else there is to tell you. They kept on asking me that sort of thing, and the inspector wrote most of it down. Where? Oh, we were in the sun-parlour. Didn't I tell you that? Eh? Yes, that's where we were. The inspector and the superintendent and me. In the sun-parlour.

"Oh, I know something else they asked me about. Yes,

look here Ronald, they're on to the state of affairs about your sister-in-law. Like hell they are. You'd better watch out there. I mean, they might make a spot of trouble over that, mightn't they? Eh? Driven to suicide, poor girl, because of being cold-shouldered and all that, you know."

"What state of affairs?" Ronald demanded.

"Why, my dear fellow, that all of you hated the woman like poison. What? You did, didn't you? Well, they're on to it all right."

"How do you mean?"

"Why, they kept asking me, had I noticed during the evening any coolness between Mrs. Stratton and any of the members of her husband's family? Had I noticed any bad blood and what's-its-name? Did I know that Mrs. Stratton was not *persona grata* or whatever you call it in this house? Had I seen a quarrel between Mrs. Stratton and her husband during the evening?"

"Well?" Ronald said sharply. "What did you say to that?"

"Oh, I didn't give you away. It's perfectly all right. Of course, I told them it was all news to me, I hadn't noticed anything; so far as I'd seen, your brother and she seemed a particularly affectionate couple; you all appeared not to be able to do enough for her. It's quite all right," said Mr. Williamson with pride. "I handed out the dope good and strong."

"I see," said Roger. "And the police are still up there? Any idea what they're doing, Williamson?"

"Oh yes," said Mr. Williamson cheerfully. "They're still taking photographs. They've been at it all the time, with the inspector popping in and out of the sun-parlour like a jack-in-the-box, trying to do two things at once."

"Did you say they're taking photographs?" said Roger, in rather a strained voice.

"That's it. There's a professional photographer there from Westerford, I believe, though how they got hold of him on a Sunday morning I don't know. Anyhow, they've got him there, taking photographs of the roof and the gallows and heaven knows what, from every angle they can think of. Seemed a bit unnecessary to me, I must say, but I suppose they think differently. Keen chaps, your police here, Ronald."

"Very," said Ronald flatly.

"May I suggest," said Roger elaborately, "that this room is open to the staircase, and Williamson has rather a strong voice?"

As he spoke, the telephone-bell rang. Ronald disappeared into his study to answer it.

Roger and Colin exchanged glances. Colin, peering over his glasses, lifted his eyebrows. In reply, Roger shrugged his shoulders. Both of them looked grave.

"I say," said Mr. Williamson seriously. "I say, Sheringham."

"Yes?"

"I say, this is really awfully good sherry of Ronald's. Have you tried it? You should. I wonder where he gets it. You've no idea, Colin, have you? Eh? Have you?"

"Ach, shut up, Osbert," said Colin.

Mr. Williamson looked surprised, but not very hurt.

Ronald appeared at the door of his study.

"Sheringham," he said, "can I speak to you for a minute in here?"

"Of course," said Roger, jumping up. He hurried across the hall.

Ronald shut the study door.

Roger did not bother to disguise his anxiety. "More bad news?" he asked.

Ronald nodded. "That was my brother on the telephone. He says the police have just taken Ena's body away from the house. They're taking her to the mortuary. I say, this is serious, isn't it?"

"It might be. Look here, Ronald. Get your brother on the telephone again and ask him to lunch here, at once. Never mind if he turns up late. It's the best excuse for having him up here. And tell him to answer no questions from anyone until I've seen him."

"Yes, I will. Thanks. David's a bit... What does it mean, Roger? That the police aren't satisfied, I suppose? Goodness only knows why not, but that must be what it means. That they've got some sort of a bee in their bonnets?"

"A bee?" said Roger unhappily. "A hive!"

IV

The lunch-gong brought the women downstairs.

Fortunately the continued presence of the police in the house was looked upon by them as part of the normal procedure, so that while lunch could hardly be called a cheerful meal, there was at any rate no spirit of general apprehension. Halfway through it David arrived, very haggard and curt, and his presence naturally added a further constraint to the gathering.

Immediately the meal was over, Roger made a sign to Ronald, who said a low word to David and carried him off. Coming back at once, he said to Roger:

"He's in my study. Shall I come along?"

"No," said Roger, and went off to the study alone.

He had been debating during lunch how exactly to convey his warning to David without appearing to know everything and yet without minimising the danger. The compromise on which he had decided had the weakness of all compromises, but it was the best one he could find.

"Look here, Stratton," he said, without beating about the bush, "you know what this means, of course, taking your wife's body off to the mortuary, and messing about on the roof, as the police have been doing. It means that they're not satisfied that your wife's death was quite so uncomplicated as it looked at first. I'm not in their confidence, so I don't know what their trouble is; but at a guess, it might be that there was last night some special motive, some particular incident or scene, such as a quarrel, which led to her taking her life and which has not yet been disclosed. Now, whether there was anything of the sort I don't know, and I don't want to know, any more than I want to know the exact details of her last moments. But if there was, and it comes to light, there's bound to be a great deal of mud-slinging over the case; and that I do want to prevent for all our sakes.

"So I'd like to impress on you that it's essential for you, of all of us, to have a perfectly simple story for the police, which can easily be supported elsewhere, so that they can understand that you didn't follow your wife up on to the roof when she ran out of the ball-room and quarrel with her there, or anything like that. You understand that, don't you?"

"Well, that's perfectly simple," David said shortly. "I—"

"Wait a minute. Let me tell you. *I* know you didn't go up there, because I was with you myself for at least ten minutes, at the bar. You remember? We were talking about the test matches and the absurd fuss the Australians made because we bowled at their leg-stumps instead of their off-stumps. I'm your alibi for that time. Then Colin Nicolson joined us, and I strolled up on to the roof for a minute or two myself—where, I may say, I saw no sign of your wife, who must have been in the sun-parlour."

"Why?" asked David curtly.

"Why?" Roger repeated.

"Yes. Why must she have been in the sun-parlour? It was ten minutes, or more. That was plenty of time for her to have done it."

"Of course," said Roger hurriedly. He had completely forgotten that his very first theory had exonerated David because of those ten minutes. Of course that was David's best defence. The doctor's report as to the time of death must be firmly taken for granted. It had been clever of David to see that.

"Of course," he repeated. "I don't know why I said that she was probably in the sun-parlour. Most likely she had done it already. Still, there's no harm in your having a margin of safety, so we'll just get it exact. I left you, and you stayed with Nicolson another three or four minutes. And then," said Roger with meaning, "you followed him straight into the ball-room, didn't you, where your brother, no doubt, and other people saw you?"

"Not at once," said David obtusely. "I went down to the bathroom first."

"No, you didn't," Roger retorted, with some exasperation. "You never went near the bathroom. You followed Nicolson straight into the ball-room. In fact, you both went together. *He remembers you did.*"

A very faint smile appeared on David's pale face. "Yes, that's right. I remember now, too. And if you want to know, I went straight up to Agatha and asked her to dance, because I hadn't been able to dance with her before. My wife," said David in an expressionless voice, "didn't like her. God knows why."

"Exactly. She'll remember that, too. And you stayed with her some time, of course, and after that you were never alone until Ronald actually saw you off the premises."

"Ronald didn't. I—"

"Yes, he did."

"Oh, all right. It all seems very unnecessary," said David wearily, "but I suppose you're right."

Roger snorted.

V

Leaving the study, Roger hurried off in search of Mrs. Lefroy. He ran her to earth in the drawing-room, detached her from a group, and led her outside the door. Time was short, and he could not mince matters.

"You remember when I took David off to have a drink, after his wife had flung herself out of the ball-room? Well, I didn't come back with him. Colin Nicolson did. You remember seeing them come in, don't you?"

"No," said Mrs. Lefroy doubtfully. "I remember David coming and sitting by me, but I think that was some time later, wasn't it?"

"It was exactly thirteen minutes after I took him out, but you don't know that. What you do know is that you saw him and Colin come into the ball-room together, and David came straight across and joined you."

Mrs. Lefroy was a rare woman. "Yes," she said at once. "I remember perfectly."

"Bless you," said Roger. "Where's Ronald?"

Ronald was discovered in the study, with David. They were not talking.

"Go home, David," said Roger. "You mustn't be here too much. We don't want to look like a conspiracy, whether we are one or not. Go home and stick to your story, and you'll be all right."

David went.

"The police have gone," Ronald said. "Shall we—"

"Damn the police," said Roger. "They'll be back soon enough."

"Yes, I'm afraid so. By the way, they've altered the place of the inquest. It's to be in Westerford now, not here."

Roger nodded. "I expected that. Now, listen to me, Ronald, because I'm going to speak very carefully." He repeated the gambit which he had already used on David.

"Yes," said Ronald. "I understand perfectly. But I don't think you do."

"I don't want to, any more than that," Roger said quickly. "All I want you to do is to look after your own alibi, because I haven't the time, and be ready to swear that you went down to the front door with your brother and saw him out of the house."

"Oh, my alibi's all right," Ronald said carelessly. "I never left the ball-room at all from the time Ena went out of it till just before David went, when I was at the bar with you."

"You didn't?" said Roger.

So it had been David after all.

"No. Heaps of people can swear to that. But, look here,

Roger," said Ronald anxiously, "are you quite sure David's is all right? Is it really cast-iron?"

"Absolutely. No, not cast-iron. Not so brittle. Wrought iron. I've just," said Roger with a smile, "been forging it."

"Ah! Well, listen, Roger," Ronald said slowly, "I want to speak carefully to you, too. I haven't said a word to David, and he hasn't said a word to me. I quite agree with you that it's much better not to *know* anything. I can see that's your line, and it's the right one. But I do just want to say this, Roger. That woman utterly deserved—well, anything she got."

"I know she did," Roger said, not without emotion. "And that's just why I'm not knowing anything at all. But I'll say this, Ronald. Everything will be all right."

"Sure?"

"Sure. You see, after all, there's no evidence at all. Not to say, evidence."

Fleeing any more emotion, Roger hurried off in search of Colin. The police might be back at any moment, and Roger wanted everything nice and simple for them when they came.

Colin was smoking his pipe with Williamson on the lawn in front of the house.

Roger called him aside and began once more.

"Colin, after I'd gone up on the roof last night and left you with David, you didn't go back to the ball-room alone. David went with you."

"But I've told you already I—"

"Colin, I haven't got much time. Listen. David went with you. Mrs. Lefroy remembers seeing you both come in together. And," said Roger with emphasis, "David himself remembers that he went in with you. David himself remembers it, Colin."

"Oh!" said Colin slowly.

"Yes, you were wrong, I'm afraid. But the lad's perfectly safe, so long as you remember just that thing."

"Of course I remember we went in together," said Colin firmly. "Haven't I told you so all along?"

"Then thank goodness that's settled." Roger mopped his brow and took a breath of relief.

"But, Roger, man, what are the police up to? Do you mean to tell me they smell a rat? What were they doing, taking photographs on the roof?"

"I don't know," Roger admitted. "But that appears to be my next job, to find out. Little did I think that the Great Detective would ever come down to detecting what the official detectives may have detected already. Well, well."

"Does it look serious, do you think?"

"No, I don't think so really," Roger said as they walked back towards the house. "It's alarming, of course, but I don't see how it can possibly be serious. They can't have anything more than the vaguest suspicions; and suspicion never even arrested anyone without some kind of evidence too, let alone hanged him. Anyhow, if the coast's clear, we'll see if we can make out what they've been up to."

The coast was clear, and the roof unguarded. Even the large constable had been withdrawn.

"Ah!" said Roger, and looked round.

At a first glance everything seemed exactly the same.

"Well, I don't know what the deuce they were at, unless they really were still worried about that chair," said Roger, and walked towards the gallows.

"Hullo!" he exclaimed in surprise. "It's gone!"

He looked round again. Undoubtedly the chair had gone. Three chairs still stood on the roof, but exactly as they had stood before. The fourth, under the gallows, had disappeared.

"Let's see if it's in the sun-parlour," said Roger.

It was not in the sun-parlour.

"Well, what on earth would they want to take it away for?" asked Colin, no less puzzled.

"Heaven only knows." Roger was beginning to feel worried, in the way that the inexplicable does worry. "I can't make it out at all. The only importance in the chair to them was its position with regard to the gallows. As an object apart from its position, I can't see how it could possibly interest them." Already such a simple act as the carrying away of the chair was beginning to look sinister. Roger felt perfectly equal to combating the known moves of an opponent, but this was an unknown one, and how can one combat that?

"Ach," Colin tried to be reassuring, "they're just daft. Trying to be too clever, that's all."

"No," Roger worried. "No, I don't think that can be it. They must have had some reason."

He stared at the roof where the chair had lain.

Suddenly he uttered an exclamation and dropped on his hands and knees, to peer intently at that same bit of roof.

"Have you found something?" Colin asked eagerly.

Roger blew gently at the ground, and then again. Then he got up and faced Colin.

"I know why they took that chair away," he said slowly. "Colin, I'm afraid we're rather up against it."

"What do you mean, man?"

"I was wrong when I said they were working just on

suspicion, with no evidence to back it. They have got evidence. Can you see faint traces of grey powder there? That's insufflator powder. They've been trying to take finger-prints off that chair, and they've found that there aren't any at all—not even Ena's."

# Chapter XII

## UNSCRUPULOUS BEHAVIOUR OF A GREAT DETECTIVE

I

"We must keep calm," said Roger, not at all calmly. "We mustn't lose our heads. We're in a nasty jam, but we *must* keep calm, Colin."

"It's the devil," muttered Colin, in a distressed voice.

"We must try to work out their moves," Roger continued, a little less wildly, "so that we can forestall them. You're the only person I can talk to freely, so you've got to help me."

"I'm with you all the way, Roger."

"You'd better be," said Roger grimly. "Because we're both of us for it if the truth comes out. In a moment of lunacy I put myself in the position of accessory after the fact, to shield someone else (I suppose one can be an accessory after the fact to a crime, by the way, without having the least knowledge of the criminal's identity? It's an interesting point); and you did the same by shielding me. I hope you realise that?"

"I'm afraid you're right. I'm an accessory to an accessory, at any rate, if there is such a position. But let's look on the bright side, Roger. Things might have been worse if I hadn't wiped those prints of yours off the chair. Worse for you, I mean."

"And possibly worse still for someone else besides me," Roger retorted.

The two were sitting in the sun-parlour, whither they had retired in some alarm after Roger's discovery on the roof, to talk the thing over. Roger had spent another five minutes, crawling about on his hands and knees round the gallows, to see whether anything else was to be read from the surface of the roof, but beyond one or two burnt match-stalks had found nothing. He had explained to Colin that the police would have done exactly the same thing, and equally, it was to be presumed, found no scratches or other marks on the surface of the asphalt to indicate that anything in the nature of a struggle had taken place there; though whether they might have found anything else, of a removable nature, could not be said.

Roger relit his pipe and continued, considerably calmer. Unlike many people, Roger found argument soothing.

"Yes, that's quite true, Colin. If you hadn't wiped off my prints, what would they have found? That officious inspector was going to test the chair for prints in any case. He'd have found mine, and presumably those of the person who carried all the chairs on to the roof, and probably several others as well. But he wouldn't have found Ena Stratton's, which he was looking for; and that might have made things more awkward even than they are now. I wonder, by the way," Roger added vaguely, "how the particular chair of the four which I chose happened to get where it was, right in the middle of the fair-way. It was the one, of course, which you knocked over."

"I didn't knock it over," Colin contradicted. "It nearly knocked me over. It was lying on its side. That's why I didn't see it."

"Lying on its side, just about half-way between the gallows and the door into the house," Roger meditated. "It might have been there, of course, when I was standing just outside the door earlier, but if so I don't remember noticing it. And it certainly wasn't there at the beginning of the evening, when Ronald took me up to show me his gallows, because we walked abreast straight across from the door. Somebody must have put it there later. I wonder if that has any significance?"

"Well, there was a chair missing from the picture," Colin pointed out.

"Exactly. Could the murderer have been going towards the gallows with it, intending to complete the picture, and then been alarmed or distracted, and dropped it there to make his escape?"

"That sounds feasible enough, Roger."

"Yes, but it's so easy to think of a feasible explanation of a fact, without knowing in the least whether it's the right one, and without probably realising how many other feasible explanations of the same fact there may be. That was the trouble with the old-fashioned detective-story," said Roger, somewhat didactically. "One deduction only was drawn from each fact, and it was invariably the right deduction. The Great Detectives of the past certainly had luck. In real life one can draw a hundred plausible deductions from one fact, and they're all equally wrong. However, we've no time to bother with that now."

"You were talking about the chair," Colin reminded him.

"Yes. It's odd that it should have been there, but I can't see that it has any real bearing on the actual crime. Though if my explanation is right, the police would have found the murderer's prints on it, though not Ena Stratton's. I'm sorry, by the way, to keep on using that term for the poor fellow who retorted on her at last in the only possible way, but there doesn't seem to be another. Executioner is too formal."

"David," said Colin carefully, "actually admitted it to you?"

"Oh, no. He didn't try, and I wouldn't have let him if he had. It just went tacitly, by default. But Ronald did."

"Ronald told you he and David had done it?"

"No, no. Ronald apparently had no hand in it. He doesn't appear to be in the least worried about his alibi. But he knows David did it. He told me with some care that David hasn't said a word to him, or he to David; but he knows all right, and I should imagine that David knows he knows. But Ronald and I took some time in explaining elaborately to each other that neither of us do know anything, and don't intend to; so that's all quite satisfactory."

"And the police don't *know*."

"No, that's our great consolation. And that's what we've got to build on. Let's try to reconstruct their ideas. They can't possibly *know* even that murder has been committed at all, let alone who did it. They may remotely suspect, but all they actually know is that there has been some hanky-panky going on. Some interested party wiped that chair clear of finger-prints; and not just the back, but the sides and seat and everything. You did wipe the seat, didn't you?"

"I polished the blessed seat!" groaned Colin.

"Don't be unhappy. It's a very good thing you did. Don't you see that with a wooden seat like that, not only finger-prints but traces of foot-prints would be looked for. The suicide theory involves Mrs. Stratton having stood on a chair. Well, with modern methods of detection it would be perfectly simple to establish whether anyone had or had not stepped recently on to the seat of that chair from this roof. The surface of the asphalt is covered with flint; quite a large amount of it would be carried up on to the seat of the chair, and pressed firmly into the varnish, and even into the wood, by the weight of the person. The knocking over the chair would displace some, but not all; and the traces of what had been displaced would be quite visible. A microscopic examination of the seat would tell all this as clearly as I've told it to you.

"And I'm not at all sure," added Roger uneasily, "that a microscopic examination, even after the polishing you gave it, won't show that Mrs. Stratton didn't stand on it at all. It's marvellous how accurate these expert witnesses are. Still, as you can understand, much better that you did polish than that you shouldn't have done."

"Well, come, that's something," said Colin, but he sounded more than a little uneasy too.

"So what do we come to then? The police know that someone has been tinkering with that chair, with or without a criminal motive. And they *may* be pretty certain that Mrs. Stratton never stood on it at all. If they are, then undoubtedly there is going to be the devil to pay; because that proves murder. But even then, looking on the hopeful side, to prove murder isn't to prove a murderer; and though there certainly would be a nasty pother, and a great deal of unpleasantness all round, I'm not at all sure that David's neck would ever be seriously in danger. Even if the police were quite, quite sure he'd done it, there's so little real evidence in the case at all that they would have an exceedingly difficult job to prove it.

"However, that's the worst that can happen, and it may not; so let's leave that possibility out of the reckoning just now, and concentrate on what is quite certain. Well, all that's really certain so far, I think, is that the police feel that there is cause for further investigation. They've made photographic records of the appearance of the roof, and they're retaining all of us here in case they want to question us further. That's all quite normal, and not so very formidable after all."

"I'm glad to hear it," said Colin.

"But what I don't quite like is the removal of the body to the mortuary. It was inevitable, if the police weren't satisfied; but it means a post-mortem—and goodness knows what that may reveal."

"But, hang it all, man, the cause of death must be obvious enough?"

"Oh, the cause of death, yes. But that's not all they'll look for. There's the question of bruises, you see. I didn't ask Chalmers last night whether he'd looked for any bruises on the body, but I don't imagine he did. Or Mitchell. In a perfectly straightforward case, they probably wouldn't. But now, of course, the man who does the p.m. will—and that may prove a little awkward."

"But why might there be bruises on the body?"

"Well, consider how it must have been done. I don't suppose Mrs. Stratton was persuaded quite peaceably to put her neck in the noose while David gave her a friendly hoist, do you? How it was actually effected I can't say, and no doubt a certain amount of guile was employed as far as possible: but there must have been some kind of a last-second struggle. Not a long one, because, so far as we know, she never screamed; and I think she would have been heard if she did. I wonder," said Roger thoughtfully, "how the devil the man did succeed in getting it done so quietly. And so quickly. He can't have been more than three or four minutes over it, at the most, so far as I can work out the times. Though it is a little doubtful just when he got back into the ball-room."

"You always say," Colin remarked tentatively, "that the psychology of the murderer is a great help in reconstructing a crime. Couldn't that apply, too, to the psychology of the victim?"

"That's a very shrewd observation, Colin," said Roger with enthusiasm. "And it interests me particularly, because it reminds me of a remark I made last night about Ena Stratton, which sounded very profound, but which I thought, as soon as I'd made it, might not bear very much examination. Perhaps it was deeper than I suspected. In fact, Colin, I believe I made it to you. Do you remember my saying that something or other, I forget now what, was significant not only of everything that had happened to Mrs. Stratton so far, but of anything that might happen to her in the future?"

"Yes, I do remember. I wondered at the time what the deuce you meant."

"To tell you the truth, so did I. But I must have meant something, surely. You can't call to mind what the occasion was, I suppose?"

"Yes, I do. It was her exhibitionism."

"Ah, was it? I said her exhibitionism was significant of anything that might happen to her in the future; and what did happen was that she got murdered. Well, could her exhibitionism have been responsible for that? I don't quite see how."

"It was the time she climbed on that beam. Can you get anything out of that? Suppose she climbed up on the gallows, and wee David swarmed up after her?"

Roger laughed. "That's taking me a trifle too literally. But it's a possible idea, for all that. That's the trouble. Any extravagant idea in that line is possible with Mrs. Stratton. But I'm afraid that if your theory were right, and David had slipped the noose over her head on top of the gallows instead of underneath them, her neck would have been broken. And there's no question of that. She died from strangulation all right. The rope was much thicker and stiffer than the ordinary hangman's rope, and the excoriations on her palms show that she tried to clutch at it, so she probably died more slowly; but her own movements would tighten the noose round her neck in a fairly short time.

"Still, you may not be so wide of the mark, Colin. It's certain, if we accept that there was no more than a very short struggle, as I think we can, that some kind of ruse was employed; and I've no doubt that Mrs. Stratton herself, and possibly her exhibitionism, dictated the ruse's nature. Still, that's beside the point. The trouble is that there must have been some violence used, if only at the last second; and violence always leaves traces.

"And if there are such traces, the suspicion of the police will be confirmed, the inquest will be adjourned to-morrow after just a formal opening for further evidence, and there'll be the devil and all to pay."

"Hell's bells," observed Colin gloomily.

"So what," said Roger, "are we going to do about it?"

## II

What Roger did about it first of all was to go downstairs and ask Ronald to find out for him when the post-mortem was to be performed and what doctor was going to perform it.

Ronald rang through to Chalmers, and learned that it was to be carried out that afternoon, by a doctor from Westerford named Bryce, and that both Chalmers and Mitchell were to be present.

"Half a minute," said Roger, and took over the receiver. "Is that you, Chalmers? Sheringham speaking."

"Oh, yes?" came Dr. Chalmers's pleasant tones.

"This man, Bryce. He's a good man?"

"Quite. An elderly man, with a good deal of experience."

"A little odd, isn't it?" Roger said cautiously. "A little odd, I mean, the police wanting a p.m. in such a very straightforward case?"

"Oh, I don't think so, really. They usually do, here."

"Coroner fussy?"

"Oh, no. But the police haven't much to do, you know, and that makes them keener when they do get anything."

"I see. You think that's all there is to it?"

"Oh, I'm quite sure there's nothing more," said Dr. Chalmers, most reassuringly.

Roger handed over the receiver to Ronald. "Ask him to ring you up as soon as the post-mortem's over, and tell you its findings," he said, "even if it is a bit unofficial. I expect he will."

Ronald put forward the request. Then he nodded to Roger, to intimate that Dr. Chalmers had agreed to do so.

Roger sidled out of the room with the noiseless

shuffle to which one feels driven when another person is telephoning.

It appeared to him that nothing further could be done until the result of the post-mortem was known.

He wandered slowly out into the garden.

The inaction irked him, for he was more worried even than he had let Colin see. That thoughtless action in adding the one detail which Ena Stratton's murderer had stupidly overlooked, might have unpleasantly serious consequences. Roger was not thinking so much of possible punishment, as of the effect on his hobby. If things did reach the point when he had to admit what he had done, the confidence of the police would be lost to him for ever; never would he be allowed to go officially detecting again. And yet he could not regret the action. Better that Roger Sheringham should be in the permanent black books of Scotland Yard than that David should suffer what blind justice would certainly order him to suffer, for an act of almost insane desperation.

But, if Roger could prevent it, things should not reach that point.

And the really important thing was to prevent the inquest from being adjourned. An adjourned inquest, in such circumstances, would mean the ears of every pressman in the kingdom cocked to high heaven. Inevitably, mud would be slung, reputations spotted, and the whole childish joke of the party twisted to fit the most preposterous insinuations. The party, and all those who had attended it, would be "news," of the yellowest description. If it could possibly be done, that must be stopped.

But how?

Time was so infernally short. The police had somehow got to be convinced that very day that there was no ground for further inquiry: that the case really was as simple as it had looked at first. And with that damning chair in their possession, Roger did not see how on earth he was going to convince them of anything of the sort.

Besides, the trouble was that he himself, for all he knew, might be suspect. It would only be justice, and not merely poetic justice at that, if he were. He tried to remember what his attitude to the police had been, and theirs to him. Had he for instance appeared too partisan that morning in dismissing the position of the chair as of no importance? And yet the irritating thing was that it had been of no importance; none at all. Had he tried to lead the inspector too obviously last night?

Roger mounted the steps that led to the raised walk round the rose-garden, his hands sunk in his pockets, his head dropped in thought.

Yes, the attitude of the police towards him had altered. Last night the inspector had been delighted to meet him, only too eager to ask his advice and listen to his suggestions. This morning on the roof, Roger's suggestions had plainly failed to convince him. Later, when the scenes with which he was so familiar were being enacted, he had not even been consulted at all. More, it might be that he had been purposely excluded. The arrival of the police at the back door and the injunction to the maid to say nothing to the master of the house about it, might have been aimed more at Roger than at Ronald.

It was not nice to feel suspect. Roger, who had chased so many quarries with gusto, felt horrid little cold finger-taps up and down his spine at the idea of being a quarry himself.

Was it possible that the police suspected him even of the actual murder? He must not get morbid: but was it? And if so, and the fact of his having handled that chair did come out, together with the fact that he had been on the roof, alone, during the crucial time—well, Colin had put up a very nasty case against him last night; how would that case sound in open court, from the dock?

No, it was ridiculous. He was Roger Sheringham.

But still…

"Hullo, Mr. Sheringham," said a voice at his elbow. "I've been watching you pace round like a lion in a cage. I'm sorry to disturb the reverie, but I'm simply dying to know what it's about." Mrs. Lefroy was sunning herself in a little arbour let into the rambler walk.

"Then I shan't tell you," said Roger, recovering himself not without difficulty. "You brought my heart into my mouth, and nearly out through the top of my head. You really mustn't speak suddenly like that to people in the dock for murder."

"Were you in the dock for murder?" Mrs. Lefroy asked curiously.

"I was. I'm not, thank goodness, now." He seated himself on the bench beside her. The presence of Mrs. Lefroy was right. Obviously there was not the least use in brooding. "Do you mind talking to me," he said carefully, "about—about pancakes? Yes, pancakes." Pancakes are very soothing things.

"Pancakes!" Mrs. Lefroy repeated rather dubiously. "I'm not sure that I know much about pancakes. But I can tell you how to cook a chicken *à la Toulousaine*."

"Tell me," said Roger eagerly.

III

At a quarter to four Ronald Stratton, on Roger's impatient instigation, rang up Dr. Chalmers. No, the doctor was not yet back.

Roger possessed himself somehow for twenty-five minutes, but certainly not in patience.

"And they started at three!" he groaned. "Oh, ring up again, Ronald."

Ronald rang up again.

This time he was more lucky. "Dr. Chalmers has just come in? Ask him to speak to me, will you? Mr. Stratton."

In the pause, Ronald beckoned to Roger. "If you put your head close to the receiver, you'll probably be able to hear too."

Roger nodded, and put his head close to the receiver.

He could actually hear Ronald's heart thumping, and knew that Ronald could probably hear his.

Then came Chalmers's voice, just as cheerful as ever.

"That you, Ronald? I was just going to ring you up, my man. Yes, just got in."

"The p.m.'s over?"

"Oh, yes. Quite simple. Of course, the cause of death was never in doubt."

"No, no. But…"

"What is it, my man?"

"Well, did you find anything else? Bruising on the body, or anything like that?"

"Oh, yes. The body was rather badly bruised. The skin broken on both knee-caps, a large contusion on the right hip and another on the right buttock, and a bit of a bruise on the back of the head which I'm afraid we must have overlooked last night. Otherwise nothing."

"I see," said Ronald, in a dull voice.

He looked inquiringly at Roger, who shook his head. There was no need to ask anything further.

"That all you wanted to know? We shall just send in a formal report. In fact, the whole thing was nothing but a formality. Yes. Well, good-bye, Ronald."

Ronald hung up the receiver and looked at Roger.

Roger looked at him.

A bruise on the back of the head, Roger was thinking. Then he must have overlooked that, too, as well as the doctors, for he had felt the back of Mrs. Stratton's head last night for the exact purpose of finding out if there was any bump or swelling, and had detected none; it must have been too high up under her hat. In any case, that explained only too clearly why there had been no struggle or noise. David had stunned her. Roger wondered what with, and whether it was now safely concealed. David had stunned her, and she had slumped down on to her knees, breaking the skin on the rough surface of the asphalt. How the other bruises had been acquired did not matter; the one on the back of the head was the damning one. So that was how David had done it.

Roger realised that he was still looking at Ronald, and Ronald at him. And he was pretty sure that the thoughts which had just been chasing each other through his own mind, had equally been chasing themselves through Ronald's.

Aloud he said:

"That's a bit of a nuisance."

"Yes," said Ronald.

## IV

Dr. Mitchell's house was of cheerfully modern red brick, with a small garden in front full of flowering shrubs and a glimpse down one side of a lawn and rose-bushes at the back. It stood in a pleasant green avenue, and Roger had had no difficulty in finding it, on the instructions Ronald had given him. He had asked Ronald to drop him at the Westerford cross-roads, whence he could make his way to Dr. Mitchell's on foot, as he considered that it might be unwise for Ronald to drive all the way to the house. For all anyone knew, Ronald might now be under police suspicion, and he must not appear to be trying to tamper with the medical evidence.

For that matter, so might Roger himself; but people in Westerford could not recognise him as they could Ronald, and Ronald's car.

He waited for Dr. Mitchell in a somewhat severe room with an official-looking desk in one corner of the room and, rather incongruously, a piano in another.

"Why, Sheringham, this is a surprise. Delighted to see you. Come into the other room and have some tea."

Dr. Mitchell, no longer Jack the Ripper but a thoroughly respectable practitioner in a lounge suit, was obviously pleased to see him.

Roger, however, had no time for tea, though his conscience felt a little uneasy as he tried to detach the doctor from the young woman waiting in the next room, who would certainly be cursing him heartily for the next fifteen minutes.

"Thanks, very much, but I'm rather in a hurry. Can you spare me a couple of minutes, or are you in the middle of tea?"

"Not a bit. Sit down. You've not come to consult me professionally, surely?"

Dr. Mitchell seated himself at the official-looking desk, and Roger took a convenient chair.

"No. At least, not exactly. I just wanted to ask you one or two questions about Mrs. Stratton."

"Oh, yes?" said Dr. Mitchell, quite pleasantly but quite non-committally.

"You may know," Roger began, "that I've done a good deal of work at one time and another with the police?"

"Of course. But you don't mean to tell me you're interested in Mrs. Stratton's death from that point of view?"

"No, no. What I was going to say was that, having worked so much with the police, I know the signs; and quite between ourselves, I'm pretty sure," said Roger frankly, "that they're not altogether satisfied about Mrs. Stratton's death." He had worked out with some care the best way of approaching Dr. Mitchell.

A slightly worried look appeared on the other's face. "Well, to tell you the truth, Sheringham, I was a little afraid of that myself. I don't know what's in their minds, but calling for a post-mortem and so on—"

"I think I know what's in their minds," Roger said, with a confidential air. "It's this. They suspect that something is being kept back from them which the coroner ought to know. They think it very odd, you see, both that Mrs. Stratton should have taken her life at a party where everything ought to have been bright and gay and—"

"Alcoholic depression," put in Dr. Mitchell.

"That's a good point," Roger said gratefully.

"I was going to suggest it in my report as a contributory cause. I suppose," said Dr. Mitchell a little uneasily, "this is all quite between ourselves?"

"Oh, entirely. And I think we'd better be quite frank, as you'll understand in a minute. So I'll say at once that the other thing which the police find curious, as the inspector himself told me," said Roger, not altogether accurately, "is that David Stratton should have warned them about suicide so pat before it happened, when he'd never done such a thing before. You knew about that?"

"Yes, I heard that last night. But I don't quite see the idea."

"Why," said Roger, producing his old ace of trumps, "they suspect that there was some direct cause for Mrs. Stratton doing what she did, beyond just general depression and melancholia, and they suspect a conspiracy among all of us to hush it up."

"But what kind of direct cause?"

"Oh, a violent quarrel between herself and some other person, probably her husband. Or a scene of some kind. Anything like that."

"But we can give evidence that there wasn't."

"If we get the chance!" Roger cried. "But you know what the procedure is when the police are suspicious. The inquest is adjourned for further evidence, after just a formal identification of the remains. And you know what happens then. The newspapers get hold of it."

Dr. Mitchell nodded. "I see the point."

"Precisely. It wasn't the kind of party that anyone will want to advertise, seeing that it ended in a real death. You can imagine the amount of mud-slinging there would be. And no one who attended it would escape. It's to the interest of all of us to see that the inquest is not adjourned to-morrow and that everything passes off smoothly and quickly. And I imagine that is to the interest of you and Chalmers as much as anyone."

Dr. Mitchell sighed. "My dear Sheringham, if you just knew the ridiculously tiny things which give offence in a doctor! Yes, I should think it is in our interest."

"Very well, then. I'm working to do that and dispel the police suspicions, and I want you to give me all the help you can."

"Anything I can do, that isn't *too* unprofessional, I certainly will."

"That's good. I thought of going to talk it over with Chalmers, and then I remembered that I'd had a chat with him last night but not with you. Besides, I know the evidence he is prepared to give on one very important point, and I didn't know your opinion. Chalmers considers that Mrs. Stratton was a suicidal subject. Do you?"

"Yes, undoubtedly."

"Good. Even though it's a stock remark that the people who talk about suicide don't commit it?" Roger ventured.

"That may be true of the normal person. But Mrs. Stratton wasn't normal. I'm prepared to back Phil up in that, too, by the way. Well, it was obvious. No, I think Mrs. Stratton must be excepted from that stock remark. She was quite irresponsible and likely to act on any wild impulse."

"Well, that's quite satisfactory. Now, you agree with Chalmers about the time of death? I think he puts that somewhere round about two A.M. Within half an hour, anyhow, of her leaving the ball-room."

"Yes. It's very difficult to say, you know, especially in the case of sudden death, and with the complication of the cold night air; but it was certainly within an hour of her leaving the ball-room, and quite probably half an hour."

"The sooner," said Roger airily, "the better."

Dr. Mitchell looked interrogative.

"You saw her state of mind when she flung out of the ball-room. Without giving all the details, we can certainly tell the police that she left in a raging fury, after working herself up over nothing at all. Any impulse might have been present in her mind then. The longer the time of death is delayed, the longer the time for reflection, and the less the impulse."

"I see what you mean," said Dr. Mitchell slowly. "Yes, perhaps an hour was rather an over-statement on my part. After all, Chalmers has been practising longer than I have. He may quite probably be right in cutting it down to half an hour."

"As an outside limit. It may quite well have happened immediately?"

"Oh, yes; quite well."

"Good again. Now, another point. You made your report to the inspector last night. Have you made one to the superintendent yet?"

"Yes. I was intending to go down to see him this afternoon, but he came to me instead, directly after lunch. He told me about the post-mortem at the same time."

"Yes? And what did you report to him?"

"There was nothing to add, really, to what I'd said to the inspector. He asked a good many questions—"

"He did, did he?"

"Yes, but I had to keep telling him I couldn't give him any more information till after the p.m."

"Of course. Now, I understand this afternoon you found a good deal of bruising on the body, and particularly one place on the back of the head?"

"Yes, we did. Not a very bad one, and it was hidden under the hair, just at the back of the scalp; though I don't think we'd have missed it last night if we hadn't both been so whacked."

"Yes."

Roger paused. Now that he had come to the really crucial part of the interview, he was not quite sure how to proceed. Somehow Dr. Mitchell had got to help him to explain that bruise away, and yet he could not even hint to the doctor why. But Roger was sure that the police would draw precisely the same deduction from it as his own; and while the body bruises were damning enough, the stunning bruise might be fatal. Somehow a convincing explanation of that bruise had got to be found—*must* be found, before there could be any hope of achieving anything else at all.

"Yes," he said at last, taking the bull by the horns, "and how do you account for the presence of that bruise on the head, Mitchell?"

"Well," said Dr. Mitchell bluntly, "I suppose someone, must have given her a knock on it."

Roger looked at him in distress. This was about as bad as it could be.

"Is that the only possible explanation? I mean, it looks so much like that quarrel which we know didn't take place," he added feebly.

"She must have had a bang on the head, to cause a place like that," Dr. Mitchell pointed out, with reason.

"Yes, but couldn't she have banged it herself?"

"Oh, she could have, undoubtedly. But do people bang themselves on the back of the scalp?"

"I mean, on a low doorway, or something like that?"

"Not unless she was going through it backwards, surely."

Roger felt he was losing grip.

He was handicapped by not being able to come out into the open. It was impossible to explain that the police, suspecting not just a more complicated suicide but something far more serious, would almost certainly have been wondering if there might be just such a sign of violence on the back of the head, to explain the absence of any indication of a scuffle on the asphalt surface; for asphalt marks very easily, and if a scuffle had taken place, traces of it would undoubtedly remain. And here just such a sign was.

"Well, isn't there any way she could have got it without having it inflicted on her by another person?" he asked desperately. "And for that matter, the body-bruises, too?"

Dr. Mitchell looked serious. "I quite see what you mean, Sheringham, but there's no getting away from it: she does look as if she'd been knocked about a bit. Bryce himself said so, and he's sure to put it in his report. He actually said: 'Hullo, who's been knocking Ena about?'"

"Hell," said Roger despondently.

Then suddenly he turned on the other a face full of excitement.

"Mitchell! Were the knees of her stockings torn?"

"The knees of her stockings? I don't believe they were. No, I'm sure they weren't, because one was stuck to her knee-cap with a spot of dried blood, and there had been no sign before we turned it down. Why?"

"Because that explains everything," said Roger happily. "All the bruises. Shall I tell you where she got that mark on the back of her head? From the grand piano."

"The grand piano?"

"Yes, in the ball-room. Good lord, what an idiot I am. Of course her knees couldn't have been bruised on the roof, because the asphalt would have torn her stockings. But what will break the skin underneath thin silk, and yet not injure the silk? Moderate friction against a polished wood surface. In other words, we both saw Mrs. Stratton bruising her knees, and all the rest of her—if we happened to be watching. Now, have you got me?"

"That Apache dance she did with Ronald!"

"Of course." Roger beamed at his pupil. It is so much better for the pupil himself to voice the obvious conclusion. That means that he will take it for granted afterwards that he thought of it for himself, without any prompting; and consequently he will stick to it like glue.

"By Jove," Roger followed this up, "and I remember now seeing her get up off the floor once by the piano, rubbing her head. Did you see that?"

"No, I can't say I did."

"Oh, yes," said Roger with enthusiasm, who had not seen it either, but was determined that Mrs. Lefroy should have, and Ronald himself, and Colin. "She rubbed her head and said, 'Oo-er, that was a nasty bump; do it again, Ronald,' or something like that, you know."

"Well, that's the explanation, undoubtedly," agreed Dr. Mitchell, equally relieved.

"Yes. And I suppose," added Roger, with a passing qualm of anxiety, "that all the bruises are accounted for in the same way?"

"Oh, certainly. She came down once or twice very heavily. I thought at the time that she must be getting hurt, but she seemed to like it."

"Precisely. And that's another point for the coroner's jury. They'll be quite ready to believe that a person who liked getting hurt would enjoy the idea of suicide. And so, for that matter, she did. Well, that's most satisfactory. Did you say something just now, by the way, about a cup of tea?"

Dr. Mitchell rose with alacrity.

## V

Roger almost danced in again through the front door of the Stratton house. Everything was going splendidly. Only one snag now remained, and that depended not on the police but Colin.

But before even breaking the good news to Ronald, Roger hurried straight upstairs to the empty ball-room. And there he did a very regrettable thing.

Closing the door carefully behind him, he chose a nice nubbly piece of moulding on the lower edge of the grand piano and, going down on his hands and knees, rubbed his head carefully against it. There is a certain amount of grease on every head of hair, and Roger contemplated with pleasure the faintly dull patch he had caused on the brilliant shine of the varnish; he would have liked a nice black hair to add to it, but unfortunately such a thing was not available.

It would have been unkind, Roger felt, seeing that the police would probably look for it, not to gratify them with a nice bit of evidence.

Then he went down to look for Ronald and Mrs. Lefroy and tell them what they remembered seeing. The questionable ethics of all this simply did not occur to him—any more than did the notion that Ena Stratton might really and truly have banged her head on that grand piano.

# Chapter XIII

## WIPING THE SLATE

I

At twenty minutes to six Roger, no longer losing grip, was closeted with Colin Nicolson in Ronald's study, with what looked like an uphill job in front of him.

"Every other point is cleared up," he pleaded. "Every single one. There's only that chair left. If we can clear that up, too, there's not only no case left, there isn't even any more room for suspicion."

"And you want me to go to the police and admit I wiped the prints off the chair, Roger?"

"Yes."

"Nothing doing," said Colin firmly.

"But you must, man!"

"Must nothing. I wiped your prints off that chair to save you from getting into a nasty jam, Roger, through your own silly carelessness. I'm not going to put myself in a jam over it instead."

"But don't you see—"

"What I see is that you ought to have wiped the prints off yourself. So go and tell the police you did, you old rascal."

"But I can't!" wailed Roger. "I'm too well trained to destroy evidence. They'd smell a rat at once if I told them I'd done such a thing."

"Ach, rubbish!" said Colin rudely. "You're afraid to take the blame, that's all. You think it would put you in bad with the police for the future."

"And so it would."

"Well, I can't help that. You should have thought of that before you interfered. No, no; this is your pigeon, Roger. Nothing to do with me at all. Nothing at all."

"Look here, Colin," Roger said desperately, "if you won't own up like a man, I'll tell the police myself that you did wipe that chair."

"Right you are. And I'll tell them that you moved it."

"But you can't! That would give David away, and we've got him absolutely covered."

"Then you tell them you wiped off the prints yourself."

Roger groaned. Colin was being excessively Scotch. But Roger could not but admit to himself that Colin had reason. He had performed an action which Roger ought to have performed for himself, and he did not see why he, and not Roger, should have the blame.

Nevertheless, Colin must not be allowed to have reason. It looked like finishing Roger with the police for ever if he were.

"Look here, Colin, if I can think up some excellent reason for you to have done it, won't you—"

"No, I won't, Roger, and that's flat."

"Oh, blast," said Roger.

There was a knock at the door.

"Come in," called Roger morosely.

Mrs. Lefroy's head appeared round the lintel.

"Oh, Mr. Sheringham, Ronald asked me to let you know that the police are here again. He's upstairs with them, in the ball-room."

"Thank you. No, don't run away, Mrs. Lefroy. Come in and see if you can persuade Colin to be noble. I can't."

"Oh, Colin, you will be noble, surely."

"Don't you try your wiles on me, Agatha. I'm proof against all that sort of thing."

"I'm afraid he is, Mr. Sheringham. What is it you want him to do?"

"Only tell the truth."

"Well, that would be a nice change, for some of us," said Mrs. Lefroy pleasantly. "I don't think I've ever undertaken to tell so many lies in my life."

Roger looked at her eagerly. "You wouldn't tell one more, would you?"

"What would one more be among so many? I mean, what one in particular?"

Roger hesitated. Mrs. Lefroy really knew nothing, whatever she might think. Was it wise to let her see how very serious things actually were?

"Shut up, Roger, you ass."

Roger took his decision. He would have trusted very few women to this extent, but Mrs. Lefroy really was different.

"Would you say that you'd wiped the back of a chair on the roof last night, and incidentally the finger-prints off it,

Mrs. Lefroy, when you know perfectly well that you never did anything of the kind?"

"Ach, Roger, come now. You can't ask her to do that. Do it yourself, man."

"Is it important, Mr. Sheringham?"

"One might almost say that it's vital."

"And Colin won't?"

"No."

"But I tell you there's no need, Agatha. Roger can say it himself. There's no necessity at all for me or you to put ourselves in hot water on his account."

"It isn't on my account," Roger snapped. "You know that perfectly well."

"Mr. Sheringham must have some good reason for not saying he did it, Colin."

"Of course I have, but Colin won't see it. The police would be more suspicious than they are already. They'd know I would never destroy evidence like that without knowing what I was doing; and that would make them do just what I want to prevent them from doing, and that is, ask themselves just what I was playing at. What I want is for someone to come forward and say he did it, who might never have realised what an important action it was. You understand that, surely? Because Colin doesn't."

"Ach, yes, I do; but they wouldn't believe that I didn't know what I was doing, either. I did know, jolly well."

"Now you're shifting your ground."

"Well, it's true enough."

"Anyhow, don't quarrel any more, you two," said Mrs. Lefroy soothingly, "because I'll say it. I can, quite conveniently, because I actually was on the roof last night soon after Ena had been found."

"You were?" Roger said in surprise. "I didn't know."

"Yes, I was. I'm afraid I didn't tell the inspector so last night, because it didn't seem of the least importance; but as it happened, I wasn't in the ball-room when Colin came down to keep us penned in. I was... Anyhow," said Mrs. Lefroy, "I heard a lot of commotion on the stairs, so I went straight up to the roof. Osbert was there, and he told me what had happened."

"Osbert's never mentioned that."

"I don't expect," said Mrs. Lefroy, "that he remembers very much about it. But he probably would if I reminded him."

"That's excellent."

"Yes. So what exactly is it that I'm to confess to? Something about a chair, did you say?"

"It's like this, Mrs. Lefroy," Roger explained rapidly. "You know there was a chair lying under the gallows, which Mrs. Stratton must have used. For a certain reason which I needn't go into, Colin gave that chair a polishing with his handkerchief—thereby, incidentally, rubbing off any fingerprints that might have been on it, including Mrs. Stratton's own. The police have discovered that the chair has been wiped, and are choosing to put a sinister interpretation on the fact. It's essential that someone should own up to the wiping, laughing heartily and without the faintest notion that the act might be considered a serious one. That's what I want you to do."

"Well, that seems quite easy," Mrs. Lefroy said.

"I do like a woman who doesn't ask a lot of unnecessary questions," said Roger with enthusiasm.

"Yes, but there seems one rather necessary one. Why did I do such a thing?"

"Why, indeed?" Roger said thoughtfully. "Yes, it's essential to have a really good reason."

"And one that will bring in the seat, as well as the back," added Colin.

"Yes, the seat. I do wish—by Jove, I've just remembered something. That's a bit of luck."

"What?"

"Why, I was rather worried about that seat, wasn't I? But it's all right. I stood on it myself. So even if you did polish it a bit, that's bound to show. And now I come to think of it, the polishing's all to the good. It will have left the traces of slightly gritty feet; but it will have destroyed any awkward contrasts between flat heels and high ones. Yes, that is a bit of luck."

"I'm glad there was some use in what I did," Colin said dryly.

"Do you know that I'm absolutely dying to ask a thousand unnecessary questions, Mr. Sheringham?" said Mrs. Lefroy. "I should like you to know that, because I'm not going to ask a single one of them."

"I'll tell Ronald what a magnificent woman you are," Roger promised. "He may have some idea, but he can't realise fully."

"Agatha's a grand woman," Colin agreed. "But why did she wipe that chair?"

They looked at each other. It was very difficult to imagine why Mrs. Lefroy should have wiped the chair.

"It couldn't have had jam on it, or anything like that?" asked Mrs. Lefroy, not very hopefully.

"A wee dicky-bird?" suggested Colin.

Roger groaned.

"You wiped it so thoroughly," he said. "Why should anyone want to wipe a chair thoroughly on a roof?"

"Because of smuts," Mrs. Lefroy said promptly. "After all, my dress was white."

Roger looked at her with admiration. Then his face fell.

"But you weren't going to sit on it. For one thing, it was on its side. For another, you wouldn't have been going to sit on that particular chair."

"Yes. I came over queer, and had to sit on the nearest chair."

"If you came over queer, you wouldn't have bothered to wipe it. Besides, what did you wipe it with? The skirt of your white dress? Not very convincing, I'm afraid."

"Ach, Agatha never wiped it at all. Osbert wiped it for her, with his handkerchief. The man was as tight as a lord. He won't know whether he wiped fifty chairs last night or not."

"Colin," said Roger, "I believe you've hit it. But wait a minute. Did Osbert wipe it on its side? Hadn't he the common politeness to pick it up?"

"Oh, yes," said Mrs. Lefroy. "But I knocked it over again when I got up."

"Then why hasn't it got Osbert's prints on it?"

"Oh! Well, I picked it up myself, before he wiped it. And it hasn't got my prints on it because I was wearing my velvet gloves."

"So you were," Roger said happily. "And you asked Osbert to wipe it because it made a smutty mark on your white velvet glove when you picked it up."

"Naturally I did. And I was just able to stand up, queer though I'd come over, till he'd done it. And all that fits beautifully, because there I was, actually on the roof with Osbert, while you and Ronald were with Ena downstairs. I'm afraid it was rather morbid of me to go and examine the gallows so soon, but there, I'm not ashamed of that."

"This," said Roger, "looks to me like a very pretty piece of work. We'll rehearse it once, just to make sure that the details are perfect, and then we'll tell Osbert. Now, Mrs. Lefroy, you're you, I'm Osbert, and Colin isn't there. Here are the gallows, and this is the chair. We three have just gone down, and you've come up, to find Osbert in possession. He's told you what has happened, and you've walked over to the gallows. Yes, here's the rope, you see."

"How dreadful," murmured Mrs. Lefroy. "Was she really—Oh, Osbert, I feel horribly faint. I must sit down." She picked up the chair. "Oh, look at my glove. Have you got a handkerchief, Osbert? Just wipe the chair for me, will you?"

Roger wiped the chair. "There you are."

"Thank you." Mrs. Lefroy sat down. "Oh, dear. No, I'm all right, thanks. It will pass in a minute. Yes, I'm better now. But I think I'll go down. Who's going to tell the others? Oh, dear, I can't think how they managed these skirts. I've knocked the chair over. Well, it doesn't matter. We'd better go down, Osbert. I must see if I can do anything."

"Excellent," Roger applauded. "Yes, that seems perfectly natural. Colin, do you think you could find Williamson and lure him here?"

Colin nodded, and went off to do so.

"Dear me," said Mrs. Lefroy, "I suppose this is all quite unprincipled, isn't it, Mr. Sheringham?"

"Quite," said Roger cheerfully.

## II

Mr. Williamson looked bewildered.

"What's that? I'm upsetting the police? What do you mean? I haven't upset any police. Eh? Have I?"

"I may be wrong," said Roger unctuously, "but I have an idea that you've worried them a little. By wiping that chair for Mrs. Lefroy last night, you know. I think you ought to tell them about it, in any case."

"Wiping a chair? What? I never wiped any chair for Agatha last night."

"Osbert!" exclaimed Mrs. Lefroy, much pained.

"Well, when did I wipe a chair for you?"

"Really, Osbert. When I joined you on the roof, after they'd taken Ena down. You must remember."

"Remember wiping a chair for you? I'm blest if I do. What's it all about, eh? What do you mean?"

"Well, you remember my coming up on the roof, don't you?"

"Did you? Yes, I believe you did. Yes, I remember."

"And you told me what had happened."

"Yes. Well?"

"And I came over rather queer."

"Did you? Did you?"

Mrs. Lefroy turned to Roger. "Well, it isn't much good if Osbert doesn't even remember what he did," she said, with proper indignation.

Roger looked serious. "Don't you really remember, Williamson?"

"I remember Agatha coming up on the roof, yes. At least,

vaguely. But I don't remember what I did. I mean—anyhow, what's it matter?"

Roger's gravity deepened. "I'm afraid it may matter quite a lot. You see, you destroyed some rather important evidence."

"I did? How the dickens did I do that?" Mr. Williamson looked decidedly alarmed.

Roger set about deepening the alarm. "Look here, this is rather awkward. You'd had one over the eight last night, you know."

"Two over the dozen, *I* should say," suggested Mrs. Lefroy offensively.

"I wasn't drunk, if that's what you mean," Mr. Williamson demurred with indignation.

"No," Roger said with great emphasis. "You weren't drunk. Whatever happens, the police mustn't get the idea you were drunk. If they once get that notion into their heads, they'll think we were all drunk. Then they'll begin talking about drunken orgies, in the course of which a death occurs, and for all we know the whole lot of us may end up in the dock for manslaughter."

"The devil we might!" squeaked Mr. Williamson. "I say, Sheringham! I say, you don't really think that, do you?"

"I certainly do. So the best thing is for you to remember quite clearly what you did last night, and then own up to the police like a man. After all, it's quite a simple thing, and I don't suppose they'll do more than give you a formal wigging. Perhaps not even that."

"But look here, what did I do?" asked Mr. Williamson desperately.

Roger told him.

"Now do you remember, Osbert?" asked Mrs. Lefroy.

"Well, not altogether," said Mr. Williamson unhappily. "Vaguely, you know. Tell me again, Agatha. You asked me if I'd got a handkerchief…"

Mrs. Lefroy told him again.

Then she told him a third time, to make sure.

Then Roger told him all over again.

In the end Mr. Williamson remembered it perfectly, for himself.

III

Roger paused for a few moments outside the ball-room door, and frankly eavesdropped. From inside came the sounds of a gruff voice, followed by Ronald's lighter tones. Evidently an inquisition of some kind was in progress, but it was impossible to make out the words of question and answer.

Roger opened the door and went into the room. After him sidled a sheepish Mr. Williamson. Besides Ronald and his interlocutor there stood, a little apart, Celia Stratton, looking distinctly worried, and Inspector Crane, looking apologetic.

"Ah, here is Mr. Sheringham," said Ronald in tones of unmistakable relief. "He'll bear me out. Roger—"

"If you'll excuse me, Mr. Stratton," interrupted the owner of the gruff voice, a larger person running somewhat to girth, whom Roger instantly and correctly put down as the local superintendent of police, "if you'll excuse me, I'll ask the gentleman myself. Mr. Roger Sheringham?"

"That's me," Roger said cheerfully. "And you, of course, are Superintendent—?"

"Jamieson is the name, sir. Pleased to meet you," said the

large man, without, however, very much enthusiasm. "I was asking Mr. Stratton about the quarrel which preceded Mrs. Stratton's departure from this room. We have already learned from Miss Stratton," said the superintendent sternly, with a glance at the obviously distressed Celia, "that such a quarrel took place. I should be glad to have your version of it."

"Celia exaggerated it," Ronald said quickly to Roger. "I've told the superintendent—"

"Mr. Stratton!" boomed the superintendent, so ferociously that Inspector Crane looked even more deprecatory than before. "Yes, Mr. Sheringham?"

"But there was no quarrel," Roger said blandly.

The superintendent bent his formidable brows. "Then how do you account for the fact that Miss Stratton admits that there was a quarrel, Mr. Sheringham?"

"I didn't 'admit,'" Celia said with spirit. "You speak as if I was in the witness-box. I told you perfectly willingly that—"

"Please, miss!" The superintendent held up a hand like a bread-trencher. "Mr. Sheringham?"

"I can't quite see what the confusion is about," Roger said pleasantly. "What happened was perfectly simple. There was no quarrel, and nothing approaching a quarrel. Mr. Stratton and Mr. David Stratton and Mrs. Stratton were indulging in a little horse-play, when Mrs. Stratton, without the slightest warning, lost her temper and banged out of the room in a fury. There was no time for a quarrel, or anything like that."

"Umph!" grunted the superintendent, in a disappointed kind of way. Obviously this information exactly coincided with what he had heard from another source, and his disappointment was due to his failure to make more importance of it. "Then why," he asked, suddenly rounding on Ronald, "did you deny that any unpleasantness had taken place at all?"

"Damn it, Superintendent," Ronald said hotly, "don't be so beastly offensive. If you want me to answer your questions, kindly put them with ordinary politeness."

"Shut up, Ronald," barked Roger, noticing with alarm the growing tinge of puce which was overspreading the superintendent's already inflamed countenance.

"I've a good mind to ring up Major Birkett and ask him to come along," Ronald grumbled.

Roger deduced that Major Birkett might be the Chief Constable.

"Major Birkett has already been communicated with," said the superintendent, with something of an ominous ring in his voice.

"Yes, well, that's really all that happened, Superintendent," Roger said smoothly. "Mrs. Stratton flew into a raging fury over simply nothing at all, and almost threw herself out of the room. You can get confirmation of that from anyone who was in here. And of course, as you've seen, it's a matter of considerable importance."

"What is a matter of considerable importance, Mr. Sheringham?"

"Why, I mean the state of her mind when she went up on the roof. That's very suggestive, isn't it? But that's not really my province," added Roger cunningly, remembering his hints on this matter to Dr. Mitchell. "You must ask one of the doctors whether that would have been likely to influence her immediate actions."

"Thank *you*, sir," returned the superintendent shortly, as

one to say that he knew what he must ask the doctors and what he need not. Not a pleasant person Superintendent Jamieson, thought Roger, realising now who it was that had caused all the trouble.

Roger considered it time to lead the conversation to his objective.

He strolled over to the inspector. "By the way, Inspector," he said in a casual voice, "you were interested this morning in the position of that chair right under the gallows. I've been amusing myself by tracing its history, if you'd still like to hear how that happened."

Roger had purposely addressed the inspector and not the superintendent, as if the matter of the chair and everything connected with it were far too insignificant to interest that august person; but behind him he could almost hear the superintendent creak as his large body stiffened into attention.

"Indeed, sir?" said the inspector eagerly. "Yes, I should like to hear that."

"Well, Mrs. Lefroy's skirt caught it when she got up from it, and knocked it over. You remember she was wearing one of those old-fashioned balloon-skirts."

"Mrs. Lefroy *sat* in that chair?" uttered a slightly stifled voice behind Roger. "She *sat* in it?"

Roger turned round. "What? Oh, I see what you mean. The smuts, and her white dress. But of course she didn't sit down till *after* the chair had been wiped."

"The—chair—had—been—wiped?" repeated the superintendent, spacing his words with pregnant blanks.

Roger looked surprised. "You knew *that,* surely?" he said, in tones just scornful enough to stimulate without scourging.

"Surely you knew that Mr. Williamson wiped the chair for Mrs. Lefroy?"

The superintendent flung himself round so suddenly that Mr. Williamson leapt back in alarm. "*You* wiped that chair?" he roared.

"Y-yes. I mean—well, why the devil not?" retorted Mr. Williamson, regaining courage as he found himself still alive. "Eh? Why shouldn't I? You wouldn't want her dress spoilt, would you?"

"What did she want to sit down at all for?"

"Because she came over queer," replied Mr. Williamson with dignity. "I mean, she felt faint. Eh? Why shouldn't she? What? It was pretty unnerving, wasn't it? Why the dickens shouldn't she feel faint? *Eh?*" said Mr. Williamson aggressively.

The superintendent turned to his inspector. "Crane, go down and bring Mrs. Lefroy up."

"Inspector!" said Ronald Stratton gently.

"Yes, Mr. Stratton?"

"Give Mrs. Lefroy Superintendent Jamieson's compliments, and ask her if she would oblige him by coming up here for a moment."

Roger shook his head. It does not pay to irritate the police.

"And now, Mr. Williamson," said the superintendent grimly, having taken no apparent notice of this exchange, "I'd be obliged if you would be kind enough to tell me what the blazes you did with that chair that's given us so much trouble."

"Trouble?" said Mr. Williamson, with innocent astonishment. "Why trouble? What's it got—?"

"What did you do?" barked the superintendent rudely.

Mr. Williamson told his story.

He told it well. Roger, listening to his pupil with admiration, awarded him full marks. There is nothing like implicit belief in one's fact to present a convincing result. Mr. Williamson had not the faintest doubt of any of his facts. His air of mild indignation that anything so ordinary as to wipe a chair for a lady should have given offence to the police could not possibly have been assumed.

Mrs. Lefroy seconded him with the true art that conceals art.

"What's all the fuss?" she appealed to Celia. "Oughtn't I to have felt faint, or what?"

"Don't ask me," said Celia. "I'm simply lost."

"Finger-prints?" repeated Mrs. Lefroy wonderingly a moment later, after another glimpse of the superintendent's heart. "I'm afraid I never thought of them. Why should I? Or foot-prints."

"Oh, yes, talking of foot-prints," Roger put in glibly, "were you able to verify the presence of grit on the chair-seat, Superintendent, or had Mr. Williamson in his zeal for Mrs. Lefroy's frock polished all that off too?"

"Oh, he managed to leave a trace or two," replied the superintendent grumpily.

Mr. Williamson summed it all up in a thoroughly dignified manner.

"If I really did anything I shouldn't have done, I apologise; but I still can't really see what the hell all the trouble's about. Eh?"

It was for Roger, however, to administer the final jab. It was a nasty little underhand job, for not only did it wound, but it managed to transform what must have been considered by its perpetrator as the keenest efficiency into a miserable piece of bungling.

"I noticed," said Roger airily, "that you'd had the chair removed, and I couldn't imagine why. It wasn't until I made inquiries myself and heard how the chair had been wiped, that I wondered whether the absence of finger-prints might possibly be worrying you; but even then I could hardly believe that it was so, or you'd have made the same elementary inquiries as I did, and found out what had happened. I must tell Moresby about that, at Scotland Yard. He'll be amused. Why, Superintendent," Roger added with a light laugh, "you'll be telling me next that you don't know where all the bruising on the body came from!"

The superintendent appeared to have been stricken dumb, but Inspector Crane was able to ask:

"Did you anticipate bruising on the body, Mr. Sheringham?"

"Anticipate it? What happens when you bang the back of your head against the lower edge of a grand piano?" Roger patted affectionately the piano in question. "What happens when someone picks you up and throws you violently on the floor? Do you bruise or don't you—especially if you happen to be a woman, Inspector?"

A last ray of hope lit for an instant the superintendent's darkening face.

"What's this? There was a struggle of some kind, then?"

"A struggle?" said Roger, with fine disgust. "No, man! An Apache dance!"

IV

The police had gone, finally, and Roger was shaking his head at Ronald Stratton in the study. As it was Sunday evening, the party was not changing; and the rest were having their cocktails in the drawing-room. Roger, however, had taken his host down to the study to tell him what he thought of him.

"Really, Ronald, you shouldn't have lost your temper with the superintendent, you know," he chided, rather unhappily. "You've made an enemy of the man now, and it simply doesn't do to put the police at enmity—especially in such a delicate case as this," Roger added with meaning.

"I suppose so," Ronald admitted. "But I simply couldn't help it. I can't stand people trying to bully me."

"Tchah!" said Roger.

"You surely don't think it can have done any harm?" Ronald asked.

"I hope not, sincerely. But the trouble was, you see, that I had to back you up to a certain extent, with the result that I treated the man as an opponent, instead of as a possible ally."

"But does that matter?"

"I suppose not, really. Yes, I suppose everything is all right now."

"You don't sound very certain, Roger?" said Ronald Stratton, not without anxiety.

"One never can be quite certain, with the police," Roger replied, rubbing it in. "Still, I think they haven't many doubts left about suicide now. At least, I don't see how they can have. But for all that," added Roger thoughtfully, "it wouldn't be a bad idea to strengthen the case for it a little more still, if we can."

"As how?"

"Well, just an idea that occurred to me. We've got plenty of evidence that Mrs. Stratton was chatting about suicide most of the evening, but if the police are still suspicious they may be pleased to consider all our evidence tainted. Can't you produce something that can't be questioned, on that point? A letter, for instance. The record of the written word is so much more convincing, you see, than the mere report of the spoken one."

"I see the idea," Ronald nodded. "But I'm afraid she's never written to me on those lines. But she might have to Celia."

"Run and ask your sister," Roger suggested.

Ronald ran.

"No," he reported. "Celia hasn't got any letters like that. But what about David?"

"Ring him up and ask him," said Roger.

Ronald rang up his brother.

David, it transpired, could produce nothing, but thought that if any such letters existed they might have been written to a certain Janet Aldersley.

"Lives in Westerford," Ronald explained. "Ena's particular friend and confidante about the brutality and general iniquities of her unworthy husband."

"Get out the car," Roger said briskly. "There's half an hour yet before dinner. We'll go and see her."

"Right you are," agreed Ronald, impressed.

Miss Aldersley lived in a large house on the farther side of Westerford. Ronald was able to arrange an interview with her without disturbing the Aldersley parents. She was tearful, and much impressed by the idea that she might be of help.

Roger explained the object of the visit.

"If you had any such letters," he said smoothly, "it would help to shorten the proceedings at the inquest, I fancy, and any way in which we can do that will of course help, too, to lessen the scandal, Miss Aldersley."

"It's too dreadful," sobbed Miss Aldersley, who was fair and fluffy and of a type to be impressed by her late friend's histrionics. "Poor, poor Ena! How could she ever have done such a thing?"

"Yes, but has she ever written to you of it in her letters?" Roger asked patiently.

"Oh, yes. Often, poor darling. But I never thought she would really ever do such a thing. Oh, I shall never forgive myself, never. Do you think I could possibly have prevented it? You don't, Mr. Sheringham, do you?"

Roger was tactful, and set about obtaining possession of the letters.

Miss Aldersley, convinced at last that she would only be serving her dead friend's best interests by handing them over, agreed without much difficulty and went off to find them.

Roger carried them away with him in triumph.

"Don't take them to the police," he said, as he gave them to Ronald in the car a minute later. "I don't trust them. Take them round to the coroner yourself, directly after dinner. He'll probably be quite glad of the chance of a private word with you, too, as he knows you personally."

On such small details, Roger told himself with some satisfaction, is the unassailable case built.

But calling in on Colin that night for a last word before going to bed, Roger found that a certain uneasiness still remained with him.

"We've got our stories all pat," he said, sitting on the bed and watching Colin brush his hair, "but we must allow for the unexpected. I don't think the police are likely now to ask for an adjournment to-morrow; but after Ronald's attitude, if they have by any remote chance got something up their sleeves for us, they'll have been keeping it darker than ever."

Colin looked round from his dressing-table. "But what could they have up their sleeves, man?"

"Goodness knows. But I wish now I'd played that superintendent a little more tactfully. Ah, well, we must just sit tight and know nothing, that's all. If only that David doesn't let us all down..."

# Chapter XIV

## INQUEST ON A VILE BODY

I

THE CORONER SHUFFLED HIS PAPERS.

"Well, gentlemen, that being so, we'll proceed to hear the evidence. Mr. Stratton, will you...? Mr. David Stratton, I should have said. Yes. Now, Mr. Stratton, I quite realise that this is a very painful occasion for you. Very painful, indeed. You may be sure that we won't trouble you more than necessary, but it is my duty to ask you a few questions. Now, let me see. Yes. Perhaps the best thing would be for you to tell us exactly what led up to this distressing event, yes."

Roger held his breath.

He need not have been alarmed. David gave his evidence clearly and without faltering. He spoke in much the same abrupt, almost jerky tones as those with which he had first answered the questions of Inspector Crane, but now they appeared nothing but a cloak for nervousness.

The coroner was as kind to him as possible, and led him in a way which, Roger considered, might have given a suspicious superintendent of police some pain. (Ronald's call on the coroner the previous evening had been an excellent move.) After telling his story David was asked a few questions about his own movements; but only, it seemed, with the object of finding out why he had not followed his wife out of the ballroom and whether, had he done so shortly afterwards, it would not have been possible to avert the tragedy; to which David frankly replied that his wife very often behaved in an odd way, and he had no anticipation at all that this performance in particular might have serious consequences. As for ringing up the police-station later, he had learned a long time ago from Dr. Chalmers that his wife could not be held to be always strictly accountable for her actions, and being worried over her disappearance had thought it best to take this precaution; he had never done so before, because the occasion had never arisen. Altogether, Roger thought admiringly, David could not have carried greater conviction had he been innocent.

"Yes," clucked the elderly little coroner. "Quite so. This is very distressing for you, Mr. Stratton, I know, but I am bound to ask you. With regard to what you say about your wife's behaviour at times…"

David gave instances, shortly and with obvious reluctance. Mrs. Stratton had been subject to profound fits of depression; she was accustomed occasionally, in company, to drink for effect, though it was impossible to call her a drunkard; she often lost her temper over trifles, and would then rave and storm in a quite unbalanced way; she would worry for days over the most insignificant things; and so on.

When at last David was released, Roger felt that the worst was over.

And evidently the police had not asked for an adjournment, so perhaps no surprises might be expected after all.

Ronald Stratton followed his brother, and he, too, gave nothing away. Confirming David's account of Ena's behaviour at the party and her loss of temper over their horse-play, which Ronald manfully admitted to have been mistaken with so touchy a subject, he told of the anxiety about her disappearance which had resulted in the prolonged search, and of the finding of the body. He spoke with sincerity and frankness, and obviously created an excellent impression on the jury.

Questioned by the coroner, he not only agreed with David's estimate of the dead woman's mental instability, but conveyed the impression, without actually saying so, that David had been loyally minimising this lack of balance, which in reality was a great deal more pronounced than he had suggested. He added further examples of her strange behaviour.

Celia Stratton confirmed this, and added that when staying with David she had frequently been distressed to hear his wife shrieking at him in their bedroom till all hours of the morning, like a mad woman.

"Like a mad woman?" repeated the coroner deprecatingly. "You're sure that isn't too strong an expression, Miss Stratton?"

"Not in the least," Celia retorted firmly. "If you'd heard her, you'd understand. She used almost to yowl, one might say, as if she'd completely lost control of herself."

"Dear me," said the coroner sadly. "Very painful, indeed."

Roger privately thought that Celia had overdone it a trifle, but there was no doubt that the idea must be getting home to the jury that Ena Stratton had been anything but normal.

As Celia was about to leave the stand, the coroner added one more question:

"If you realised that your sister-in-law was really so seriously unbalanced as this, I wonder you did not advise your brother to consult an alienist about her, Miss Stratton?"

"But I did!" Celia retorted indignantly. "Of course I did. My elder brother and I both wanted him to do so. But he said he'd already consulted Dr. Chalmers, who had advised him that though his wife was unbalanced to some extent, it couldn't be considered pronounced enough to warrant sending her to a home just yet, though that might come later."

"I see, I see," hastily agreed the coroner. "Yes, we can hear all about that from Dr. Chalmers himself, yes."

Roger smiled and blessed the ways of coroners' courts. In a court of law, governed by the rules of evidence, Celia's last statement would not have been allowed even to reach completion; and it was a useful one. But not perhaps, Roger reflected, for Dr. Chalmers, who stood a chance of getting hauled over the coals for negligence.

Roger also noticed, with considerable interest, that so far not a word had been said about chairs.

He himself was called next.

Asked to do so, he described glibly enough the part he had played in the scene that followed the discovery of the body.

"In consequence of a communication made to me by Mr. Williamson, I called Mr. Ronald Stratton quietly out of the next room and accompanied him up to the roof, followed by Mr. Williamson."

"Yes. Just a moment, Mr. Sheringham. What was this communication that Mr. Williamson made to you?"

"He told me that he had found Mrs. Stratton," amplified Roger, who had thought he had achieved rather nicely the official phraseology.

He continued his story.

"And I should like to say, Mr. Coroner," he said unctuously, "that I take full responsibility for the cutting down of the body before the police arrived."

"Of course. Quite so. Yes. You had naturally to make certain that life was extinct. Of course. Yes, Mr. Sheringham? And then?"

Roger went on.

Not a word was said about chairs.

"Quite so. Your experience, of which we have all of course heard, was of great service. We can be sure that everything was done in a perfectly regular and proper manner. Yes. Now, Mr. Sheringham, you have heard the evidence that has been given regarding the state of Mrs. Stratton's mind. Did you yourself notice anything unusual in her behaviour?"

"Yes. My attention had been called to Mrs. Stratton earlier in the evening, in consequence of overhearing a remark made by Mr. Williamson to Mr. Ronald Stratton." Roger paused provocatively.

"I think you may tell us what the remark was, Mr. Sheringham. We are not bound by the strict laws of evidence here, you know."

"Mr. Williamson said: 'Is your sister-in-law mad, Ronald?'"

Laughter in court.

"Ah!" said the coroner, not without a smile himself. "Indeed? That is very interesting. We will hear from Mr.

Williamson himself about that. And that caused you to observe Mrs. Stratton closely, Mr. Sheringham?"

"It did. With the result that I considered that Mr. Williamson's question, though put in a somewhat exaggerated form, was not without foundation."

"What did you see that led you to that conclusion?"

"I noticed then that Mrs. Stratton was evidently suffering from a mild form of exhibitionism. She wished to be attracting notice all the time." Roger cited the climbing on the beam and the Apache dance, a reference to which he had been anxious to make, and added a reference to his conversation with Mrs. Stratton on the roof, in the course of which she had threatened suicide.

"I'm afraid, however, that I attached no importance to this threat. I put it down as being part of her general desire to impress."

"Are you still of this opinion?"

"No, I think now that I was mistaken. Not so much from what did actually happen later, as that I believe now that Mrs. Stratton was actually more unbalanced than I suspected, and so was ready to carry her mania of being important to still greater lengths."

"You think, then, that she would even carry it to the length of suicide?"

"In sufficiently picturesque circumstances," said Roger grimly, "yes, I do."

He was allowed to stand down.

Still not a word about chairs.

Roger was really surprised. He had expected without fail a question or two regarding the position of the chair when the body was being cut down, or at the very least its presence, but the questions had not come.

His uneasiness began to return. Were the police keeping something up their sleeves after all concerning that chair?

Mr. Williamson was the next witness, and Roger regarded him with an apprehensive eye. He had had no time that morning to rehearse Mr. Williamson again in his part, and beyond a hurried injunction to refer to Mrs. Lefroy if his memory failed him in any detail of the chair-wiping, had spoken no more to him about it since the previous evening. And it was quite too much to expect that Mr. Williamson also would be allowed to get away with it in silence.

Roger remembered now that Mr. Williamson's reply to this injunction had been a little curious. What had he said? Something about it being all right, he had had it out with Lilian. Roger felt still more apprehensive. What on earth had Mr. Williamson meant by that? Roger had been careless in not finding out at once. Perhaps devastatingly careless. Had Mrs. Williamson got hold of her husband and undone all the good work by informing him that he had never wiped a chair for Mrs. Lefroy at all? But how, for that matter, could Mrs. Williamson possibly know that he had not?

In the meantime Mr. Williamson's evidence had been proceeding.

"How did I find the body, eh? Well, you see, we were all looking, and I wondered if anyone had looked on the roof, so I went up there. And then I found her, you see."

"But what called your attention to her? I understand that other people had already searched on the roof."

"Oh, well, I don't suppose they'd bumped into her. That's what I did, you see. I bumped into her. Eh? Yes. And she seemed a bit heavy for a straw figure—and that," said Mr.

Williamson, also achieving the correct phraseology, "aroused my suspicions."

The coroner took him briefly through the resulting alarm and the attempt to render first aid, and then, reverting to the question to Ronald Stratton which Mr. Sheringham had overheard, asked Mr. Williamson what had prompted it.

"Well, I'd just been talking to her, you see," said Mr. Williamson uneasily. "I mean, she'd just been talking to me."

"And what had been the nature of the conversation?"

"Why, she'd been talking about her soul," explained Mr. Williamson, his slight diffidence giving place to indignation. "Eh? Popping down double whiskies nineteen to the dozen, and talking about her soul, and whether it wouldn't be better to put her head in a gas-oven and finish it all off. What? Well!"

Under cover of the resulting laughter Roger, who was sitting between Ronald Stratton and Colin, whispered to the latter:

"That was a good touch. He couldn't have done that better if we'd rehearsed him. Carried conviction."

"Let's hope he says his real lesson as well," Colin whispered back.

The coroner, quelling the laughter indulgently, questioned Mr. Williamson further about the conversation, and gently underlined the undoubted fact that Mrs. Stratton had been contemplating suicide even before the scene in the ball-room.

"He's made up his mind all right," Ronald Stratton whispered happily to Roger. "I thought he had, last night."

Then at last came the series of questions which Roger had been awaiting.

"Now tell me, Mr. Williamson. When you went back to

guard the roof after the body had been taken downstairs, did anyone join you up there?"

"Yes, that's right," said Mr. Williamson affably. "Mrs. Lefroy did."

"Yes, and what happened?"

"What happened? Well, I told her, you know, and showed her the gallows, and the end of the rope, and all that."

"Yes. And then?"

"Eh? Oh, she came over queer. Is that what you mean? She felt a bit faint, I suppose. Women do sometimes," explained Mr. Williamson with kindness.

"Yes. Quite understandable. And when Mrs. Lefroy felt faint?"

"Well, she pulled up a chair or something, and I wiped it for her with my handkerchief," said Mr. Williamson bravely.

"Yes. Why did you do that?"

"Because she asked me to. Hadn't any idea I oughtn't to have done it," mumbled Mr. Williamson contritely. "Very sorry, and all that."

"It didn't occur to you that it was the chair on which Mrs. Stratton might have stood?"

"No, I'm afraid it didn't. Eh? Never occurred to me, I'm afraid. No."

"Well, perhaps you mustn't be blamed very much for that, in the circumstances, though it's a safe rule not to touch anything at all in the vicinity of any sudden death."

"Eh? Oh, I see. No. Yes, I mean."

"In any case, where was this chair when you saw Mrs. Lefroy pick it up?"

"Where was it?" repeated Mr. Williamson vaguely. "Oh, somewhere in the middle of the roof, you know."

Roger did not alter his position. Only a slight tightening of the muscles all over his body evidenced the emotion that was filling him. He felt as if the eyes of everyone in court were staring at him, and not by look or movement must he give himself away.

Colin was less sensitive. In a voice which Roger shudderingly felt must be raucously audible all over the court, he whispered:

"Ach, the madman! That's just torn it."

Mr. Williamson, it seemed, had not learned his lesson after all.

## II

Mrs. Lefroy and Celia were sitting together on the other side of the court. Celia had insisted that it would be unwise for Mrs. Lefroy and Ronald to sit together. Roger now cursed the decision, for he was unable to lean across Ronald and whisper new instructions. All he could do was to try frantically to catch Mrs. Lefroy's eye.

But Mrs. Lefroy's eye refused to be caught. She was looking intently at Mr. Williamson, with an expression of nothing but intelligent interest. Roger could only hope desperately that the interest was intelligent enough. If Mrs. Lefroy did not contradict Mr. Williamson's ghastly blunder, and sustain her contradiction, then everything must be up with the case for suicide.

Roger hardly heard the few questions which remained for Mr. Williamson to answer, though he did notice in a dull way that the coroner not only refrained from any sort of comment regarding the position of the chair, but asked nothing more about it at all. Roger would much rather that he had probed.

Silence was too ominous. It could only mean that the coroner had been primed on the point by the police, and the inquest would be adjourned after all. And yet the odd thing was, Roger now remembered, that the superintendent had not asked Mr. Williamson anything about the position of the chair either; all he had appeared to be concerned about yesterday in the ballroom had been the wiping of it. The position, which was far the more important matter, had simply not been mentioned. What the devil *were* the police up to?

And yet Roger, in all fairness, could hardly blame Mr. Williamson. It had been impossible to impress on him yesterday that the chair had been lying under the gallows, except by inference and more or less casually. But Roger had mentioned it, even if casually, so many times that he was sure it had sunk in. Well, it had not sunk in. And now everything depended on Mrs. Lefroy. She at any rate would have the intelligence to realise what, after all, had only been hinted to her too.

"Mrs. Lefroy," called a voice from somewhere.

Roger held his breath.

## III

The coroner looked at his notes. Superintendent Jamieson, who had a chair just behind him, came forward and whispered something in his ear. The coroner nodded.

"Yes. Now, Mrs. Lefroy, will you tell me what happened after Mr. Williamson had shown you where the body had been found?"

Mrs. Lefroy had given very brief confirmation of the main events of the evening, but not having spoken once during the whole party to Ena Stratton had been unable to help in more personal matters.

"Yes, certainly," she said, in a calm, clear voice, and went on to perjure herself gallantly on behalf of her fiancé's brother. "It was a great shock to me, and I felt very upset. I felt faint, and wanted to sit down. There was a chair lying on the roof near and I picked it up. I was wearing white velvet gloves, and I saw that the chair had marked them. I thought it might be smuts, on the roof. I was wearing a white satin dress, so I asked Mr. Williamson to wipe the chair for me before I sat down on it, and he did so. I understand now that the chair shouldn't have been touched, but I didn't think of that at the time."

"Yes. You heard, no doubt, the remark I made to Mr. Williamson on that point. It might, in a different case, be very serious indeed, you know."

"Yes, I see that now," agreed Mrs. Lefroy contritely.

"And this chair that you picked up. It was lying on its side, then?"

"Yes, it was lying on its side on the roof."

"Whereabouts on the roof?"

"I should think," said Mrs. Lefroy brightly, "somewhere about the middle of the roof."

"Oh, my heaven!" groaned Roger inwardly to his immortal soul, and buried his head in his hands.

## IV

"If you're called," whispered Roger feverishly to Colin, "say the chair was under the gallows when you came up on the roof. Never mind about the explaining. Say that!"

"I will not," Colin whispered back. "And have us all landed for perjury and heaven knows what? No, I will not."

"Mr. Nicolson!" came the voice of doom.

V

"But your efforts at first aid elicited no response?"

"No, none."

"No. And then?"

"I went down to keep the women in the ball-room so that they shouldn't see the body as Mr. Stratton and Mr. Sheringham carried it downstairs."

"Yes, exactly. An admirable precaution. Now, when you went up to the roof, Mr. Nicolson, did you notice a chair lying there?"

"Yes."

"Where was it?"

"It was about in a line between the gallows and the door on to the roof, but perhaps rather nearer the gallows than the door."

"I see. Did anything in particular cause you to look at it, or did you just casually notice it?"

"I didn't notice it at first. I stumbled over it. That's how I remember it being there."

"Oh, indeed? You stumbled over it?"

"Yes. As a matter of fact, I barked my shin on it."

"Really? Is that so? Perhaps you would show me the place? I'm a medical man myself, you know, and..."

"Oh, but it's nothing." Colin came round the table and solemnly pulled up his trouser-leg; the coroner as solemnly examined the slight scar thus displayed.

"I see. Yes. Nothing very serious, as you say. Still, it's advisable always to treat a wound with proper care, however slight it may appear. Yes. This chair, then—how far would you estimate its distance from the gallows?"

"About twelve to fifteen feet."

At last the coroner came out in the open.

"Was it too far, in your opinion, from the gallows, for Mrs. Stratton to have kicked it there when she—er—*if* she launched herself into eternity?"

"Yes."

"Thank you, Mr. Nicolson. That is all. Eh, what's that? What? The doctors want…? Yes, very well, very well. I'll take the medical evidence next. Dr.—Let me see, yes, Dr. Chalmers first, please."

Colin sat down again, quite calmly, next to Roger.

"I suppose you know," Roger whispered savagely, "that you've hanged David Stratton—nothing more nor less than hanged him?"

## VI

The evidence of all three doctors was flawless.

Dr. Chalmers and Dr. Mitchell both agreed that death must have taken place very soon after Mrs. Stratton left the ball-room, perhaps within a few minutes, almost certainly not more than half an hour; Dr. Bryce had no doubt at all that the bruises on the body could have been caused, and he appeared to take it for granted that they had been caused, by the very violent Apache dance in which, he understood, Mrs. Stratton had indulged with Mr. Ronald Stratton. It was quite evident to Roger, listening moodily, that the three doctors had had a conference last night, at which the ideas he himself had been at pains to plant in the mind of Dr. Mitchell had borne unanimous fruit.

Lovely words and phrases, such as "egomania," "alcoholic depression," "acute melancholia," "suicidal subject," "post-mortem staining," filled the admiring court-room.

Mrs. Stratton had been as mad as a hatter, and the doctors did not hesitate to say so. Unfortunately, however, they were equally firmly agreed that it would have been totally impossible to certify her, or put her under restraint in any way except with her own consent. And mad though she had been, she had not been as mad as that. Not a single awkward note marred the excellent doctors' discourse.

But Roger found small solace in his foresight. Little good all that was now, when Williamson, Mrs. Lefroy, and Colin between them had taken his beautiful case for suicide and torn it into little shreds under his nose.

Well, he had done his best for David Stratton. The man had deserved a second chance, and Roger had given him one. Anything that happened now must be his own responsibility.

The coroner was mumbling something.

"...one more witness, before we go on to the police evidence, with which I shall conclude this inquiry. Mrs.—yes, Mrs. Williamson, please."

Roger looked up. He had not expected Mrs. Williamson to be called; she had played so small a part in the proceedings. What could they want her for? Just confirmatory evidence about the party, no doubt; though goodness knew they had had enough of that, one would have thought, already.

"I do not propose to ask you any questions about the earlier part of the evening, Mrs. Williamson. I think we are quite clear on that. I want you just to tell the jury one thing. Did you go up on Mr. Stratton's roof at a certain time that night?"

"Yes."

Roger stiffened. My heavens! he thought, appalled, she saw him do it!

"What time was that?"

"Just after Dr. Chalmers and Dr. Mitchell had gone." Roger looked at Colin. "What on earth…?" he whispered. Colin shrugged his shoulders.

"Yes. That would be just about an hour after Mrs. Stratton had left the ball-room, would it not?"

"I think so, yes."

"Yes. Did you go up for any particular reason?"

"No. I just wanted to get away from people for a bit. I wanted to be alone, in the night air."

"Yes, yes. Of course. Very understandable. Now, will you explain very carefully what you did on the roof, Mrs. Williamson, if you please."

Roger and Colin again exchanged glances of surprise.

"I stood for a minute or two, enjoying the cool air; and then I climbed up the ladder on to the upper roof. I—"

"Yes. Just one minute, please, Mrs. Williamson. I think I had better explain to you, gentlemen—we shall get it in evidence later, from Superintendent Jamieson, but I think I had better explain to you now, that Mr. Stratton's roof is rather a peculiar one. Apart from the large flat portion with which we have been concerned so far, there is another and smaller flat part, formed by roofing in the space between two gables which run across the end of the large flat portion. There is a small flight of iron steps fixed close to the door out on to the roof, by which access to this upper part may be obtained; and it is that staircase to which the witness is referring. Yes, Mrs. Williamson?"

"I climbed up the staircase on to the upper roof, and stood there for a moment or two, looking at the lights of London in the distance which I could just see from there. The night was so beautiful that I thought I would take a chair up there and sit for a few minutes, alone. I didn't wish to be disturbed, and I thought no one would be likely to find me up there. I went down the stairs again to get a chair, and saw one lying under the gallows. I picked it up and was on my way back to the staircase, when I heard my husband calling, so I put the chair down and went in again."

"Yes. Do you remember where you put the chair down?"

"It must have been between the gallows and the iron staircase, but I don't remember exactly where."

"The iron staircase being next to the door into the house. The point is, gentlemen, that we have to establish that the chair which we have heard from three witnesses was lying in the middle of the roof was actually the chair which Mrs. Williamson tells us she moved from underneath the gallows, and that explains why it was not in that position later. Yes, Mrs. Williamson. You say that you put the chair down. Did you put it down carefully, or did you drop it?"

"I put it down carelessly, and I heard it fall over behind me, but I didn't wait to pick it up."

"Exactly. Now we know, from the medical evidence, that Mrs. Stratton must have been dead when you picked the chair up from close beside her. You did not realise that?"

"No," said Mrs. Williamson, with an unfeigned shudder.

"You did not, in fact, know then that she was missing at all?"

"No."

"You said that the chair was lying under the gallows. Can you amplify that at all? Was it under one beam of the gallows for instance?"

"No. So far as I remember it was just about under the middle of the triangle."

"In your opinion, could Mrs. Stratton have thrust it there, in the event of her having made use of it for the purpose of hanging herself?"

"Oh, yes; easily."

"Thank you, Mrs. Williamson. That is all."

Roger was clutching Colin's arm in a frenzied hold.

"Colin! Do you realise? It *was* suicide. She did do it, after all," he whispered excitedly, under the hum which accompanied Mrs. Williamson back to her seat. "We've had all our trouble for nothing."

"I never did believe it was that poor wee David," returned Colin stolidly.

## VII

The verdict never actually had been in question.

The coroner's summing-up was brief and kind. Missing an opportunity which would have brought joy to many of his tribe, he did not find it his duty to deliver a lecture to Ronald Stratton on the morbid compliment which that gentleman had thought fit to pay his distinguished guest, though he did feel bound to point out that the matter of suggestion on an unbalanced, impressionable mind could not be disregarded. Having got that off his chest, he proceeded to sum up the evidence in such a way as to indicate his own opinion quite unmistakably and suggest that, in such a simple case, any other opinion was impossible; as indeed, on the evidence that had been heard, it was. The mentality of the dead woman only underlined the obvious conclusion.

"After all, gentlemen," the coroner concluded, "all you have to do is to satisfy yourselves first as to whether Mrs. Stratton died from the effects of strangulation, and if so whether that was brought about entirely by her own unaided effort. If you are satisfied on those two points there is, practically speaking, only one verdict you can return."

The jury returned it.

# Chapter XV
## LAST GLIMPSES

I

Roger and Colin were walking back from Westerford to Sedge Park for lunch. There would have been room for them in the Williamsons's car, but after a short but fervent conversation outside the court-room, Roger had decided that he had a great deal of emotion to walk off. He had also decided that Colin should help him to walk it off.

"She told the police yesterday morning!" Roger was declaiming. "Happened to go up on the roof to see what that husband of hers had been up to, and told the superintendent himself. But did she think of saying a word about it to me? Oh, dear no."

"Why the dickens should she?" Colin asked reasonably.

Roger, however, was in no mood for reason. "Well, she might at least have mentioned it to Ronald, or *somebody*. 'Didn't think it was of the slightest importance!' My religious aunt!"

"Come now, Roger, don't take it to heart."

"Yes, but think what terrible bloomers we might have

made. It was only by the grace of heaven that I didn't speak up this morning and burst out with the chair being under the gallows all the time we were cutting the body down. I should certainly have said so if I'd been asked."

"Then you'd have committed perjury," Colin pointed out with equanimity.

"No, I shouldn't."

"How's that?"

"Because I didn't take any oath—as you or anyone else could have seen if you'd been using your eyes. Nor, it may interest you to know, did Mrs. Lefroy."

"Ach, don't quibble, man."

"It isn't a quibble. Still, we needn't go into that now. The point is that if Lilian Williamson had only mentioned that one enormous fact, Ronald wouldn't have thought his brother a murderer, I should have been spared a great deal of unnecessary work, and many consciences would have been saved some nasty hard knocks."

"Not yours, at any rate, Roger. You can't knock something that isn't there."

"And it was suicide after all. Well, I'm glad, really."

"And what's more, the police have known it perfectly well ever since yesterday morning."

"Yes, and all their fuss was simply due to your wiping of that chair, which we see now to have been as unnecessary as it was officious."

"The less you say about my reason for wiping the chair, the better. I did catch you napping that time at any rate, Roger."

"Yes, you did," Roger admitted handsomely. "Almost as badly as I thought I'd caught my supposed murderer. But my goodness, for real officiousness commend me to that inspector. Fancy wanting to play about with insufflators in such a proved case of suicide. Just like a child with a toy. I see now, by the way, that when Ronald and I were on the roof the next morning and he was pretending to be so worried about the position of the chair, that was just a blind. He'd put the insufflator over it already and, of course, had gone all excited about the result, and wanted to hold us off till he'd told the grim news to his superintendent."

"Who realised that, though the cause of death might not be really in doubt, there'd been some hanky-panky, and meant to get to the bottom of it."

"Exactly. And proceeded to give us all a man-size dose of alarm and despondency. Well, I suppose he thought it was his duty, so he did."

"It's lucky," said Colin thoughtfully, "that I didn't listen to you when you wanted me to say the chair was under the gallows from the beginning."

"As it turns out," Roger said coldly, "it is."

"And it's lucky that all that rigmarole you made up about Agatha coming over queer and Osbert doing the Sir Walter Raleigh act with his handkerchief, didn't lead to something pretty serious, Roger."

"No doubt, now," said Roger, still more coldly, "it is."

"And it's lucky," Colin meditated further, "that Osbert had the sense to mention it to Lilian in their bedroom last night, *and* get the muddle straightened out, *and* speak of it to Mrs. Lefroy this morning so that she was able to make her version square with theirs. Agatha's a grand woman. She saw the point at once."

"And I suppose it's lucky," said Roger, quite frigidly, "that none of them thought of mentioning it to me?"

Colin considered this.

"Well, that did prevent any further complications, didn't it, Roger?"

He looked hopefully at his companion.

But Roger had frozen himself into an arctic silence.

In any case, there was not much that he could say.

II

In the drawing-room Celia Stratton, Agatha Lefroy, and Lilian Williamson were twittering excitedly.

"My dear, I could simply never face it again. It was too dreadful. Came over quite queer, I did, as soon as I sat down again."

"My dear, you were marvellous. My dear, was my hat really straight? It felt as if it slipped all down over one ear."

"My dear, you looked perfectly all right. And so terribly composed. Anyhow, that's where your hat ought to have been. My dear, did I sound the most *ghastly* idiot?"

"My dear, you were wonderful. Did I…?"

"My dear, you…"

"My dear…"

III

In the study Ronald and David Stratton were lapping up a much-needed glass of sherry.

"Well, cheer-oh, David."

"Cheer-oh."

"Thank goodness that's over."

"Yes."

"Feeling O.K.?"

"Top-hole."

"Everything in the garden lovely?"

"Absolutely."

"Well, thank heaven it's all settled. And no doubt about suicide after all."

"After all?"

"I believe Sheringham had some kind of cock-eyed idea at one time that you'd done it."

"Done what?"

"Strung Ena up. I wondered if you'd gathered."

"Oh, that's what he was driving at. I did wonder."

"He was going all out to do the noble, and save you from the gallows."

"Decent of him, if he really thought that."

"Dam' silly idea, though."

"Oh, I don't know. I'd often thought of something like that. But I should never have had the guts."

"Well, she saved you the trouble. Have another spot?"

"Thanks, I will."

"Cheer-oh!"

"Three cheers!"

## IV

In the garden Mr. Williamson wrestled with a problem in ethics. Could a fellow be said to have committed perjury when he had sworn, in perfect good faith, to a thing which he couldn't remember but which someone else had remembered for him?

Or couldn't he?

Mr. Williamson was quite worried about it.

## V

In his surgery Dr. Chalmers took down the jar of chloroform-water and filled up the medicine-bottle in his hand. It was annoying that the coroner should have kept them hanging about so long on just the day that his dispenser was away with a bad cold; it had put him badly behind-hand with his list.

Well, the inquest had all gone off very nicely. Dr. Chalmers had never anticipated that it might not, but it was pleasant to have got it over.

The post-mortem had been rather horrible, but that could not be helped.

Well, it had been a good job, neatly done. Dr. Chalmers had never for one moment regretted it. But he was a little surprised that he should not have had a single qualm, either of conscience or alarm. He had always understood that murderers went slinking about the place, starting violently when anyone addressed them. Dr. Chalmers, on the other hand, had only felt rather pleased with himself; he would never have thought himself capable of such an admirable deed, and found some satisfaction in the knowledge that he had been.

But of course there had never been the faintest risk.

He replaced the stopper in the chloroform-water jar, and put the jar back on the shelf, corked and labelled the medicine-bottle, and wrapped it up neatly in a piece of white paper.

"Phil!" came a long-suffering voice from down the passage.

"Hullo?"

"Aren't you coming in to lunch to-day at all?"

"Coming, dear."

Dr. Chalmers went in to lunch, of which he proceeded to partake with a hearty appetite.

Dr. Chalmers was not an imaginative man.

## VI

At half-past six that evening Mike Armstrong presented himself in the tiny sitting-room of Margot Stratton's tiny flat in Bloomsbury.

"Hullo, darling," said Margot with enthusiasm.

"Hullo."

"Had a good day?"

"Not bad. I brought an evening paper. There's a paragraph about the inquest on Ena."

"Oh! Let me see it. Where?"

Mike Armstrong indicated the paragraph. Margot read it quickly through.

"'Suicide during temporary insanity.' Well, that's all right," she said with obvious relief.

"Not so much of the 'temporary.'"

"No."

Margot dropped the paper on to her knees and stared at her fiancé.

"That means it's all finished?"

"Yes."

"They're quite satisfied? I mean, they're sure it was suicide?"

"Well, obviously."

"You're certain they won't be making any further inquiries?"

"Shouldn't think so. Why should they?"

Margot did not answer directly. Instead, she said:

"Darling, I didn't tell you, but I nearly died when that man came round here last night."

"That inspector bloke? Why? He said it was only a routine inquiry. They're bound to interview all the people who were there."

"I know. But I was afraid he'd want me to give evidence to-day."

"Well, there wasn't any evidence you could give that wasn't covered already by other people's."

"Wasn't there!"

"What do you mean?"

"Darling, if I don't tell someone, I'll burst. You can keep a secret, can't you?"

"I hope so."

"Yes, I know you can. Well—Ena didn't commit suicide at all!"

"What?"

"You see, I know she didn't."

"How do you know?"

"Will you swear never to breathe a word of this to anyone?"

"Yes."

"Well—Phil Chalmers tried to kill her."

"*What!*"

"I happen to know he did."

"How? Why?"

"Because she was going to split to the K.P. about Ronald and Agatha, and because she's been giving David such a hell of a time lately."

"But how do you know all this, darling?"

"Darling, I'll tell you. You know when I was looking for

you just before the Chalmers went last night? Well, I went up on the roof."

"Yes?"

"Darling, you will keep quiet about this, won't you?"

"Of course."

"Well, I stood just outside the door and called. At first I thought there was no one there. Then I heard someone saying 'Margot!' in a choky sort of voice. I looked round, and still couldn't see anyone. And then I saw Ena. At least, I didn't recognise her at first, but it was Ena. My dear, *where* do you think she was?"

"Can't imagine."

"My dear, hanging on the rope! Actually hanging there!"

"What?" said Mike incredulously. "My dear girl, she couldn't possibly have spoken if she'd been hanging."

"But she wasn't hanging on her neck. She'd got hold of the rope above her head, and pulled herself up, to take the weight off her neck. She was clinging on the rope—my dear, it sounds awful to say it, but she really was—just like a monkey on a string."

"Good lord!"

"I started running towards her, of course, but she called out to me, still in the choky voice, to bring the chair. I looked round, and there was a chair lying on the roof close to the door, so I took that with me and put it underneath her, and she let herself down on to it."

"Well, I'm blessed."

"That's what I was nearly dying about when that man was here, you see. I thought someone *must* remember how she was able to pull herself up on to that beam in the drawing-room, and see that of course she could pull herself up on the rope too. But luckily no one seems to have thought of it."

"Good lord. Well, what happened?"

"Well, she stood there, with the rope still round her neck, puffing and panting for a bit—and then she began to let fly!"

"Let fly?"

"My dear, she was simply *livid*. With rage, I mean. I suppose she was frightened, too, but mostly it was rage. The things she was going to do! Apparently we were all in it—Ronald, David, Agatha, Celia, everyone, quite apart from Phil. She seemed to think there'd been a regular conspiracy to kill her, and Phil had been sent up to do it. Anyhow, she was going to ring up the police that instant and give Phil in charge for attempted murder, and stop Ronald and Agatha getting married, and make David wish he'd never been born (as I should think he'd done ever since he married her, poor devil!), and heaven only knew what not else.

"My dear, in a way of course it was terribly funny, though she wouldn't have seen that, of course. I mean, the way she was standing there, breathing out fire and slaughter, with the rope still round her neck. She was far too frenzied to do more than loosen it a bit, or else she thought she made a fine impressive picture like that. The lamb and the slaughter, you know."

"But I can't think how she hadn't choked already, before she could catch hold of the rope at all?"

"Oh, well, you see, it was rather thick and stiff. She said something about that—something about her fine brother-in-law having made a miscalculation, and if the rope hadn't been too thick to make a quickly-running noose she'd have been a dead woman already."

"Well, what happened then?"

"Well, I stood it for a bit, till I began to feel damned sorry I'd come along at all. David had been rather pouring his heart out to me, you see, during the charades, and heaven knows I hated the woman enough before that for myself. Besides, I'd like to do Ronald a good turn, and it would have been a jolly good turn if I'd gone straight down again instead of giving her that chair to stand on. She said herself she couldn't have lasted for another half-minute."

"So…?"

"So I cut into the tirade and said she must be talking nonsense. Phil would never have done such a thing. That made her more angry still, and she said that Phil jolly well had done such a thing. She'd been talking to him, and he'd dared her to stand on the chair and put her head in the noose, and when she did it he just pulled the chair away from underneath her and now she was going to ring up the police and give him in charge for attempted murder, and that would be that. So…"

"Yes?"

Margot hesitated. "I like Phil, don't you?"

"Yes, he's a good sort."

"Yes. And… Darling, you would love me whatever you knew I'd done, wouldn't you?"

"I expect so."

"Sure you would?"

"Positive. What did you do?"

Margot coughed in a rather deprecatory way.

"Well, darling," she said simply, "I pulled the chair away again."

THE END

*Mystery in the Channel*
by Freeman Wills Crofts

*Mystery in White*
by J. Jefferson Farjeon

*Portrait of a Murderer*
by Anne Meredith

*Santa Klaus Murder*
by Mavis Doriel Hay

*Secret of High Eldersham*
by Miles Burton

*Serpents in Eden*
edited by Martin Edwards

*Silent Nights*
edited by Martin Edwards

*Smallbone Deceased*
by Michael Gilbert

*Sussex Downs Murder*
by John Bude

*Thirteen Guests*
by J. Jefferson Farjeon

*Weekend at Thrackley*
by Alan Melville

*Z Murders*
by J. Jefferson Farjeon

## Praise for the British Library Crime Classics

"Carr is at the top of his game in this taut whodunit...The British Library Crime Classics series has unearthed another worthy golden age puzzle."
—*Publishers Weekly*, STARRED Review, for *The Lost Gallows*

"A wonderful rediscovery."
—*Booklist*, STARRED Review, for *The Sussex Downs Murder*

"First-rate mystery and an engrossing view into a vanished world."
—*Booklist*, STARRED Review, for *Death of an Airman*

"A cunningly concocted locked-room mystery, a staple of Golden Age detective fiction."
—*Booklist*, STARRED Review, for *Murder of a Lady*

"The book is both utterly of its time and utterly ahead of it."
—*New York Times Book Review* for *The Notting Hill Mystery*

"As with the best of such compilations, readers of classic mysteries will relish discovering unfamiliar authors, along with old favorites such as Arthur Conan Doyle and G.K. Chesterton."
—*Publishers Weekly*, STARRED Review, for *Continental Crimes*

"In this imaginative anthology, Edwards—president of Britain's Detection Club—has gathered together overlooked criminous gems."
—*Washington Post* for *Crimson Snow*

"The degree of suspense Crofts achieves by showing the growing obsession and planning is worthy of Hitchcock. Another first-rate reissue from the British Library Crime Classics series."

—*Booklist*, STARRED Review, for *The 12.30 from Croydon*

"Not only is this a first-rate puzzler, but Crofts's outrage over the financial firm's betrayal of the public trust should resonate with today's readers."

—*Booklist*, STARRED Review, for *Mystery in the Channel*

"This reissue exemplifies the mission of the British Library Crime Classics series in making an outstanding and original mystery accessible to a modern audience."

—*Publishers Weekly*, STARRED Review, for *Excellent Intentions*

"A book to delight every puzzle-suspense enthusiast."

—*New York Times* for *The Colour of Murder*

"Edwards's outstanding third winter-themed anthology showcases 11 uniformly clever and entertaining stories, mostly from lesser known authors, providing further evidence of the editor's expertise...This entry in the British Library Crime Classics series will be a welcome holiday gift for fans of the golden age of detection."

—*Publishers Weekly*, STARRED Review, for
*The Christmas Card Crime and Other Stories*